Acclaim for Little Oslo

Little Oslo was a pure delight to read. It is a journey into a Wisconsin valley that is filled with memories, mystery, and redemption. But *Little Oslo* is more than just a story. It is a mystery that brings hope and faith, baseball and bicycles, and most importantly, the good news that people can do the right thing.

Pastor Rick Hoyme, Bishop, ELCA Northwest Synod of Wisconsin

I loved *Little Oslo*. It has wonderful characters. My favorites are the Judge, even though he doesn't know the name of the substitute secretary who has worked for him two summers, and Jake who cares deeply for his grandmother. The book rightly compares his love to that of the Boy's love for Santiago in *The Old Man and the Sea*. I also loved the ending. It is strong—very strong.

Karen Speerstra, Publisher and Author,
Nautilus Book Award Gold Medal Winner

Master storyteller Bill White invites us into a terrific mystery seen through the eyes of seventeen-year-olds Jake and Candy and a cast of colorful characters in the book *Little Oslo*. White keeps us guessing up until the end. The book is wonderfully written and is a great read.

Dave Keilitz, President of the American Baseball Coaches Association

Little Oslo is a book I couldn't put down! It's an engaging, heart-warming, coming-of-age story in a small Wisconsin town in the 1950s. I was captivated by the strong intergenerational relationships built around family, friends, church, baseball, and the local café, Little Oslo. But tension challenges some of these relationships as Jake and friends set out to solve a local mystery. The resolution to the mystery speaks of love, trust, and redemption.

Beth Lewis, President & CEO, Augsburg Fortress

Little Oslo, a great read, is a story of redemption and grace. It wonderfully describes the character and culture of growing up in a small town in western Wisconsin. It tells how a community's values and relationships can foster and frame the people who spend their entire lives there.

Shawn Pfaff, Mayor, Fitchburg, Wisconsin

I was totally hooked by page six. White has written an honest and moving account of people and places he clearly knows and loves. This small-town story is at once hilarious and poignant. It rings true with the intricacies of baseball, racism, redemption, first love—and a mystery you can really sink your teeth into. I laughed and I cried and I cheered for Jake. White has reminded me what reading a novel should feel like.

Bill Wilson, Executive Producer, The Santa Clause Films

Also by William R. White

Speaking in Stories
Stories for Telling
Stories for the Journey
Fatal Attractions: Sermons on the Seven Deadly Sins
Stories for the Gathering
In Over Our Heads: Meditations on Grace

Little Oslo

Little Oslo

A NOVEL

WILLIAM R. WHITE

HPA | HUFF PUBLISHING ASSOCIATES

Publisher: Huff Publishing Associates, LLC
Minneapolis

Cover design: Hillspring Books, Inc.

Library of Congress Control Number: 2014906194

Hardcover ISBN: 978-09895277-3-6
Paperback ISBN: 978-09895277-4-3

Bible quotations are from the King James Bible.

For Sally

About the Author

 Bill White retired in 2011 after serving forty-six years as a pastor, including the last twenty as Senior Pastor of Bethel Lutheran Church, Madison, Wisconsin. At Bethel he was the lead speaker on the TV program "Worship at Bethel," viewed by 30,000 people weekly over a six-station network. He graduated from the University of Wisconsin-Eau Claire, where he met his wife, Sally. The Whites have two grown children and three grandchildren and live in Madison. In retirement he spends time as a writer, speaker, and the director of "Partners for Puerto Rico," a program that matches churches in the U.S. with churches in Puerto Rico.

Author's Note

Little Oslo is a work of fiction. The major towns, villages, and characters are all products of my imagination. The answer to the most frequently asked question is, "No, this is not highly autobiographical." Jake is much different than me. Though the mistakes in this book are mine alone, I did gain insights from a number of friends: former district attorney Denis Vogel, Hall of Fame baseball coach Dave Keilitz, professors Marilyn Zorn and Sue Knight, and publisher/author Karen Speerstra. My children, Scott White and Sara White, read the manuscript and made helpful comments. Sally White, to whom I dedicate this novel, also was a careful reader. She has listened patiently as I have told stories for more than fifty years. Finally, I appreciate the work of my editor, Susan Niemi, and publisher, Bill Huff, for their time and dedication.

Contents

The Invitation

CHAPTER 1

On a Saturday in May, as I was about to climb in the back end of the Sunbeam bread truck to fill an order, I heard a woman screaming. I turned and saw her jumping and pointing at a car without a driver that was slowly rolling down a long hill just outside the main business center of Wahissa. I dropped the bread pans and started running after the car. As I ran, I yelled to stop a pickup that was trailing it.

Thirty yards away, just before the hill began a sharp decent, I reached the runaway car, opened the door, and managed to swing into the driver's seat. I grabbed the wheel, steered the car toward the curb, and pressed the brake. The car came to a stop a foot away from a parked truck.

I sat quietly for a moment, listening to my heart thumping, then set the emergency brake, took the key out of the ignition, sighed deeply, and stepped out onto the street. Moments later I was not alone. The pickup that had stopped for the screaming woman was the first to arrive. Other cars, sensing something dramatic had just taken place, stopped on both sides of the street. Moments later the chief of police arrived with his siren blowing and red light flashing.

The woman, whom I recognized as Mona Mellem, ran from the pickup and hugged me so hard I almost lost my breath. "Jake, you are a hero!" she yelled in a voice that could easily be heard blocks away. "You saved my car! You prevented an accident!"

During the next few minutes the street filled with vehicles and pedestrians wanting to hear the story. The last person to arrive, driving his pickup down the sidewalk to avoid the traffic jam, was Moose, Mona's husband. Together they owned the town's most popular restaurant, Little Oslo. The big man slowly removed all six foot four inches of himself from his Chevy. Moose was wearing his trademark outfit, a blue apron worn over a white T-shirt and red corduroy pants, topped off by a sailor cap. After he received a summary of what had happened, he cocked his head and said, "You are one lucky woman Mona Mellem. You turned your sedan loose across the street from the fastest person at Wahissa High. Jake Joseph just saved your biscuits."

I tried to get away, to get back to the Sunbeam truck where Farley, my boss, would be impatiently waiting, but Moose grabbed me by the arm. "When you finish the bread route stop by the restaurant. I've got a plan for you."

I remember that day as if it were yesterday, though almost four decades have passed. As I look back I realize it was the day that the summer of 1952 began, a summer that for me didn't come to a close for thirty-six years.

. . . .

My job on Saturdays during the school year was to help Farley deliver Sunbeam bread. He'd swagger into a store or restaurant like he was a five-star general, and I'd follow like his aide. He'd peer at the shelves before he looked off in the distance like he was developing a plan to attack Normandy. Finally, he'd bark out the orders: "Ten white, seven wheat, ten hamburger, six dogs, and a dozen sweet rolls."

My job was to hustle out to his truck, fill the order, and lay it at his feet. If we were in a store he would then stock the shelves carefully, making certain that his bread was better positioned than the *enemy's* bread. If we were in a café he would assign me to position the bread and buns carefully on the shelf with the Sunbeam name facing out.

Farley's route primarily covered Wahissa, but after we hit the big grocery stores and the major restaurants, like Little Oslo, we drove to the country where we serviced a number of smaller general stores. It was during these longer rides that he dispensed his advice on education, love, politics, and the business world, advice that was worth exactly what he charged for it. Store owners quietly told their patrons, "Farley is a blowhard with an opinion on every issue." It was true, but he was a nice blowhard.

On that Saturday in May, despite the delay, we finished the route early, which meant I arrived at Little Oslo while the booths were still full. "I can't talk until the buzz is over," Moose explained to me while I was sitting at the counter. "Dogs or a burger? They're on me."

After I ordered two chilidogs and a Coke I sat at the only empty table in the restaurant. Though I had been in the café dozens of times, I had never thought much about how the restaurant looked. On each side of the front door was a circular booth in front of a large bay window. Two rows of tables ran the length of the café, all the way to the back where the counter was located. Behind the counter was the kitchen, easily viewed by everyone. The side walls were filled with travel posters of Norway. Though the restaurant bore the name of the capital city, the posters were of rural scenes, fjords, mountains, and ski jumping.

Before I swallowed the last bite of my dog, Moose approached me while changing his apron. "Mona's right," he said. "You were a hero this morning. But what I want to tell you is that I have a job for you this summer. Charlotte will be gone starting the first of June and won't be back until the last week in August. You'll work from 6:00 a.m. each day 'til the buzz is over, about 2:00 Monday through Saturday. I'll let you off if ya gotta play ball. I'll pay you a buck an hour, plus tips. That's as much as I pay Charlotte, so stay hush about your salary, understand?"

As I look back I realize Moose never asked me if I wanted to work at Little Oslo, and I never said I would, but we both knew I would show up at 5:55 a.m., June 3, 1952, the Tuesday after Memorial Day.

. . . .

Looking back almost four decades later, I don't remember anything significant that happened in the classroom during the last month of school, but there were plenty of important events after school—concerts, ball games, and prom.

Prom was something most guys dreaded. Like weddings, it was primarily designed for females. Five years later no guy remembered what he wore to prom or who was king. Girls could describe their dresses to the last detail and they all envied the queen.

I had been going steady with Candy Paulson since the previous August, so naturally I took her to prom. Candy was five foot five with long blond hair and deep blue eyes. She was pretty, athletic, and very smart.

Going steady was a trade-off. On the plus side it saved me from the thing I dreaded more than death, asking a girl for a date. Going steady meant I had someone to go with to movies and parties. On the other hand it meant I had to go to prom and homecoming. It meant coughing up money for flowers plus an expensive night at a restaurant. Did I mention that it was the girl who chose the restaurant?

May also meant lots of baseball games. The song says "April showers bring May flowers," but if you are a seventeen-year-old baseball player you don't think about the flowers, you think about postponed games. April showers bring May doubleheaders. It doesn't rhyme, but that was the way I saw it.

. . . .

The last couple of Saturdays I worked for Farley, he felt even greater urgency to train me in the way of life. Most of it had to do with Candy. "You really ought to break her in," he kept telling me. "If you're even thinking of marrying that girl you ought to find out what she's really like. You've got to open the hood and look at the engine. You wouldn't buy a car without driving it, would you?"

I insisted that Candy wasn't a car, but he did get me thinking about why we hadn't been more intimate. When I tried to touch her in special places she said we had to wait. I don't recall asking her how long we were going to wait, but wait we did.

I would have pressed the issue more had I not heard Pastor Hauge warn us about "intimacy without permanent commitment." Outside of my family he was the most influential man in my life. A big man who stood six foot two, he was both kind and wise. If Jesus Christ walked the earth I figured that he would look and act pretty much like Pastor Hauge.

. . . .

On June 3 I arrived at the restaurant at 5:50 a.m., eager to begin. There were already a half dozen men eating their breakfast, and Moose looked at me like I was late. "These are mine," he explained nodding at the men at the counter. He took off his sailor cap, pointed with his massive arm, the one with an anchor tattoo slightly below the left sleeve of his T-shirt, and said, "You'll cover the tables, but before you do, eat something. The buzz starts in twenty minutes and you won't be able to grab a bite until after nine."

I quickly discovered that he was right.

At precisely 6:10 a group of five men in white entered Little Oslo in solemn procession. The quintet, led by my math teacher and baseball coach, Swish Ewing, were all teachers. They had painted houses together for eight years, operating under the name *Michelangelo's Pals*.

In college most of my friends were surprised to hear that we called all of our coaches by their first names or nicknames. I can't explain it except to say everyone in Wahissa addressed them this way with no disrespect shown. Swish, an outstanding math teacher, earned his name playing minor league baseball where he either hit a home run or struck out.

Right behind Swish came Woody Carlson, the shop teacher, who was the line coach for the football team and the only teacher at Wahissa High School who had played college football. I'm not sure I have ever met a man as strong as Woody. He had massive shoulders and arms the size of tree truncks. He lived across the street from the high school and could be seen mornings, with his shirt off, doing chin-ups in his garage. A friend swears he counted Woody doing fifty-three one morning in the dead of winter. Though his real name was Elder, he got his nickname from all the carvings on his shop floor.

Following Woody into the restaurant were three other painters, who not only had a common profession, but were also coaches at either the junior high or high school.

Moose reserved one of the big bay window booths for the Pals so they could go over their daily assignments. "You handle them," he said. "You don't need to take any orders; they all want the combo (eggs and pancakes). Have their thermoses filled with coffee—no cream—and have them ready by quarter to seven. We don't charge them for the mud."

I put my head into the back kitchen and started to order, but was cut off by Cookie, "I know, five combos," he grumbled. A few minutes later Moose explained that Cookie was having a bad day. By August I discovered that what Cookie was having was a bad summer or a bad life. He grumbled his way through every day.

At 6:30 a group of bankers and real estate agents arrived, and exactly at 7:00 Sheriff Silver claimed the other bay window booth along with several of his friends. Somewhere between 7:00–7:30, the Doctors Quincy (Richard and David), along with two friends, a pharmacist, and a lawyer settled in. All morning people arrived in little groups. Seldom did anyone come in to eat alone.

The biggest gathering took place for mid-morning coffee, about 10:00. We moved most of the tables together in the middle of the room for fourteen to sixteen downtown businessmen. They were easy to serve. We simply put out several pots of coffee, three to four glasses of chocolate milk, and several orders of toast with peanut butter and jam.

At 10:20 they began to "guess the number," to see who paid for everything. The loser from the previous day picked a number between one and one hundred, writing it on a piece of paper placed carefully under one of the coffee pots. The men (there were no women in the group) guessed a number. The one who picked the number would inform each guesser whether his number was high or low. The next person who gave a number had to stay under the highest number and above the lowest. Eventually someone would guess the number and become the loser. The loser paid the bill, plus a ten percent tip.

Some of the same men who ate breakfast were back at 10:00 for coffee and at noon for lunch. It appeared to me that they spent more time at Little Oslo than in their offices or businesses.

About 11:30 the noon crowd began to appear. Often that was the first time that we served women. I didn't know why Moose called the busy times *the buzz* until my first day. It quickly became clear. The noise sounded like a buzz, with a dozen conversations taking place simultaneously. I guess you could also say that Moose and I buzzed around from table to table as fast as we could.

Little Oslo was probably the only restaurant in the county that served Scandinavian cuisine year-round. We featured lefse, a tortilla-like Norwegian potato bread, Swedish pancakes, and Swedish meatballs.

Around Christmas we sold lutefisk for lunch. Lutefisk lovers, though small in numbers, drove long distances to eat cod that had been soaked in lye. Most people had two objections to lutefisk: the smell and the taste. The aroma that was emitted during preparation was so revolting to people like me that Cookie prepared it in a small room vented into the back alley, thus preventing the smell from invading the restaurant. As for the taste, it produced many serious arguments. Some found it delicious. Most, like me, concluded that it tasted like boiled rubber. Friends and foes alike refer to it as "the piece of cod that passes all human understanding."

Moose and I worked the floor alone until shortly before noon when Mona joined us for the noon buzz. She stayed through the afternoon. Moose left for a short time and got back in time for closing, which was about 4:00.

Mona was a terrific waitress and an even better person. She always dressed in a sailor suit and had her hair in pigtails. Moose, who was exactly one foot taller than his five foot four wife, was gruff and tended to talk much more than he listened. Mona, who was a bit heavy, was a wonderful listener and approached each table as if they were her only customers. The people at her tables didn't just consider her their waitress, they thought of her as their friend.

Cookie, who stood a shade under five foot seven, was pencil thin and sported a tiny mustache and a goatee. He had retired after twenty years in the army and had lived with his mother until she died two years earlier. Moose said Cookie was usually waiting by the back door when he arrived around 5 a.m. and stayed until closing. He belonged to no organizations and attended no civic functions. Moose once said he brought soup to Cookie when he was sick and found his cupboards and refrigerator nearly empty. He ate all his meals at Little Oslo, which was his life.

As Moose had promised, I was free to go after the buzz, which was close to 2:00. I either rode home on my bike or stopped off at Ham's Standard Station, where most of my high school buddies hung out. Ham's was not only a great place to catch up on all the Wahissa gossip, it was an educational center. We didn't have sex education in the school curriculum, but we had Ham's. At Ham's we learned about menstrual cycles, bra sizes, and contraceptives. Unfortunately, at least fifty percent of the information proved to be erroneous, but it was free.

At the end of the first week Moose handed me a check for forty-nine dollars for a six-day week. When I added in my tips I had made a total of sixty-three dollars. Since Moose didn't take out taxes or social security I was feeling rich.

The Jewelers

know it is hard for people living at the end of the twentieth and beginning of the twenty-first centuries to imagine the days before TV. It is even hard for me, writing almost four decades later, to remember all the details of those days in the early '50s. Had I not kept a journal I would not have been able to string together even a few chapters.

On Wednesday and Sunday nights in the summer, 900–1,000 people came to Wahissa Stadium to watch the Jewelers, our city's semi-pro baseball team, play against area teams. One year when the Kansas City Monarchs, the pride of the Colored Baseball League, barnstormed through town more than 2,100 people flooded the grounds. They filled all of the bleachers, stood along both foul lines, and sprawled on the small hills on either side of the infield. Local baseball historians claimed that Satchel Page pitched the first two innings.

I attended Jewelers' games from the time I was five. When I was in grade school I ran with a pack of boys who chased after foul balls. We returned each ball to the concession stand in exchange for a nickel. On a good night I could retrieve three or maybe four balls, enough for a soft drink and a candy bar.

When I was a little older I arrived early and waited with my friends in the parking lot for the players to arrive. We offered to carry their bats and gloves from their cars to the dugout. Then, when we weren't chasing foul balls, we sat in the stands and cheered them on, calling them by their first names.

You can imagine my excitement when, in the second week of May 1952, I received a phone call from Smokey Barnes, the longtime Jewelers' coach. "Jake," he growled, "I want you to play for us this summer. I'll start you in left field and bat you seventh. We both know you've got to work on your defense. Whatdaya say?"

"I'd love to play with you this summer. When do we start practice?"

"You can't join us until your season is over. State high school rules. Our first game is the fourth of June."

"Where can I get a schedule?" I asked.

"I'll drop one off with your dad tomorrow. That'll do it for now."

Since I had led my high school team in hitting as a sophomore, I had hoped Smokey would invite me to play the summer of '51, but the phone call never came. Now, following my junior year, I had a chance to fulfill one of my dreams.

The Jewelers was composed mostly of players from the Wahissa area, though two fellows who grew up in town and moved away also played on the team. Though the core remained the same, a few changes on the roster took place every year when guys went off to college or took jobs outside the area. The left fielder from the previous year had joined the Navy after Christmas and created the opening I would fill.

Smokey came to all the high school home games and watched for players that could help the team. In the summer of '52 the only other player from the high school team that Smokey invited was Cam Taylor, who was scheduled to pitch and play in the infield. We were both seventeen, playing on a team of men who ranged in age from nineteen to thirty-four.

My time on the high school team was split between the outfield and catching. I was a bit disappointed that Smokey wasn't going to give me an opportunity to catch, but he told Dad that he thought my arm was too weak to play behind the plate in the Western Wisconsin League.

I loved playing in Wahissa Stadium, which was built on the site of an abandoned rock quarry on the west side of town. A rock ledge formed a shield behind home plate and created a sound stage that made each crack of the bat sound like an explosion.

In addition to seating behind home plate, there were bleachers that held 700 on the third base side and a small hill down first base where people sat on the ground.

Wahissa Stadium was a right-hand hitter's dream. It was a mere 330 feet to the foul pole in left and 350 in dead center before taking a crazy angle and ending up at 390 down the line in right.

In right center a tower remained from the quarry days. I was told that the quarry foreman sat in the top of the tower and had a perfect 360-degree view of all the roads in the area, which allowed him to keep track of his trucks while having total control of the quarry. When they closed the quarry they locked the building. Somehow a key to the tower reached the hands of one of the young guys. He made a copy, and those two keys were passed down from class to class as a small town ritual for years.

Guys used the tower to play cards, drink beer, and take a girl for a quiet night alone. If a guy had a particularly intimate evening with his girl he would say that he *towered* her. We all assumed that the city owned the building and turned a blind eye toward its use for youthful fun and games. At the top of the interior steps was a door with a window. If anyone was using the room and didn't want to be disturbed, he pulled a red curtain over the window and no one bothered him.

The goal of all the heavy hitters, both from Wahissa and the visiting teams, was to hit a ball that would strike the tower. Several sluggers came close during batting practice, but old-timers said no one had ever come within thirty feet of hitting the brick building during a game.

The Jewelers got their name from the sponsor, Ted Town, who owned Town's Jewelry. Ted was not only the sponsor for the team, but also its chief cheerleader. He sat directly behind the Jeweler's dugout on the third base side in a box that he built for himself and his family. He chattered constantly through the entire game. His wife, embarrassed with his cheering, seldom sat with him.

My arm may not have been strong enough to catch, but it was slightly better than average from the outfield. I was blessed with very good speed and, despite Smokey's comment, prided myself in my fielding. My one trouble was judging line drives hit directly at me. I had missed two screamers in a single game during the high school season. Evidently Smokey was at that game.

I figured the main reason he wanted me was that I led the team in batting average and stolen bases. Though I didn't hit for power, I usually made contact. I only struck out once during the short high school season and hadn't been thrown out trying to steal.

Though very few position players were paid in the league, most teams paid their hurlers. Harden, a river town about twenty miles southwest of Wahissa, found a pitcher, Dick Lombardo, somewhere near Rochester, Minnesota. After his second season, when he threatened to play ball closer to his home, a job was created for him at the State Bank of Harden. He continued playing baseball for Harden nearly twenty years, which was long after I had hung up my cleats. Lombardo married a local girl and made Harden his home. He retired from the bank as a vice-president.

Lombardo was perhaps the finest pitcher in the league. He had an electric fastball and threw a wicked palm ball that served as a change of pace. When it was working you saw hitters lunging at the ball or tapping it weakly to one of the infielders. He was also the batter Harden's opponents most feared. He struck out often, but he could hit the ball a country mile. When he wasn't pitching he would either catch or play first base. He loved playing in Wahissa Stadium with our short left field.

Duck Lake, bankrolled by a wealthy printer, usually hired a pitcher out of Madison. Smokey claimed that no Duck Lake pitcher played two successive years, but they always found someone very capable.

The Jewelers, who generally competed for the championship with Duck Lake and Harden, relied on Buck Hardy, who owned a general store in Paradise, an unincorporated village nine miles south of town. Buck had a fine fastball, a sharp breaking curve, and was just wild enough that most batters didn't feel comfortable digging in on him. He was tall and thin. He had reached Class A ball as a professional, but decided to move back to our area when he married Pearl Yittri, a local girl whose dad owned the Paradise General Store. As a wedding present Pearl's father turned the store over to Buck. When Pearl's father died it was re-named Buck's General Store.

Buck was nearly the equal of Lombardo as long as he kept himself under control. His big problem was what players called *rabbit ears*, his inability to shut out what opposing players were saying about him. If the other team heckled him you could almost see his temperature rise. That, of course, is what they wanted and the reason players would taunt him. He was known to retaliate by deliberately throwing at an opposing batter, which generally set off a fight. People were still talking about the altercation that took place several years earlier between the Jewelers and Duck Lake. It began when Buck hit their first baseman with a fastball. The first baseman charged the mound and threw the first punch. Buck also threw a punch, which hit the man so hard several of his teeth broke.

Just as Harden, Duck City, and Wahissa usually led the league, Kickapoo City, Ft. Prince, and Browntown normally finished near the bottom. In the past these teams hadn't found any pitching talent and relied on the same position players year after year.

Smokey believed that to win the title you had to sweep the poorer teams and split against Duck Lake and Harden. That meant that he would save Buck for the big games and rely on other hurlers for the lesser teams. If possible he would pitch Buck no more than six or seven innings in any game. For example, he would start him on a Sunday and use him for an inning or two of relief the next Wednesday. His goal was to pitch him no more than nine innings a week. I don't know why no one thought about pitch counts as they do today, but Smokey went strictly by innings.

One of our backup pitchers was Mo Johnson. Though he had a nice curve ball, he relied primarily on his knuckle ball. When the knuckle ball was floating he was nearly un-hittable. Two major problems limited the number of appearances for Mo. First, his knuckle ball worked best when he threw into a light breeze. At Wahissa Stadium he needed a west wind. When there was no breeze the ball arrived at the plate flat and slow. It was like hitting a ball off a tee.

The second problem was that when the knuckle ball was working, it was not only *un-hittable*, it was also *un-catchable*. Our catcher tried everything he could to hold onto the ball. Frequently he just tried to knock it down, retrieve it, and throw it back to Mo. The problem was when the hitter missed a third strike the catcher often did, too. On his better nights Mo's knuckle ball was like a butterfly with hiccups. It was not uncommon for the opposition to have a fourth or even fifth out. Years later Bob Uecker, the radio announcer for the Milwaukee Brewers, told folks that it wasn't all that difficult to catch a knuckle ball. "You simply go back to the screen where it will stop rolling and throw it back to the pitcher." Unfortunately, that was often the way we handled Mo's baffling pitch.

At the center of the team's batting order were the Zitzner brothers, LaVern and LaVon, who played in the outfield. The brothers farmed together specializing in beef cattle. Not only did they breed cattle, they butchered and sold directly to area supermarkets. The Zitzners both had good gloves, though neither was very fast. They excelled in their hitting. They both hit for power and had led the team in runs batted in the past three years.

At the only practice I could attend, Smokey asked me if I would mind pitching on occasion, but we both knew good hitters could maul what passed for my fastball. We agreed that I'd be used only to face one or two right-handed batters in a relief situation. He also changed his mind and suggested that I may be used to give the catcher a break. It must have dawned on him that I was the only person on the team with prior catching experience.

Our first game of the year was Wednesday, June 4, at Ft. Price. Smokey figured this was a gift from the folks who made the schedule, because Ft. Price and Browntown, our second game, were the weakest teams in the league.

These first games served as spring training for most of the Jewelers. Smokey's plan in the first game was to pitch Buck three to four innings and use relief pitchers the rest of the way.

The Jewelers got off to a quick start against Ft. Price when the first seven players who came to bat hit safely. I was batting seventh and singled with a man on third. The eighth hitter struck out and our first baseman grounded into a double play. When I came back to get my glove Smokey was muttering, "Should have had you running, Jake. You could have kept us out of the double play."

Nearly everything went according to plan that first night. Our pitcher threw a scoreless fifth and had two outs in the sixth when the Ft. Prince first baseman came up to bat. After throwing two fastballs in a row past the big man, our pitcher hung a curve ball that the big man hit on a line to left. I slid over two steps and was ready to catch it about head high when fear struck me. I realized that the ball was at least two feet over my head. I jumped, but was still inches short. The ball rolled all the way to the fence. Later dad summarized things well when he said, "The only thing that prevented an inside the park home run was that the runner was slower than the wrath of God." I ran to the fence and threw the ball to our shortstop who was in the perfect cutoff position. We held him to a triple. The next batter struck out to mitigate the damage I had created.

As I ran slowly toward our dugout after the third out each of the infielders slapped me on the back saying, "No damage done, Jake. We're okay." I quickly looked to Smokey who glared at me as if I had just let in the winning run in the seventh game of the World Series.

Though they scored two runs in the seventh our guys shut them down in the eighth and the ninth. We had our first victory.

I rode home with Mom and Dad, who brought Candy to see the game. No one mentioned the error in left field. Dad, who was a pretty fair ballplayer a few years back, saved his comments for what he thought was a real problem. "The only two guys on the team with good speed are you and Sherm," he said. "Cy is a mere shadow of the player he used to be. The last twenty pounds have slowed his feet and his bat."

Candy looked at me for a comment, but I was still hurting over the misjudged fly ball. Further, I didn't want to talk about my teammates. The truth was Cy was a liability. Before I could comment Dad said what I was thinking. "The team would be better off if Smokey would have invited Tim (my cousin) to play. He could help out in right field and he's a far better fielding first baseman than who we have."

The next morning at breakfast I asked my high school coach, who was one of the Pals, if he had a bag of used balls I could borrow. "Batting or fielding practice?" he asked with a smile.

"Both," I replied.

"I'll leave it at your dad's garage at noon, when I take my break," he replied. "Don't beat yourself up over one line drive."

"I don't want to incur the wrath of Smokey," I said.

"Don't worry about Smokey," Swish said. "Your problem was the lights. You're accustomed to playing in daylight. It's hard to adjust to lights, particularly if they haven't been focused right. When you do work out make sure you do it with the lights on. You can ask the recreation department to leave them on after the softball game at night. I assume you'll ask Tim to hit balls to you. By the way, your spot is not in danger. Without you Smokey has no speed at all." He looked over his shoulder at Sherm who was busy eating his pancakes. "I'll be surprised if Smokey doesn't have you batting lead-off in two or three games. It won't make Sherm happy, but it would be best for the team

That night I took the bag of balls Swish had left and asked if I could use the field following the last slow pitch game. Tully, the head of the recreation department, said it was no problem and told us how to turn the lights off when we were done. For forty minutes my best friend and cousin, Tim, hit ball after ball to my left, my right, and straight at me. He hit towering fly balls and pop-ups. But mostly he hit line drives. About twenty minutes into the exercise I began to see the ball like it was daytime.

A few days later we opened our home season against Browntown. Our pitchers held Browntown to only two runs until Mo took the mound in the fifth. It didn't take very long to see that his flutter ball had no wings. Fortunately for us, an east wind was blowing hard enough from left field to hold up three fly balls. I caught two balls about 310 feet from home, and one was a foot over my head at the fence. I was sure I could hear Smokey breathe a sigh of relief way out at the fence. After the game Dad said that the ball that came to the plate was so tantalizing that the Browntown batters were nearly coming out of their shoes when they swung. Rather than swing for a solid hit they all decided that this was the night to show off their power. Without the wind there would have been at least three Browntown home runs.

Buck came on in the eight and didn't allow a single base runner in the final two innings. With a little help from Mother Nature we were now 2–0 in conference play.

The Bang at Vang

CHAPTER 3

We traveled to Kickapoo City for our third game of the summer and discovered that the Chiefs, a perennial cellar dweller, were a much different team than in past years. They had picked up a sponsor who had developed a strain of corn that was blight free. It sold all over the Midwest with a concentration in Wisconsin and Iowa, and it helped make him a wealthy man. Herman Getter was tired of his hometown being the league doormat and decided that the best way to give back to the community was to provide a solid team to entertain people during the summer. He traveled as far as Madison to find pitching talent. He hired a sweet left-hander, Curt Baaken, who could either go power or finesse. Baaken had a good fastball, curve, and change-up. Next, Herman induced a big power hitter from Boscobel to play first base and recruited a fancy fielding shortstop from Prairie du Chien who batted in the number one slot.

We played them even until the seventh inning when Baaken wore out. They brought in their starter from the year before and we exploded. Our shortstop singled to start the inning and LaVon Zitzner hit a 1–1 pitch over the left field fence. LaVern followed with a home run to dead center field. I was hit when a curve ball got away from the pitcher. The right-hander had a big leg kick, which allowed me to steal both second and third. I scored when our first baseman drove me in with a single. Buck shut them down in the last three innings, and we went home with an 8–4 victory. We were 3–0 for the season.

. . . .

I discovered that Saturdays were not much different than week-days at Little Oslo, except none of Michelangelo's Pals showed up. Evidently the teachers were committed to working a five-day week both in the classroom and with a paintbrush. A few more women joined their husbands around midmorning so that by noon the restaurant was filled with people standing in line for Swedish pancakes.

Swedish pancakes differ from the American flapjack by being thinner, more like the French crepe. They don't rise and are folded over. Little Oslo served them with a variety of fresh berries in the summer and frozen berries the rest of the season. I understand that the purists insisted on lingonberries, while others preferred cranberries. At Little Oslo strawberries were the berry of choice, though in July raspberries were served. After the berries were tucked in the folded cake they were sprinkled with powdered sugar and served with lots of real butter. If people insisted, we provided warm syrup, which again alarmed the purists.

On the second Saturday that I worked, most of the Sheriff's table, which Moose called the *Silver Table*, had ordered by 7:15. It usually included five merchants, including Ken Brown, a man I learned to dearly love. Ken owned a number of apartments, including a complex behind Piggly Wiggly. That morning the only person missing from the Silver Table was the Sheriff himself.

As I was taking orders I heard one of them say, "Sid had a bad night. Someone got messed up at the Vang Tavern. Guess he was there 'til the wee hours."

I didn't catch more of the conversation since I had to take the orders to the kitchen. Cookie asked me what was going on, and I shared what I had overheard.

Several of the early crowd were ready to check out when Sheriff Silver came in slowly and sat in his usual chair on the outside of the booth. "Hell of a night," he said shaking his head. "Hell of a night."

Those who had just paid their bills sat down again, and most of the room turned their chairs to face him.

"Never in my life have I seen anyone beat up like that," he continued before lapsing into silence. Nobody spoke. Hardly anyone breathed.

He broke the silence saying, "His face was a bloody mess. One of his arms was broken and all five fingers on his right hand hung dangling. It was as if a machine crushed them." He shook his head several times, "Cept it wasn't a machine. It was a man. A very powerful man. Somebody beat the snot out of Lloyd Swenson, and we ain't got a clue."

At Cookie's urging I moved slowly toward the Silver Table with a coffee pot, doing my best not to get in the way. The Sheriff saw me standing off to his right, looked at his empty cup, and then nodded to the pot I was holding. "And I'll take the combo," he said in a near whisper. "Over easy with the eggs."

I filled his cup and headed to the kitchen to give Cookie the order, but he waved me off. Like everyone else, he had heard every word the Sheriff uttered.

"Ain't got a clue," the Sheriff repeated shaking his head. "We interviewed everyone at the tavern. Wasn't anyone there big enough or strong enough to mess Lloyd up like that. He ain't a small man. Nobody saw nothin' happen. Did someone just slip in and out of Vang without being seen?"

"I assume it happened outside," a man dared to say.

"You assume correctly," Sid nodded. "It appears Lloyd went out to take a leak. At least his fly was open when we found him. He had wandered back by a grove of trees. Someone coldcocked him. He must have gone down with the first blow. I figured he got hit with a big fist, but he could have been hit with some tool. We'll know better when the crime lab gets done. But his fingers . . ." he shook his head and said nothing for a few moments before he concluded, "crushed, mutilated."

"Was he hit on the left side of his face, indicating it was a right hander?" someone asked.

"You get that question from the movies?" Sid said with half a smile. "Truth is he had gashes on both sides of his head. One eye was completely swelled shut. Whoever beat him is equally powerful with his right hand and his left."

"Is it life threatening?" someone asked.

"Hell, no. The 'ol ticker is beating steady, and he is fully conscious. Doc Quincy says he should recover just fine, but it will take time. A lot of time. Now we've got a job to do. We've got to find whoever did it."

"What about tire tracks?" asked a man at the counter.

"Hard to tell. Cars came and went all night. We put floodlights on the area and saw dozens of tracks. We weren't able to sort it all out. I'll bet half of 'em were Firestones. We've got a crew out right now looking in the daylight. Friday nights are busy in Vang, probably 150 people there at one time or another. It could be as many as eighty or ninety cars comin' and goin'. I don't spect tire tracks will solve this."

"You got a motive?"

Sid's laugh was kind of hollow. "We got dozens of 'em." If it weren't so brutal not a soul in the bar would have felt sorry for Lloyd. Half the guys there admitted to hating the bum. He drives a milk truck out of Paradise, and most of the farmers can't stand him. He's undependable. Never know when he'll pick up your milk, and he's got a filthy mouth. Spreads terrible gossip about everyone. Nearly everyone in the bar can tell a story of when Lloyd offended him. He wouldn't win any popularity contest, that's for sure. This one is going to be a pistol to solve."

The room remained silent waiting for more information, but there was nothing more coming from the Sheriff.

Back in the kitchen Moose said, "He's already said too much. I've never heard Sid run off at the mouth like that. He usually keeps everything hush hush."

I just nodded and delivered an order.

When I returned Cookie whispered to me. "It's a part of a plan. Sheriff uses Little Oslo for rehearsal before he talks to the newspapers. He sees how it goes here and then rewrites his script. I got a hunch that he wants the word to go out that the guy who did this has him buffaloed. Figures it will make him cocky. Silver's not one to blow off like this, 'cept in here. In here he talks more than Moose knows, because Moose doesn't pay attention most of the time or he's too busy talking himself. In public Sid normally will say, 'We'll get this thing figured out in a few days,' even when he ain't sure. This time he wants everyone out there to believe he's stumped. It's part of a plan, just wait and see."

When I got home about four, Dad was sitting in the porch sipping Mom's homemade soft drink, a combination of lemons, oranges, and 7 Up. He waved at me to join him. Mom must have seen me coming because no sooner had I landed on the porch than she came out with a cold glass for me and a plate of cookies.

"I'll bet you got an earful this morning," she said sitting down. It was clear they were both hoping that I'd share what I had heard. Dad called it *The Bang at Vang* and informed me, "Just so happened I was in Vang this morning. They can't talk about anything else. What do you know?"

I excitedly told them everything I heard and concluded by recalling, "The Sheriff said that they don't have a clue. It has to be someone unbelievably strong."

You didn't want to be in a hurry when you were talking with Dad. He would frequently announce his intention to speak by clearing his throat and saying, "Well . . . ." Then we would wait forever for him to actually say anything. Dad's brother Jumpy's theory was that Dad was rehearsing the next two or three sentences before he spoke. This time was no exception. Finally he said, "There's a lot of speculation about the identity of the man. They're calling him Superman. People in Vang have a number of candidates in mind." He then looked outside and said nothing.

My mother believed her role in life was to act as Dad's prompter. "Such as . . ." she suggested.

"Such as one or more of the Eggen brothers. Some think that up to two of the Eggens are involved. Actually, there are three of them. Two bachelor farmers who live together up on Vang Ridge. They're big strong men. Then there's Herb, the married brother, who farms alone. He's probably the strongest of the three. Lloyd picks up their milk, or at least he is supposed to."

"What does that mean?" Mom asked. "He is supposed to pick up their milk."

"Well," Dad began. This time he got going on his own. "From everything I hear he is the most unreliable milk driver in the county. Not only is he late, there've been days when he doesn't come at all."

"Is it a problem to miss a day?" Mom continued.

Dad laughed and then stared off in space. "Yeah, yeah it is," he finally said. "It is a problem for the cheese maker if he can't start his work on time and an even bigger problem if he doesn't have milk to work with." He thought a bit longer, "And Lloyd usually exchanges empty milk cans for full ones. Not all farmers have enough cans for two days."

Mom nodded and switched subjects, "Are the Eggens the only ones who have a reason to beat that poor man?"

"Not really," Dad said slowly.

This time I tried to get him to hurry his giddyup. "You got some names in mind?" I inquired.

"I couldn't find anyone who spoke a good word about him. It isn't hard to imagine that someone decided to settle old debts." Dad didn't speak for a couple of moments as he again looked off in space. "I can't imagine Herb beating on any man. I don't know about the other two. There are some other guys in the area who are as strong as bears. Axel Dunhouse is a huge man. He lives closer to Paradise, but has a piece of property near Vang. People say he's as mean as a badger, particularly when he's drinking. Superman doesn't have to live in the area. A lot of people show up in Vang on a Friday night from a long way off. People say that folks come from Browntown, Duck Lake, and even La Crosse. Mostly for the music."

"Sheriff Silver says that there are a lot of people with a motive," I added.

Dad nodded and after a pause concluded, "That's what I heard as well."

"I talked to some women who said it was frightening to think that a man like that is on the loose," Mom said.

"That's nonsense," Dad retorted with unusual speed. "Women in Wahissa have nothing to fear. This took place fifteen miles away at a bar around midnight. Superman isn't going house to house. Women," he said shaking his head. "They can build an epidemic out of a single sneeze."

Mom looked embarrassed and passed the cookies.

For everyone's sake I thought I should change the subject. "Dad, what do you know about Lloyd? He hauls milk, but what else? Where does he live? Is he married? Does he have kids?"

Dad again looked off in space before he spoke, "He . . . he doesn't live anywhere near Vang, though I suspect that he must have grown up in the area. People in Vang talked like they knew him. He actually lives over by Paradise. Up on a ridge." Dad said. "It must be three, four miles from Buck's store. Small house. No paint. A couple of cars up on blocks in the yard. He's married. I know that because his wife works at the Vang General Store. Maybe that's why he was there. I don't know anything about children."

"Anything else?" I asked, knowing you had to pump Dad to find out what he knew.

"Not that I can think of," he said, before he went into one of his trances. I'd seen this before and it usually led to something worthwhile. Finally he said, "Except . . ."

"Except what?" my mother asked.

"Except, Lloyd is a ballplayer, or was. He was quite a hitter at one time. He may have played for Harden, or was it Kickapoo City? It seems to me he was an outfielder. Not long ago someone mentioned his name. Someone I know told me he played against him at one time. Lloyd hit a fastball out of the park. Who in tarnation told me that?"

"All I can think of," Mom said thinking out loud, "is that he won't be able to work for some time. I hope his wife has a good enough job to take care of the family until he heals."

Just then cousin Tim came walking up from his house with his bat and glove. He waved them in the air, a silent invitation to work out. I grabbed the bag of balls the coach had loaned me and waved good-bye to Mom and Dad. As it had always done, baseball was taking me away from the difficult things in life that I didn't like to face.

Topps 1952

CHAPTER 4

My best friend in 1952 was my cousin Tim. In fact, thirty-six years later he is still my best friend, though we live ten hours apart. Our dads were brothers, business partners, and also best friends. The business was an oil and gas company that they built from the ground up. Jumpy Joseph, Tim's dad, delivered heating oil to homes in Wahissa and several smaller towns. My dad, Skip, delivered gas to farms all over the county, helping farmers fuel their John Deere and Farmall tractors. Our mothers split a job, both working half time as receptionists and bookkeepers for Joseph Brothers Oil and Gas Company. Even though Tim and I were best buddies, I couldn't imagine us being business partners. Our dads, however, loved every day they worked together. I never heard either speak ill of the other. Though the women weren't intimate friends, they liked and respected each other.

At the time that Dad and Jumpy started Joseph Brothers, they purchased a small farm at the edge of Wahissa. Jumpy and Melinda moved into the farmhouse while Dad and Mom built a house just up the hill, perhaps 150 yards away. All of the gas company buildings were located close to Jumpy's place.

Tim and I, born exactly thirty days apart, sang in church choir; were both starters on the football, basketball, and baseball teams the last two years in school; and spent a lot of time just talking. Though my dad was three inches taller than his older brother, Tim and I were both six foot one. In school Tim focused on math and science while I preferred history and literature.

Since he was twelve, Tim had worked summers at Crash Johnson's body shop. When Moose told me that my job would end about 2:00, Tim arranged to start work at 7:00 so he could finish by 3:00, and we could have late afternoons together.

My late afternoon hangout was the lounge that was over the big garage where Dad and Jumpy parked the green and white Joseph Brothers Oil and Gas trucks. The building could hold five vehicles and had a lift where they could change oil and do minor repairs. The two-office suite where Mom and Melinda worked was on the south end of the garage.

Jumpy had built a cement basketball court next to the garage. He and Dad had spent several Saturdays crafting the second floor into a room we called the *Loft*. It had a couch, refrigerator, two comfortable chairs, a ping-pong table, and a radio. The room also had a space heater that allowed us to hang out three seasons of the year.

That first week in June we set two days aside to organize our baseball cards, nearly filling the ping-pong table with the various stacks. We organized our cards and talked baseball nonstop. Of course we also talked about girls. The truth was sports and girls were all we talked about anytime we were together.

I was an only child, but Tim had two siblings, Karen, two years younger and Mark, who at seven was eight years younger than his sister. For the first five years of his life the whole family called Mark

Whoops for pretty obvious reasons. When he went to kindergarten we figured that he needed to use his given name.

Most afternoons Tim and I played basketball, ping-pong, listened to the radio, or just talked. Evenings, when I wasn't playing ball, were spent with Candy. I could reach her place by bicycle in less than five minutes. Tim, on the other hand, dated nearly every pretty girl in Wahissa. A major portion of our time together was spent talking about the girl he was dating, the girl he used to date, or the girl he hoped to date.

Candy's summer job was at the Wahissa County Court House. She moved from department to department, filling in for support staff who were on vacation. One week she would be in the County Treasurer Office and the next the Register of Deeds. She also helped out in the offices of Social Service and the district attorney.

She preferred working for Judge Erling Swiggum, the county judge. The *Judge*, as most people referred to him, was a popular figure who usually won elections without opposition. He was a small man, perhaps five foot six, who dressed in dark suits in the winter and white cotton suits in the summer. Most women thought he was handsome. Most men found him entertaining. Nearly everyone liked him. He was almost always people's first choice to act as master of ceremonies at a public function.

Candy was scheduled to work three weeks for the Judge, who was seldom in his office. He scheduled very few court cases in the summer because, in his words, "The crime rate in the country is rather low."

Working for Judge Swiggum was an exercise in anonymity. Though this was her second summer subbing in his office, Candy was quite sure the Judge did not know her name. In addition, she was told not to identify herself when she answered the phone. "Just answer, 'Office of the Circuit Judge.' If anyone asks for me you are to say, 'Judge Swiggum is in his chambers and is not available at the present time.' If they ask you to identify yourself say, 'This is Judge Swiggum's secretary. If they ask when I will be in say, 'I don't have the Judge's calendar in front of me right now.'" Most people got tired of trying to reach the Judge and stopped calling.

I would have found her job frustrating, but Candy preferred to think of working for the Judge as a game, which she called *Diversion*. The goal was to divert as many phone calls as possible.

For Candy, who loved to read, working for Judge Swiggum was a dream job. She enjoyed working alone, and she loved her hour for lunch, which she normally spent outside under one of the courthouse oaks reading a novel. Judge Swiggum left the office early each afternoon. He gave her neither an assignment nor a destination and, in a day before cell phones, he never left a forwarding number. As soon as Candy could no longer hear his footsteps heading down the corridor she shut the door, moved a stack of folders to the counter in front of her desk so that people could not see her from the hall, and began to read without being observed. She closed her book only when the phone rang or someone knocked on the door.

Most of the departments greeted Candy warmly and treated her like a friend. They had special treats the first day she subbed, and they frequently had a potluck lunch on her last day. The one agency that had neither treats, nor any laughter, the one agency she would have preferred to avoid, was Wahissa County Social Services, directed by Margaret Gamble. Mrs. Gamble, a small square woman who wore a permanent frown, barked out orders and tried her best not to smile at anyone, or so it seemed.

Candy recognized that Mrs. Gamble had a difficult job because people in her department often had dual supervisors. One of her employees worked part time for Judge Swiggum, another for the Department of Health, and two others for the district attorney. Unfortunately Candy worked three weeks in Mrs. Gamble's office, the first week of June and the last two weeks of August.

· · · · · · ·

During the first week of summer Tim and I spent most of our time working on the groundbreaking 1952 Topps baseball card set. In addition to the player's picture and the team logo, each card listed the player's complete major league record. It was the first time that such information could be found on the back of a baseball card. By today's standards the 1952 set wasn't that great, but in 1952 they were a dramatic departure from earlier cards. The pictures themselves were colorized black and white photos, an amazing feat at that time.

There were a total of 411 cards, each of them numbered. Both Tim and I had bought nickel packs all spring, but we hadn't had time to organize them. He wanted to organize them by number, and I wanted to organize them by team. We compromised and organized them by number. (That was the way we compromised on most issues.)

Tim printed numbers on a piece of paper, which we scotch-taped to the table. We unwrapped the cards and then lined them up starting with number one. Shortly after we began that afternoon we discovered that we had both cards #1 and #411.

Card #1 was Andy Pafko, a favorite of every Wisconsin boy. We were proud that Andy was born in Boyceville, Wisconsin, though we didn't have any idea where Boyceville was located. We also knew that in 1951 the Cubs traded him to the Dodgers, which was high treason in our part of Wisconsin. Tim and I decided that "the trade" called for a shift in allegiance. We abandoned our dads, who were lifelong Cubs fans, and cheered for the Cardinals. These, I might add, were the days before Wisconsin had a major league baseball team.

We carefully placed the cards in numerical order, putting all of the doubles in a special pile. We used the doubles to trade with other collectors. We ended up with three Andy Pafko cards, but kept all of them. You could never have too many cards of "Handy Andy." When we went off to college the cards were transferred to Tim's bedroom, under joint ownership. Thirty years later I answered the phone and heard Tim say, "Want to make a fast $450? Tim's son, Glen, was now the collector in the family and the holder of our cards. He had discovered someone who was willing to pay $1,000 for a 1952 Andy Pafko card in mint condition (only two of our three were in mint condition). Tim was calling to get permission to close the deal.

I agreed to sell and give Glen a $100 seller's fee. Who would guess cards that sold five for a nickel in 1952 would bring that kind of money in the '80s?

One of those early days in June we invited a young boy from the neighborhood, who bragged that he received $10 a week for his allowance, to join us in the Loft to do some trading. It seems strange today, but the Loft was viewed with reverence and awe by younger kids from our neighborhood. Kenny brought a stack of doubles, which included Jackie Robinson and Roy Campenella, two players he didn't like, and two rookies he had never heard of, Mickey Mantle and Willie Mays. We made about fifteen trades that afternoon with Kenny, including the four cards I just mentioned.

Our only disappointment with the 1952 Topps set was that it did not include Ted Williams, Stan Musial, or Ralph Kiner. Years later I discovered that it had to do with contract disputes. What was pure fun for two kids was a business for others.

· · · · · · · ·

Early one afternoon, the first week I was at Little Oslo, I waited on Mrs. Zahn, my English teacher. She was a tiny woman who looked like she had just stepped out of a fashion magazine. When I came to clear her table she handed me a small bag. "Jacob, I'm giving you a book," she said with a twinkle in her eye. "You ought to do more than make money and play baseball this summer."

I took out *The Old Man and the Sea* by Ernest Hemingway. "I'll start reading it this week," I promised.

Mrs. Zahn told me that she remembered that I had given an enthusiastic report on *For Whom the Bell Tolls* in junior English. At the time she told our class, "Hemingway writes novels like the newspaper reporter he has been. His style is lacking, but he can tell a story." As I held the small book in my hands she said, "This is his best work so far. I think the story will appeal to you. I'll expect a verbal report before summer is over."

In addition to the novel just mentioned, I had read *The Sun Also Rises* the previous summer. I don't remember being as excited about Hemmingway as Mrs. Zahn reported, but I was thrilled that one of the finest teachers at Wahissa High had given me the gift of a new novel.

Two nights later I began reading the book. I hadn't read more than a few pages when I thought about the irony of reading a book about fishing. In our family Mom was the only one who ever went fishing. She couldn't convince Dad or me to join her. One day she asked my seven year-old cousin Mark if he wanted to catch a few sunfish, and he leaped at the chance. It was something that the two of them loved to do together.

Fishing was too slow for me. I didn't mind being alone, but sitting in the sun waiting for the cork to plunge wasn't my idea of great fun. As I looked at the book I concluded that if there was anything more boring than fishing it was reading about fishing.

I had read about fifty pages when I finally put it down. It moved at a snail's pace. I thought, "Do I want to read this book or do I want to spend an hour with Candy?" It was an easy decision. I tossed *The Old Man and the Sea* into a corner and headed for the Paulson house.

Ken Brown

Ken Brown was a big man who did things in big ways. Though he wasn't quite six foot tall, he weighed between 230 and 270 pounds, depending on where he was on his diet. One time he got down to 200, but that didn't last very long. The summer of '52 he wasn't on a diet, so he normally plopped down at the Silver Table and nodded. A nod meant he wanted a double stack of cakes, two eggs sunny-side up, and an order of sausage and bacon. One of my first days on the job he told me, "If Dani (his wife) asks, tell her I had eggs and dry toast. Okay, Scout?"

After he paid for breakfas he always found me and stuck a $2 bill in my apron pocket. A normal tip was a quarter or fifty cents. When Ken ate regularly it meant an extra $10 a week for me.

The big guy was Wahissa's largest developer. He got his start in a little garage where he worked on cars and had a towing service. Somewhere along the way he purchased a duplex. Then he built another duplex and continued until he owned an even dozen. Next, he built Wahissa's only apartment building behind the Piggly Wiggly grocery store. Concerned that he had saturated the market, he bought land thirty miles north on Loon Lake, where he built cabins that he rented to Chicago tourists in the summer and to hunters and ice fishermen in the winter.

Once his apartment building was up he sold a fifty percent share in the garage to the Swenson brothers, who had worked for him more than a decade. Some people thought that he held on to part of it because he loved to drive the wrecker. It was quite a sight to see a man weighing 270 pounds jump out of the cab and make the connections to tow your car. "Hell," Crash Johnson once said, "it isn't out of the realm of possibilities that Ken could tow the car without the truck."

In most of his businesses Ken preferred to work with partners. I'm not sure if this was to share the risk or because he believed that business deals enhanced his friendships. He certainly was one of the most outgoing people I had ever met.

His fascination with power led to his involvement in politics. He frequently drove to Madison where he was invited to the backroom meetings where decisions were made and deals hammered out. He had been mayor for two terms in Wahissa, but he said that cured him of any desire to run for office. He was involved in every election for state representatives and state senators. No Republican statewide candidate visited Wahissa without talking to Ken first. Judges and sheriffs often ran on money that was either given by Ken Brown or raised by Ken Brown.

I knew both of Ken's children, who were several years younger than me, and I admired his very attractive wife Danielle. Everyone in Wahissa knew her as "The Lady on the Horse." She rode a golden palomino in nearly every city parade. She was a sight to behold—a beautiful statuesque woman with flowing jet-black hair astride a stunning horse that pranced sideways down the street. I had never stood next to her, but from a distance she appeared to be eight foot tall.

Although I served him breakfast nearly every morning, I really got to know Ken entirely by accident. On the third Monday in June I decided to take a bike trip down to Herrick's Hollow, the home of the finest natural swimming hole in Wahissa County. A beautiful oak spread over one part of the pond, providing shade and a terrific branch that could be used as a diving board. All the guys my age loved to swim in the crystal clear waters that were chlorine free. If you came at the right time you could swim without a suit, which felt both exhilarating and a little bit dangerous.

The final bonus of Herrick's Hollow was that you could reach it by a fully paved road, a rarity in Wahissa County.

On that fateful Monday I left directly from Little Oslo as soon as the buzz was over, about 2:15. I traveled at a pretty good clip on my Schwinn, arriving shortly after 2:45. I laid the bike on the grass, spread out a blanket, and looked at the trees that lined the banks of the river. In addition to the big oak that served as a diving board, there were several willows and two birch. Up the bank, where we often lay on the grass, was a giant cottonwood tree, one of the few in the area. In the spring when the tree was shedding it was as if there had been a snowstorm. I gazed at it and wondered how old it was and how many swimmers it had witnessed.

A few feet away two boys were dog-paddling in the hole when I arrived. Seeing no girls, I decided it was a perfect day to skinny dip. I walked across the long branch of the oak tree and dove into the water, which was about eight foot deep. A year earlier when we were swimming, Tim tossed a nickel in the hole and shouted, "Call it." I yelled, "Tails," as we watched it drop slowly to the bottom. When it settled he triumphantly yelled, "Heads." The two of us could see it from the shore; the pond was that clear.

I swam for about an hour and shortly after the two other boys left decided to ride home. I heeded the advice "Never swim alone," particularly when diving off an oak tree.

The trip back to Wahissa was slower, since it was primarily uphill. I had biked about ten minutes when suddenly the front tire of my bike went totally flat. I had nothing with me to fix it, so I started to push the Schwinn toward town. I had gone no more than a few hundred yards when a bright yellow Cadillac pulled over. There was only one such car in the county, and it belonged to Ken Brown.

"Need a ride, Scout?" he yelled through an open window.

"That would be great," I responded.

Ken got out, opened the trunk, and helped me put my bike in its massive cavern.

I told him that I loved his car. "I don't think I've seen another one like it," I marveled.

"That's because there probably isn't another like it," he laughed. "These don't come in yellow, or as I prefer to call it, maize. I had it painted at a shop in La Crosse. It isn't hard to find in a big lot. The problem is, when you're driving a bit over the limit, it isn't hard to identify who ought to get a ticket." He laughed loud and long and then continued talking nonstop until we reached the outskirts of town. "Why don't we stop at my shop?" he said. "The Swenson boys are working on a Ford that refuses to start, but one of the other guys will find time to fix the tire. We can have something cold to drink in my office while we're waiting for them to work on the bike."

I accepted his offer and we walked into an amazing room filled with the heads of at least six animals. The ones that caught my attention were an antelope, a bear, and a sixteen-point buck. "Shot 'em myself. I'd rather hunt than eat," he said while patting his ample stomach, "and that's saying something."

He told a couple of hunting stories, and then he stopped and looked at me. "We've never talked before, but I feel like I know you. First, I do business with your dad and Jumpy. Fine men, both of them. Then, I've cheered for you at basketball games and shake my head in wonder at the way you run the bases for the Jewelers. When I was young I could hit the baseball, but I was slower than molasses in January. Then, there's church. Without the Joseph family I don't think we'd even have a choir."

I responded, "I see you, too. You're there almost every Sunday."

He nodded and said, "Two things I never miss, AA meetings and church. I need both to stay alive. David Hauge saved my marriage and maybe my life. That's a fact."

I must have looked puzzled, because he opened another soft drink and pulled out a container full of salted nuts. "Do you have any drinkers in your family, Scout? I mean, alcoholics?"

Shaking my head I said, "I don't think so."

"Well, somewhere along the way you're going to meet one. I'm going to tell you my story. It may be a bit more than you'd expect, but I have a need to tell it, and it may help you some day. You'd better get another Coke because, according to Dani, I tend to be a bit long-winded."

He took off his shoes and began. "Just over two years ago, May 16, 1950, my life was falling apart. Dani and I had separated a month or so earlier. I say we separated, but the truth is she kicked me out of the house and for good reason. Not only was I getting drunk two to three times a week, she discovered that I had been seeing other women. I hope you know that I'm not proud of this. I'm just telling you the honest truth. I work at telling the truth, because telling lies is one of the side affects of the drinking life."

He took a big drink of Coke and continued. "When she kicked me out I went to AA for the first time. I'm not sure why I went, because I didn't believe they could help me. I told the boys at AA that I could quit anytime I wanted, and that I would probably have this thing licked in a couple of weeks. They told me I was full of shit, pardon my French, which made me so mad I walked out. I vowed to stop drinking on my own. What could a bunch of drunks do to help me?"

Ken shook his head several times. "You don't have alcoholics in the family, but do you know much about alcoholism, Scout?"

I confessed that I did not.

"Well, it isn't something you can beat on your own. That is the painful lesson I soon learned. You need help. Lots of help. In the next couple of weeks I made that discovery. Finally, on May 16, I went by the house to pick up some clothes, and I broke down. I sobbed uncontrollably. I told Dani that I was the biggest screw-up in the world and that I wanted to change. 'You're the most important person in the universe to me,' I told her. 'I'll do anything if you'll take me back.'

"She said, 'The first thing I want you to do is see Pastor Hauge.'

"I protested before she said, 'Did you say, *Anything?*'

"Moments later she made the phone call. Pastor was at our house in fifteen minutes. Dani led him to the den, where I was sitting on the floor crying. 'I'll leave the two of you alone,' she said, and left.

"I cried for the first five or so minutes he was in the room. Then I finally got myself together enough to say something like this, 'Pastor, I've managed to screw up everything important in this world. I've messed up my life, probably lost my wife, and humiliated my children. Have you ever met a bigger screw-up than me?'

"Of course he wasn't about to answer a question like that. He just sat there quietly and looked at me, waiting for me to say something else. Finally I asked him a question, 'Do you know what this is all about?'

"He shook his head and said, 'I have no idea.'

"'Dani and I are separated,' I explained. 'Have been for four weeks. I'm living in one of the apartments behind Piggly Wiggly. She asked me to leave the same day she found out that I had been having an affair. I don't blame her for that. When I tried to tell her the other women meant nothing to me, she got even angrier. I don't blame her for that either. Now it sounds crappy even to me.'

"I paused to give the pastor a chance to yell at me, but he didn't say a word. I continued, 'Dani thinks most of this grows out of my drinking. She is probably right.' Again, I looked to see if I could figure out what he was thinking. I couldn't, so I kept on talking. 'I have a lot to work on, and I need to stop drinking. I think I can stop, but I'm going to need some help.'

"Then I started crying again. Finally I stopped long enough to say, 'Pastor, I used to be close to the Big Guy. When I was a boy I sang in a choir, and I prayed a lot. Not now. I spend all my time making deals. I make deals for property. I make deals to buy new stores. I make deals that will help me make other deals. When I'm making deals, I think only of me. I never think of the Big Guy. I don't even think of Dani or the kids. She says that I play monopoly for a living. Maybe she's right. Maybe I'm just trying to control Boardwalk and Park Place.'

"I started crying again. Finally, I stopped and looked at the pastor. I think I had a question in my eyes, because he asked a single question. 'How can I help you?'

"I said, 'Pray for me.'

"He told me that he would pray for me and help me to pray for myself. When I told him I didn't know how he said, 'I'll teach you.' And he did.

"He prayed and asked me to repeat what he said.

"Before he left he evidently told Dani that I should not be alone that night, because she told me I could sleep in the guest bedroom.

"The next day Pastor Hauge came to the house again. We had talked for several minutes before he asked me to go back to AA. I told him they had made me mad. He told me to go back and apologize. 'Getting better starts with admitting when you have been wrong,' he told me.

"Just before he left on that second visit he told me a story. 'During World War II a small Jewish family was captured by the Nazis, but allowed to live together in a two-room apartment in a concentration camp. Every week they received the most meager of rations: some grain, a bit of stale bread, and a few grams of lard. Yet they continued to observe the Sabbath. They managed to find a piece of candle and a little food. They said the Sabbath prayers and pronounced the Sabbath blessings.'

"'Finally, the candle burned out, and they couldn't find a replacement. The father knew he could wrap a piece of string in the lard and use it as a candle, but it would mean that his family would have to live with even less food. What should he do?'

"I was about to answer when he stopped me. 'Save it for tomorrow,' he said. 'I'll see you at 9:00 sharp at my office. We'll talk about the story then.'

"The next morning I was fifteen minutes late. He asked me, 'Are you usually late for things like this?'

"I thought for a moment and said, 'Almost always.'

"He said, 'It is impolite. It shows disrespect for the person you have asked to help you. Don't do it again.'

"He said it evenly, without any anger, but I was taken back. People never talked to me that way. At first I was a little burned, but the more I thought about it, I knew he was right. Later, I decided it was a part of my drinking life, and I wanted to change it.

"I said, 'Can we talk about the story?'

"'First,' he said, 'let's talk about your life. Where do you go from here? What is next?'

"I want to move back in with Dani and the kids," I began. "I acted like a fool. I've apologized for that. Once I move back in I'll alter some of the things I do at work.

"'Bad plan,' the pastor said.

"What's wrong with it?

"'Your number one goal is to get things back to the way they were long time ago, right?'

"Right!

"'Not good,' David said. 'You want to change your life only if it helps get you back in the house with the family. You're a sick man. You've made serious mistakes. You have to want health more than anything in the world. You have to want sobriety more than you want your wife. You have to want chastity more than you want your children. You have to feed your soul more than you feed your body.'

"I said to him, 'I don't know what you mean.'

"'Right now you want to be home more than you want to be sober. Being sober is the price you are willing to pay to get what you want. Right now you will stay away from adultery, but this is just a way to get back with your kids. In other words, it is a means to an end. You need to change, regardless of what it gains you. You want to talk to God primarily because it will help you reach your goals. Maybe you are listening to me only because it will help you reach your goals. In other words, you are using God, and perhaps me. You have to want God because he is God, not because he can get you back in the house! I wouldn't be surprised if you have a timetable all worked out for this.'

"I said, 'I'd planned to be back in three weeks, four weeks at the most, if that is what you mean.'

"He shook his head. 'Do you think this is just another business deal where the terms expire in thirty days? You are talking about your wife. You are talking about the life of your family. It may take you three years to gain back her trust.'

"Three years," I shouted! "I don't have that kind of time.

"For the first time he seemed upset with me, 'What do you have to do that is more important? Dani ought to change the locks and refuse to see you, because you don't get it. You are the man who has been spending time with a woman you have no great interest in. It is called adultery, Ken. It is the breaking of a promise. It's been going on for six years and you want to fix it in three weeks. You like food, and you know that good food takes time. It takes longer to prepare beef wellington than to fry a hamburger. Why are you in such a hurry?'

"I got up and walked around the room. Finally I said, 'You're right. I have nowhere else to go. I need to slow things down and let Dani think. I need to go to AA nearly every day, and I need to pray every day and worship every Sunday.'

"We didn't talk for several minutes. Finally, I said, 'Now about that story.'

"'How do you think it should end?'

"Yesterday I would have said, 'Eat the lard and forget the candles.' Today I'm not sure.'

"The pastor said, 'The man did wrap the lard around the string and then let it dry. When the Sabbath came his wife lit it, and they said the Sabbath prayers and gave the Sabbath blessing. When it was over his son was furious. "How could you waste what little lard we have to make a candle?" he cried.'

"'Son,' the father replied, 'without food we can live for several days. Without hope, we can't live for an hour.'

"Pastor Hauge sat and looked at me for several minutes before he rose and put his hand on my shoulder as he said, 'You are a man with a big appetite, Ken, both literally and figuratively. You gobble up properties and businesses in rapid succession. In the days ahead you are going to have to learn to control your hunger. If you want me, I'll help you. Remember, this is going to take time. Don't give Dani any timetable. Our goal is to help you get healthy, no matter how long it takes.'"

Ken Brown sat back in his chair and finished his Coke. I sensed that he was done talking.

"How long did it take?" I asked him.

"I went to AA later that day and apologized. I've been sober now for eighteen months. I do it one day at a time. Dani and I started dating again on our anniversary, June 3. We decided that we were ready to start over on the first of October. Now we celebrate two anniversaries."

I thanked him for sharing the story.

He responded by saying, "Thanks for listening. I probably need to tell it more than you need to hear it. It is one of the ways I stay clean."

By now it was 6 p.m. My bike was fixed and I headed home knowing I had a new friend.

Harden

On June 17 Aunt Elaine, who liked to refer to herself as Jumpy and Skip's much younger sister, called to say that our cousin Allen had just arrived for his annual summer visit. Allen lived with his parents in Wauwatosa, a suburb just outside Milwaukee.

Elaine's husband was killed in an accident on their small farm just north of Wahissa when I was ten. He had crawled under his tractor to fix something when the front-end loader fell on him, killing him instantly. Elaine, who taught school in Wahissa, decided to sell the cattle, rent the cropland to some neighbors, and stay on the farm with her dogs and horses.

Allen, who was nineteen, attended a small private college in the Milwaukee area. From the time he was thirteen he had vacationed with Elaine for two or three weeks each summer. This year Elaine hired him to help her fix up the place. His primary task was to paint all the buildings on her property, mow her huge lawn, and help her pick berries. During the early days of July, Elaine would frequently pick a crate of raspberries a day.

"Where can Allen get a Jewelers' schedule?" Elaine asked Mom. "He wants to see Jake play."

Mom told her that she had an extra and would leave it with Elaine's mother. She could pick it up the next time she came to town.

Tim and I looked forward to Allen's visits each summer. Though he was several inches shorter than either of us, we both thought of him as a big brother. We were enchanted with his tales of city life and his dating exploits, some of which even turned out to be true. In past summers he had been a frequent visitor to our home and even hung out with us at the Loft. We also loved to take him to Ham's Standard Station where his big city yarns drew quite a crowd.

. . . .

On June 18 the Jewelers traveled to Harden to play the Eagles. Harden, located on the Mississippi River, was a thriving little town that serviced all the farms in the area including those located on the Iowa side of the river. The team was sponsored by Farmer's Bank of Harden, which was owned by Keith Bridges. Bridges also owned a boat service on the river (Bridges to the Mississippi) and had developed a subdivision with at least twenty-five homes on a bluff overlooking the mighty river.

Harden paid more of its players than any other team in our conference. The key to the team was Dick Lombardo, a Minnesota transplant, who now worked as a cashier at Farmer's Bank. Lombardo was the real deal. The summer of 1951 he threw a two-hitter and a three-hitter against the Jewelers, overpowering them with his fastball and baffling them with his change-up. The Jewelers had only five hits in the three games he pitched; Buck had three of those five hits.

Smokey picked me up and drove to Harden, talking nonstop all the way. "One of these days I might move you to the one spot," he said. "We ain't takin' advantage of your speed right now.

"This Lombardo is tough. Beat us three times last year. We beat 'em the only time he didn't pitch. Big time fastball. Nasty change. Don't think you've seen anyone who has thrown better than Lombardo. Ya got to stay back on the change. He gets everybody lunging and they hit little piddly ground balls to the infielders. Stay back. That's what ya gotta do."

Smokey wasn't big on dialog. Like Moose, he talked and expected others to listen.

"Good hitter too," he continued. "Dead pull hitter. Ya gotta play him ten, maybe fifteen feet off the foul line. No further. If you cheat toward center you'll be chasing balls to your right all night long. Another thing. The lights in left field aren't the best. As soon as we arrive move around and see where the dark spots are. It may save you an embarrassment, or worse, a couple of runs. Since that screw up the first night you've played good left field. Make sure someone hits a few balls your way during warm-ups."

He took a plug of chewing tobacco and stuck it in his left cheek. "Ya cover a lot of ground. LaVern doesn't get around like he used to."

Outside of a few monosyllabic affirmations, "Uh-huh" or "Yeah," I didn't say anything during the thirty-minute trip. The reason for being quiet was not just that Smokey didn't give me much opportunity to talk, but I was riding in fear. When he talked he'd turn to look at me and the car would cross the centerline. I stopped looking at him, figuring that at least one of us ought to be watching the road. Thankfully, he was on the right side when we met oncoming cars. I was relieved when we arrived and grateful that I had a ride back with Mom and Dad.

Since we were the first Jewelers at the park. I put on my spikes and trotted out to left field. My first discovery was that Smokey had neglected to tell me there was no left field fence. Rather, there was a ten-foot pile of stacked lumber from the foul line into right center, courtesy of a sawmill that owned the property on the other side. I later found out that a ball that landed on top of the lumber was a home run. If it hit the lumber and bounced onto the field it was in play. If it bounced onto the lumber it was a ground-rule double.

Though the sun had not yet set, the lights were on. I walked around the outfield trying to guess where the dark spots Smokey described would be. The biggest shadow appeared to be in the left field corner. I looked up and saw that the light pole for that area, built for twelve bulbs, had four missing. As I moved toward center field the lighting was much improved.

Only five of the Jewelers had hit by the time the visiting team batting practice was over at 6:30. I jogged to left field after asking my friend Cam to hit a few fungoes. Cam, who pitched and played second base, was the only other seventeen-year-old on the team. "Hit a few that are up in the air so I can figure out the lights," I said to him. "Then hit a few line drives."

Cam did as I asked, and I shagged balls for about ten minutes, discovering I could see the line drives better than the towering fly ball. By this time the sun had set, and I found that I could see better standing in the dark, than entering into it.

The game began as a pitchers' duel. No Jeweler had reached base when I led off in the third inning. By watching Lombardo carefully I had made two notations. First, when he threw his fastball he tended to fall toward third base. Second, the first pitch to the six batters before me had been a fastball.

I entered the batter's box with a plan. He wound and threw a fastball on the outside part of the plate. I quickly dropped my bat and bunted the ball to the first base side of the pitcher's mound. Lombardo was too far toward third base to handle it, and by the time the second baseman came in from the edge of the infield grass I was on first base.

Smokey, standing in the third base coach's box, wiped his hand across his chest after he touched his chin. Lombardo went to the stretch and without throwing to first even once, threw a fastball for a strike. I hardly moved. Smokey flashed the steal sign again. If Lombardo was true to form, the second pitch would be a change. I preferred to run on the slower pitch.

I took only a two-step lead off first, as if I was staying put. When the pitcher turned his head to make his throw home, I took off. I slid into second without a throw.

The big right-hander stomped around the mound as if my steal of second was a personal insult. I looked over at the bench and couldn't believe my eyes. Smokey had the steal sign on again. I couldn't remember a time when anyone on the Jewelers had been given the green light from Smokey to steal third.

If I was surprised, the Eagle infield was shocked. With neither the shortstop or second baseman playing close to the bag, I got a huge jump and stole third easily. The catcher threw late and high, the ball rolling all the way to the left fielder. I scored standing up.

The score was tied when I came up with one out in the fifth. Both the third baseman and the first baseman played in a couple of steps, but I certainly didn't have bunt on my mind. After three fastballs in a row, I lunged at Lombardo's change and hit a weak grounder to short. I was thrown out by four steps.

In the fifth inning with the bases loaded, Lombardo hit a screeching line drive down the left field line. I had shifted to the dark spot as he came up and caught the ball over my head at the fence. The runner on third tagged and scored, but we avoided a big inning.

We tied the game in the seventh when LaVon hit a towering home run to left center. In the eighth I came to bat with Buck on third and the score knotted at 2. As I left the on-deck circle Smokey called me over, "Stay back on that change," he admonished me. That advice was easier given than obeyed.

On the first two pitches, both fastballs, I swung and missed badly. On the third pitch, a beautiful change, I slapped the ball weakly to third and was thrown out. The next batter struck out. It was our best and last chance to score more runs.

The second batter in the ninth was Lombardo. He caught one of Buck's fastballs on the meat of the bat and sent it over the stacked lumber in left field. All I could do was stand and watch it soar high over my head.

The Eagle's bench poured out on the field and greeted their big man as he crossed home plate. The 3–2 win gave Harden the undisputed league lead.

It was much quieter on the Jewelers' bench. We talked nearly in whispers, vowing to do better when they came to Wahissa.

I replaced my spikes and reminded Smokey that I was riding home with my parents. As I walked across the diamond on the way to Dad's waiting car, a big voice boomed out. "You're one up on me, kid." I looked to my right to see Lombardo grinning at me. "Mark this down. That was your last steal off me this season."

I walked toward the Eagle dugout where he was changing shoes. "I think you have your math wrong," I said quietly. "The score is 1–0, Harden. Personal statistics don't mean much when you lose. You played a terrific game."

His grin was gone. "The margin could have been bigger had you not caught that shot of mine in the fifth. How in hell you were playing me so close to the line I don't know. By the way, how old are you?"

"Seventeen. See you in Wahissa, July 9."

I saw him shake his head as I walked away. I scored a run and caught a tough ball in left field, but I had been handcuffed at the plate. There was a lot to learn before the season was over.

· · · · · · · ·

Candy, who had come to the game with Mom and Dad, saw me talking to Lombardo and came to meet me. She took my hand and walked slowly back to the car with me. "You played great," she told me.

She knew enough baseball to know that she was exaggerating, but I appreciated the kind words. I had a chance to either tie or win the game in the eighth and had failed miserably.

Dad started analyzing the game from the moment we got in the car. After a few miles Mom changed the subject and started talking quietly to him in the front seat. Candy and I figured this was her way of giving us some time alone, so we took it.

She kissed me quietly on the cheek and then said, "Dad told me that Silver spent over two hours with Lloyd yesterday. The Sheriff was hoping that he got a glimpse of Superman. Lloyd told him he didn't see anything. He asked Lloyd if he remembered seeing a shadow. When he didn't answer he asked him if the guy came at him from the right side or the left, any clue that might help in the future. Lloyd could provide no information whatsoever. Dad says it isn't even clear whether the assailant is right or left-handed, because Lloyd was battered on both sides of the face. The Sheriff told dad that Lloyd was probably drunk at the time and was wandering outside to take a leak. Superman came up behind him and caught him totally off guard."

"Did he have anyone who had threatened him in the past?" I asked.

"Lloyd told him that no one had ever warned him or threatened him," she said.

"So, it was a wasted two hours?"

"They don't think the time was wasted because Lloyd confirmed much of what they thought had taken place. When you try to solve a mystery, you want to know what is true and what is false. Since he didn't dispute anything, they figure what little they know is true."

I laughed, "Spoken like one who has read more than her share of whodunits."

Dad dropped me off at Candy's place. We were both tired and had to be at work early the next day. We stood behind the walnut tree in her backyard, making it impossible for anyone to see us from the house. A few kisses at the end of the day were wonderful.

As I walked home, however, I wasn't thinking about Candy. I was thinking about the challenge that Dick Lombardo had laid on me.

Marme

Mary Catherine Joseph, Marme, was our paternal grandmother and the warm center of the Joseph family. She and my grandfather, Dave, had been married fifty-three years when he died at age seventy-eight.

Tim, Karen, and I spent nearly as much time at Papa Dave and Marme's house as we did our own for a long stretch of our life. I was clearly her favorite grandchild, though both Tim and Karen also claimed that distinction. Poor deluded souls. When the three of us were together we frequently argued about our position in Marme's pantheon. Mark was too young to participate in our ridiculous debate.

On Thursday I went to the Loft after work and waited until Tim got home from the body shop. After he showered he drove us in his car to Marme's house.

We always knocked on Marme's door and then entered before she could answer. We generally went directly to the refrigerator, opened the door to the freezer, and removed the cookie container. I'm not sure why Marme froze all of the cookies she baked since none of them had a shelf life of more than two days, but we all knew the cookies were kept in a plastic container that read "Split Pea Soup." It was always full.

Every member of the Joseph family checked in on Marme two to three times a week, and most of them immediately visited the freezer in a successful search for cookies. Dad stopped on the way home from work five nights a week, and Jumpy frequently ate lunch with her. During school Tim and I usually visited her late afternoons on the way home after practice. Aunt Elaine, a teacher, spent more time with her mom than anyone else, usually arriving in the late afternoon five days a week on her way home from school and staying for supper.

Marme had been a legendary teacher in Wahissa. She spent thirty years teaching fourth grade, taking time off to raise her own children. Hardly a week passed without an adult telling someone in the Joseph family, "Marme was the best teacher I ever had." If we were out in public with her, someone would frequently appear out of nowhere to shake her hand and thank her for helping them develop their love of reading or math in fourth grade. She followed nearly all of her students through high school, attending their plays and games and being present when they graduated. Some summers she attended as many as eight weddings of former students. "Once a student of Marme, always a friend," we Josephs said. At graduation she presented every one of her students with a poem she had written about their class, along with a card and a crisp one-dollar bill.

She had a phenomenal memory and could recite long pieces of poetry and Bible passages. On patriotic occasions it took only a little encouragement and she would launch into Lincoln's Gettysburg Address, significant portions of his Second Inaugural Address, or the Declaration of Independence. She had committed to memory dozens of psalms and scores of religious verse.

When she retired, hundreds of students attended her party. Most of them returned a crisp dollar bill, though she also received a number of fives and tens. Those who gave the larger denominations explained that the dollars had earned interest over the years.

Though none of her grandchildren had her as a teacher, in a sense we were all her students. When we were young, almost all of her Christmas and birthday gifts to us were books. Sleepovers in her house always ended with her reading a story to us. When we were little she read while Papa Dave held us. She introduced us to *The Wind in the Willows* and Lewis Carroll's Alice books. Every grandchild had heard all of the stories from the Brothers Grimm and received a copy of the tales of Hans Christian Anderson. The Anderson stories were her favorites and consequently became ours as well.

· · · · · · ·

Tim parked his car on her driveway and sprinted for the back door, arriving only seconds ahead of me. He rang the bell and swung open the door with a single motion, as we always did. He was headed for the refrigerator when he yelled, "Hello. What is this?" He started to reach for a pot that was sitting over an open flame on Marme's stove.

"Don't touch it," I yelled.

He pulled back just in time to avoid grabbing the extremely hot handle. He turned off the heat and stepped back, coughing. We both almost choked from the smell of hot metal.

"She was probably heating some water and forgot the pot," I guessed.

Two different sets of issues concerned us about our beloved Marme. First, there were far too many incidents taking place that were similar to the heated pot. Jumpy reported that when he stopped by at noon he frequently discovered that she had left the milk out of the refrigerator since breakfast or had returned from the store and neglected to refrigerate the meat. When she missed church for the first time since childbirth because she thought it was Saturday, the family began taking turns picking her up on Sunday mornings. Dad seemed to worry the most and initiated numerous conversations with Jumpy and Elaine about their mother's future.

The second concern was that she was becoming more and more frail. She would take walks to the store or to destinations several blocks away and lack the energy to make it home on her own. She insisted on walking through the woods at Nielson Park because she was a passionate bird watcher and the woods was prime birding territory.

Dad, and to a lesser extent Elaine and Jumpy, were afraid that she would slip and fall and suffer a serious injury. No one in the Joseph family was able to give her advice that she would accept. The only people to whom she would listen regarding matters of her health and well-being were Pastor Hauge and the Doctors Quincy.

Marme believed Pastor Hauge was a man of profound wisdom and compassion. "He has," she was fond of saying, "a mature man's mind in a young man's body." We knew in a crisis we could ask him to counsel with our grandmother and she would heed his words.

Similarly, she respected Dr. David Quincy, who was the Joseph family doctor. If you wanted a physician in Wahissa you were either a patient at the Quincy Clinic or with Dr. Aaron Culbertson. The Joseph family chose the Quincys over Dr. Culbertson because Dr. Aaron was rather new to Wahissa. He had only been practicing in our city for twenty-two years.

David Quincy and his father, Dr. Richard Quincy, had been a part of the Wahissa scene for nearly forty years. Dr. Dave was in the same class as Jumpy, who is two years older than Dad. He attended both college and medical school in Madison and returned home to work with his father.

Though doctors in 1952 preferred that patients visit them at their office, they all ended their day by making house calls. Marme steadfastly refused to go to the clinic. Dr. Richard had delivered her babies at home and had treated her family for every imaginable illness in their own bedrooms. Home was where she expected to meet Dr. David Quincy who assumed more and more of his father's practice each year.

Though Marme could be stubborn, she did follow doctor's orders to the last detail. More than once she announced, "Why ask the doctor to visit if you're going to ignore his diagnosis and advice?"

That June the Joseph family was divided as to seeking outside advice. Dad thought that the family needed help immediately. Jumpy was an advocate of letting things play themselves out. "She's doing okay, for now," he said over and over. "Once she gets over this little hump she'll be fine." Dad urged a consultation with either Pastor Hauge or Dr. David Quincy before Marme had an accident, not after.

Though Jumpy pleaded the case for doing nothing, he did agree that in the long run his mother should move to the Calvary Home located just south of Wahissa. A complete retirement center owned by the Lutheran Church, Calvary Home had assisted-living apartments and a nursing home. Until that day came when Marme moved, there would be lots of visits from members of the family and lots of sleepovers.

We went in the living room and found Marme sleeping in her recliner, her Bible in her lap, and her long silver hair flowing gently over her shoulders. We kissed her cheeks simultaneously, and she woke with a start. She immediately greeted us with a smile and asked if we found the goodies.

We grinned, pulled the cookies out from behind our backs, and handed her some.

As we munched we sat in the chairs in front of her and answered her questions about our jobs. She wanted to know who had been in for breakfast or lunch and whose cars needed fixing. Like an ace reporter she generally had a follow-up question. She listened to our answers as if we were providing the most important information in the world. She asked about our friends and if we had seen any of her friends. She almost always asked how Pastor Hauge was doing, even though she had seen him the Sunday before.

I told her about the Hemmingway book that Mrs. Zahn gave me. "It was rather dull," I said. "I only scanned fifty pages. The old man just sits by himself and talks to the fish."

"Jake," she said slowly, "Mrs. Zahn is one of the best teachers Wahissa has ever had. Listen to her. She has great instincts and great insights. I haven't read the book, but if Lucille Zahn thinks you will gain by reading it, read it."

After a bit of silence the conversation turned, as did most conversations in the summer time, to the subject of baseball. Dad and Jumpy, like their father, Papa Dave, followed every move of the Cubs. As I mentioned previously, Tim and I shared their passion for the Cubbies until the general manager committed the unforgiveable sin of trading Andy Pafko to Brooklyn. As a result, we became Cardinals fans. The great advantage of this switch was that we actually began to cheer for a team that won baseball games and appeared in the postseason.

Marme, however, was a fanatic devotee of the White Sox. Her college roommate at the University of Wisconsin hailed from the South Side of Chicago and facilitated her conversion. She had visited her roommate in Chicago on several occasions and attended games in Comiskey Park. A few hours in the hallowed ground of Comiskey had made her a White Sox fan forever.

I write these words on a date close to my fifty-third birthday. My sons and I have visited nearly every baseball park that currently exists. I have talked to hundreds of people who are baseball fans. I have met Cardinals fans who live in Missouri, Iowa, both Dakotas, and Wisconsin. The same is true of Cub fans. The Cubs draw followers from all over the Midwest. Yet I have met only one person who did not grow up in the Chicago area who passionately follows the White Sox. That one person is my grandmother. She was not just a casual fan, she was, as the word *fan* suggests, fanatic.

Mornings during baseball season, Marme followed a simple liturgy. Get up at 6:00 a.m. and go directly to the living room for morning prayers. By 6:15, after she plugged in the coffee, she took a twenty-minute walk. When she returned home she picked up her morning newspaper and immediately read the sports. When asked why she read the sports before she read the front page, she said, "I read the sports first so I can start with some good news." A few years later Earl Warren, the Chief Justice of the Supreme Court, said almost the same words. Neither of them would have answered that way had they lived through the sports scandals of latter years.

Marme's reading in the summer began with the box score from the day before. Her hero in 1952 was a young Cuban born player, Minnie Minoso. A day did not pass without her announcing how Minnie Minoso had fared. Minnie charmed all White Sox fans, including my grandmother.

Though I never became a rabid White Sox fan I shared my

grandmother's adoration of Minnie. He was only twenty-four in 1952, but she predicted a great future for her hero to all who would listen. Not even Marme would have guessed that Minnie's playing career would last as long as it did. He is the only player to have appeared in a major league game spanning five separate decades—1940s–80s. He hit safely in a game at age fifty-four. Unfortunately, Marme would not be alive to witness Minoso's best years.

Marme did not like the Cubs for two reasons. One, she believed that the White Sox were the team of the working class and the Cubs, owned by the Wrigleys, were the team of the snobs. Second, she disliked their radio announcer. Radio reception in the hills around Wahissa was limited to only a few signals in addition to our own station, WHAS. Many people in Wahissa listened daily to clear-channel station WGN in Chicago. It generally came in as if they were broadcasting a block away. WGN's broadcast of Cubs games was led by Bob Wilson, an announcer who was the king of the homers. In Marme's opinion the way he began, "It's a beautiful day in Chicago," was acceptable, but his cheering for the home team crossed the barrier of good taste. Each day Wilson would coo, "We don't care who wins as long as it is the Cubs." Marme preferred Jack Brickhouse, the White Sox announcer, who she claimed was fair and balanced.

Marme never tired of trying to convince her sons that they were cheering for the wrong Chicago team. "The Cubs are pitiful," she told them over and over again. "Take away Dee Fondy and they don't have a single infielder who can hit for power or average. Hank Sauer is as old as I am." (Actually he was thirty-five).

It was true that Hank, one of our favorites, was running out of gas. Though he had a great '52 season (37 home runs and 121 RBI), in three more years he would hit only .211, hit 12 home runs, and have 28 RBI.

As always, Tim and I had a great time with Marme. Yet, as we frequently did in the summer of 1952, we left with a profound sense of sadness. There were signs that the wheels were beginning to come off Marme's wagon.

The handle to her pot was cool by the time we left, though the bottom now had a crack. We took the pot with us to show Dad and Jumpy. We could replace the pot, but of course, we couldn't replace Marme.

Reading Hemingway

Our next two games were fairly easy ones. Smokey started Cam at home against Ft. Price on a Sunday and kept him in for five innings. When they scored their first run in the top of the sixth he brought in Chris, our only left-hander. With the score 8–1 at the end of seven, Smokey had Mo finish the game. Our coach was full of smiles. We had won a game, and he was able to rest his big starter.

The victory over Brownstown on June 25 was even easier. Our big first baseman got hot and had three doubles and four RBI. I scored three times and stole two bases. Smokey told me for the third time, "One of these days I'm going to move you to the lead-off position. We've got to utilize your speed." I figured the only reason he didn't make the move is that he knew that Sherm Lewison, our second baseman, would be upset that he was being moved from the one slot. Sherm, who had led the team in hitting the past three years, had started the season in a severe batting slump. Unlike past years he wasn't drawing walks. In addition he was in a consistent foul mood. Once cheery with a big smile, he now came to the ballpark with a scowl on his face.

On the Thursday after the Browntown game, shortly before noon, Mrs. Zahn walked into Little Oslo wearing a blue suit with a hat to match and sat at a booth in my section. I went to take her order and she said, "Before I have lunch I would like to know what you think of *The Old Man and the Sea*."

I told her I had to wait on another customer, but I'd talk to her about the book in just a minute. The truth was that I wasn't sure how to tell her what I really thought about it. I wanted to be honest, but I didn't want to hurt her feelings. She was hoping that I would like it, and if I told her it was boring I was afraid she would be upset.

I took my time in the kitchen thinking what I would say and then realized I didn't have time to prevaricate. I walked directly to her table and said, "Mrs. Zahn, I am honored that you selected a book for me to read this summer. You are a terrific teacher, and I plan to take senior English from you, but the truth is, I found *The Old Man and the Sea* dreadfully boring. It is the slowest book I have ever read. I laid it down after I became convinced the old man was going to sit in the boat with that fish until the summer was over. I never finished it."

Mrs. Zahn stared at me for several seconds and then a huge smile spread across her face. Without looking at the menu she said, "Jacob, I'll have an order of Swedish pancakes." As I left for the kitchen I was certain that I heard her laughing.

When I reached the kitchen I tried to remember if I had ever heard that sound from her before. I recalled her standing straight and tall in a perfectly tailored dress before our English class with a slight smile on her lips, but I could not recall her laughing.

My palms were moist and my heart was beating wildly by the time I gave Cookie the order. Was she laughing with me or at me? Thankfully my entire section of the restaurant was filled with folks demanding my attention, which didn't allow me time to fret too much about what I just said to Mrs. Zahn.

When her order was ready I returned to her table, certain that she would have more to say. I was not disappointed.

"Jacob," she said slowly, "I have two things to say. First, I'm disappointed that you did not like the book. I hoped it would interest you. It is clearly Hemmingway's best work thus far. After a promising start as a novelist, his last two books were quite disappointing. I think with the book I gave you he returns to his place as one of the country's premier writers. This book has a chance to be a classic. Not all books are full of action. Unlike say, *The Caine Mutiny, The Old Man and the Sea* deserves to be read slowly. Slow reading allows you to think about the symbolism that he uses."

Mrs. Zahn looked thoughtful before she continued. "I don't expect most juniors," she paused before she continued, "I should say, seniors, to appreciate Hemmingway. I just thought that with what is happening to your grandmother, you might approach it differently."

I must have looked baffled, because she explained. "Jacob, Marme is one of my heroes. She is, or ought to be, an inspiration to everyone who ever has spent a day teaching in Wahissa. I love her with all my heart. I know how much your family adores her. In a way your friendship with Marme is similar to the friendship between the boy and the old man. Not many people your age have cared deeply for an older person. I thought that you might find some parallels. I hoped you would find yourself in the book. Obviously I was wrong.

"I have a second comment. You have Marme's forthrightness. She would be proud of your answer. If she didn't like something, she told you. It appears you are a chip off the old block. I hope this honesty carries over into my classroom. We have far too many students who appear to have no opinion, choosing to guess what the teacher is thinking and then parroting it. If you do end up in senior English this fall please speak your mind. By the way, I'd like coffee, black, with my pancakes."

· · · · · · ·

After the buzz I rode my bike to the park where I ran wind sprints. I did fifteen sets at forty yards before I ran the hill. I lost track of the number of sprints because my mind was on Marme and Hemingway.

I arrived at our house about 3:30, found the Hemmingway book, and headed for the Loft. Before I began to read I looked out the window and wondered if what I was about to do was because Mrs. Zahn had convinced me it was a good read or because she had shamed me. I wasn't sure and opened it. Though I began with uncertainty, I knew that I didn't want to be like most juniors or seniors. Maybe I was reading it to convince myself that I wasn't average. Did that make me a snob? I didn't know.

I looked at the book and was surprised it was only 127 pages. I remembered it being much longer. As I began reading I was amazed how little I remembered about the book, though it was less than three weeks earlier that I had read it. I must have had my brain in neutral. The first thing I noted was that the friendship between Santiago, the old man, and the boy was special. Mrs. Zahn was right, it was similar to the relationship Tim and I had with Marme.

Putting the book down I went to the window and looked toward Marme's house. I had never thought about my friendship with my grandmother. Didn't all grandsons love their grandparents? Perhaps not.

When I picked up the book again I read the section about the old man's admiration for the "Great DiMaggio." I looked to the cabinet where Tim and I stored our baseball cards. We had an entire section reserved for the Yankee Clipper.

At 5:30 Tim climbed the ladder and plopped himself in his overstuffed chair. "Crash needed an extra set of hands with a Chevy this afternoon," he said with a sigh. "I bet I'll put in fifty hours this week. The work is backed up and people are anxious to get their cars back."

"You'll be so rich by the end of the summer that you'll be able to buy the garage from Crash," I teased.

"I don't bank as much of my check as you do," Tim countered. "A night with Candy is inexpensive compared to the girls I date. I always figure that the first time out you have to impress them. Do you put your entire check in your savings account?"

I wasn't comfortable talking about money, but I decided to tell Tim what I was doing. "I bank my entire check and a bit of my tip money. I spend the rest of the tip money," I told him. "But you are right, a date with Candy is pretty inexpensive."

"You're making a buck an hour, right?" Tim asked.

"Right, but I promised Moose I wouldn't tell anyone. That's all he is paying Charlotte. What does Crash pay you?"

"Eighty-five cents an hour," Tim said. "I think I ought to be making a buck."

"You are worth at least a dollar an hour," I agreed. "You work harder than I do. You ought to talk to Crash about it."

"I don't have any idea how much Crash makes, so it isn't easy talking about money," Tim said. "I'm grateful that I have a job and that he allows me flexible hours." We sat without speaking for several minutes. Then I closed the book, noting that I was on page seventy. I knew I could finish it in another hour and a half. As I put the book down Tim saw the cover and said, "I thought that book was totally boring."

"I was wrong," I confessed. "The truth is, it's fascinating, but confusing. One minute I think it is a religious book with the old man as a Christ figure. The next moment I think it is a totally secular book about how we all have to struggle against the cruel world. I'm going to finish it tonight. You want to read it when I'm done?"

Tim shook his head. "Sounds to me as if you were right the first time. The whole thing sounds boring. You know my theory—summer is a perfect time to avoid reading books. If God wanted us to read in the summer he never would have made eighty degree days without clouds in the sky. By the way, I think supper is ready at your house. Do you want to go to the movies tonight? They've got a John Wayne film, *The Quiet Man*, playing."

"No," I answered. "I'm going to finish the book and then go over and see Candy."

· · · · · · ·

When I walked in the kitchen I could see that supper was ready, but Mom and Dad were not. The dining room table was filled with piles of 45 rpm records. My dad had been near Duck Lake and heard that Harmony Music had a sale of used discs. Harmony

Music supplied bars and restaurants with jukeboxes all over the three-country area. A couple of times a year they held a sale of records they no longer needed for their machines. Sometimes people stopped selecting the record, but more frequently they had simply bought too many. Dad had picked up a stack of 45s that included "Tennessee Waltz" by Patti Page, "Mona Lisa" by Nat King Cole, "Cry" by Johnny Ray, and two of Hank Williams favorites, "Cold Cold Heart" and "Hey Good Lookin.'" Mom didn't care much for country music, and they were sorting out the ones they'd keep and the ones Dad would drop off for Jumpy and Melinda.

It didn't look like they could finish dividing the records before we ate, so Mom moved the meal into the kitchen. We were having steak. The truth was, we had steak three or four nights a week. Beef was inexpensive in our area. Each fall Dad and Jumpy bought a beef cow from the Zitzners and "went halves" on it. We had roast, steak, or hamburger six nights a week.

On the rare occasions that we went out to eat we always ordered chicken, which seemed a major change from our diet. On Christmas and Easter we had ham. The rest of the time our diet was centered on beef.

Those were the days before every home had a freezer. We rented a freezer at the Wahissa Locker, where they butchered the beef and then cut and packaged it to fit our families—three steaks per package for us and five for Jumpy's crew. In addition to steak there was roast and lots of hamburger. When the locker folks finished their work, Dad and Jumpy would go down and sort through the packages. Dad said it was only fair that Jumpy got more because he had a larger family, though I'm not sure Mom agreed.

I finished my steak and excused myself, heading to my room to finish *The Old Man and the Sea*. It took me longer than I expected to read the final fifty-seven pages, so it was a bit late when I parked my bike at Candy's place. She was in the backyard playing catch with a couple of the neighbor boys. It was a pity that we didn't have girls' teams in 1952. Candy would have been a star in basketball and softball.

When the boys went home and we were walking toward her

house, Candy's dad drove into the yard in his brown police car. She ran over and kissed him and asked, "Did you have a good day?"

"Spent the day working on the Vang case," he said shaking his head. "It was almost two weeks ago and we are no closer to solving it than we were the night it happened. But," he said stretching, "I don't need to do police work at home."

After he went into the house Candy and I found our places on the porch, in a corner where neither the neighbors nor her parents could see us. I kissed her before I asked her the question of the night, "What do you know about *The Old Man and the Sea?*"

"I thought you gave up on that book," she said with a grin.

"That was before I talked with Mrs. Zahn today." Slowly I told her about my encounter with the teacher and then began to summarize the book.

"The book is about this old Cuban fisherman Santiago and a giant marlin," I began. "The old man has gone nearly three months without catching a fish, which leaves him broke. He is so unlucky that the parents of his fishing companion refuse to let their son, who is called 'the boy,' fish with him. They tell the boy that he has to go out with fishermen who are successful.

"The boy, however, is totally dedicated to the old man and visits him at night and manages to get food to him in the morning. They love to talk baseball. The old man's favorite player is Joe DiMaggio, who he calls 'the great DiMaggio.'

"Most of the book, it is only 127 pages, is about this one fishing expedition. The old man leaves one morning and rows far from shore. Too far. While he is out he hooks the biggest fish he has ever caught, a fish so big and so strong that it tows the boat out further. The old man struggles against this fish for two days and two nights."

Candy interrupted, "So what does Hemmingway write about during this two days and two nights? It sounds boring."

"It really isn't, once you get into the story. He tells us what the old man is thinking and describes the action of the old man against the fish. This kind of fishing isn't like throwing a bobber out and catching a bluegill. The old man fishes with his entire body. He uses his arms and his torso. Sadly, he isn't prepared for a three-day battle. He doesn't have enough food or water or equipment."

"So," Candy asked, "this is a big macho thing. Man against fish. Hemmingway is this big hunter who wrote about fighting bulls and living in the wilderness. He's a boxer and a tough guy."

"This book isn't like that," I explained. "The old man respects the fish. He admires him and talks to him like a worthy adversary. There is a different tone in this book than in *The Sun Also Rises*."

"How does it end?" Candy asked, eager for my long story to draw to a close.

"Are you sure you want to know the ending? You may want to read it yourself."

"Jake, I've told you a dozen times that knowing the ending doesn't bother me," she said.

It was true. Candy was the only person I knew who often read the last chapter of a mystery long before she finished the book. She said she didn't want to invest her interest in people who were going to be dead. She also claimed that knowing the ending slowed her down and let her appreciate the style of the writer.

"Okay. The old man finally lands the fish and kills it by stabbing it with a harpoon. He straps it to the boat and heads home, dreaming of the money he will make when he sells it. Then the book really gets eerie.

"On the way into shore, sharks begin to attack. They had followed a trail of blood left by the marlin. Santiago fights them off and kills a number of them, maybe five, but in the end the sharks devour all but the head of the marlin. When the old man gets to land he is so weak he can hardly carry the mast. Finally, he falls asleep in his shack. He remains an unlucky fisherman."

"What did Mrs. Zahn say about the novel," Candy inquired?

"She told me she thought I would like it because it was about the friendship between an old person and a young person, kind of like my friendship with Marme. And she suggested it was filled with metaphors, things I would only understand if I read it slowly and thoughtfully."

"And?"

"She's right. It is full of metaphors, but it is a very confusing book. For example, the old man talks about how much he needs salt, while he is surrounded by salt. If he only lets some salt water dry on something he'd have all the salt he wants. You'd think a fisherman would know such things."

Candy said, "I have two things I want to say to you. First, Mrs. Zahn has seen what we all see—you have a very special relationship with your grandmother. In fact, I don't know anyone who connects with their grandmother like you do. She is the reason that you are secretly thinking about being a teacher. Am I right?"

I thought for a moment. "I guess I am thinking about being a teacher. And a coach. Perhaps Marme is the reason. I've never thought about it."

"The second thing I want to say is Hemmingway is sharper than you are giving him credit for. If collecting salt was as easy as you make it out to be his character would have done it." She paused and then said, "But you have something more to say, don't you?"

I told her I did. "Hemmingway is forever comparing Santiago to Christ. He describes Santiago's cry as a noise a man might make when a nail goes through his hand and into wood. Obviously he wants us to think of Jesus. The old man carries the mast the way Jesus carried his cross. He sleeps face down with his arms out straight and his palms up. More Jesus. What I don't know is if his comparisons are positive or negative. I'm not sure where he is going with it. The whole book ends up negative. Is he suggesting that the entire life of Jesus is negative? I read a prayer of Hemmingway once that went, 'Our Nada, Our Nothing, who art in heaven. Nada is your name.' There certainly is no resurrection in this story, no hope. The old man fails. Life is the craps."

"Are you going to talk to Mrs. Zahn?"

"I don't think so. I'm going to think about it, and if you read it, I'm going to talk with you about it. How is that for a plan?"

Candy said, "I have a better plan. My plan is for you to forget the book for a few minutes, close your eyes, and kiss me. I think this whole conversation has gone on too long."

When it came to great intellectual arguments Candy was a very practical woman.

Kid Hill

riday after work I rode my bike over to see Marme. I wanted to get there early because Candy and I were going to a movie that night. Three blocks from her house I saw Marme sitting under an oak tree in someone's front yard. Even before I got off my bike I called out to her, "Hello sweetheart. How are you doing?"

I dismounted and approached her. It was then that I could see that she was quite pale. She looked at me with a vacant stare that I had never seen before. For a moment I was afraid that she didn't know who I was. "Do you know me?" I asked.

She took two deep breaths and spoke while shaking her head. "Jake, I'm exhausted. Don't bother me with any ridiculous questions."

I started to mount my bike again and go for help. "You stay right here and I'll go get Jumpy to give you a ride home," I told her.

"You'll do no such thing," she said, her voice rising to command. "I'll sit here until I've regained my strength and then you can walk home with me."

We sat under the oak tree for several minutes while the color seemed to slowly return to her cheeks. Then she said, "Give me a hand so I can get up."

I did as I was directed. Before she began to walk a gleam came to her eyes. "Give me a ride home on your bike, the way Karen rides with you."

I protested, "Marme, Karen usually has shorts on when she rides behind me. You have a dress." She always wore a dress.

"Is there anyone in town who will be offended by looking at the legs of a seventy-eight-year-old woman? There are bigger problems to face than this."

I mounted my bike and Marme pulled up her dress, climbed on the back, and wrapped her arms around my waist. I showed her where she could put her feet. Though she shifted her weight a couple of times, we managed to traverse the last few blocks without incident. That night when Mom brought her dinner, Marme told the whole story laughing all the way and managing to ignore the minor detail—that she was worn out from her walk.

Candy and I had planned to go to a movie, but when Mom was talking to Marme in the living room I called to tell her I wanted to stay with my grandmother that night. She immediately told me that was the right thing to do and asked if she could join us. I thought it was a terrific idea and urged her to come immediately after supper. "Marme has an early bedtime, I reminded her."

By the time we ate supper Marme was laughing and telling stories. She threw her arms around Candy when she arrived as if she was a long lost friend. Again, she told of riding home on my bike, ignoring any mention of her exhaustion. Soon she announced she was tired and went to bed, pausing long enough for full hugs.

Candy and I sat on the front porch and talked until after ten. She had borrowed the family car, so I kissed her good night and headed to bed myself.

That night, in the room next to Marme, I cried shamelessly. We were slowly losing the most wonderful woman I had ever met.

The next morning I found her puttering around the kitchen when I came downstairs at 5:40. "No need to make breakfast for me," I told her. "I'll grab something at Little Oslo." I kissed her good-bye and headed for work, knowing that her two sons would be with her most of the morning.

. . . .

When I walked into Little Oslo that Saturday, June 28, exactly two weeks after The Bang at Vang, I knew something was wrong before I got through the door. The air was heavy and the restaurant was eerily quiet. I wasn't sure what the problem was until I looked over at the Silver Table and saw the Sheriff. He was at least twenty minutes early, and he sat staring at the floor.

I quickly put on a blue apron, grabbed a pot of coffee, and poured him a cup. "Do you want the combo?" I asked.

He didn't hear me until I repeated myself, and then said, "Sure. Whatever."

A few minutes later as his table began to fill I heard the voice of one of his friends, "Another bad night, Sid?"

"Another beating," the Sheriff sighed.

"At Vang?" someone asked him.

"No," this was near the Paradise Dance Hall. "Same M.O. Some pour bastard got the piss beat out of him. Broken arm, mutilated fingers. His face is a mess. About the only difference was that it was his left hand this time." Before anyone could ask, he answered the big question by shaking his head and saying, "Not a clue."

"Anybody we'd know?" Ted Towne asked.

"When I was a deputy I arrested him once for disorderly conduct. Name's Richard Hill. He goes by the name of Kid. You probably remember him. He played some ball for Duck Lake a few years ago."

"Fine ballplayer, left-hander," Ted Towne recalled, "with a terrible temper. I remember he almost got in a fight with Buck when a fastball drove him back from the plate. After he blew off his mouth Buck threw the next pitch right at him. He bailed out just as the ball broke across the plate for the third strike. Prettiest screwball I've ever seen," he said slapping his knee. "Seems to me he screamed at Buck for the next fifteen minutes."

There was an awkward silence as Ted discovered what everyone else knew, this wasn't the right occasion for a baseball yarn.

The whole room was again listening. "You figure it was the same guy, right?"

Sheriff Sid nodded. "Sure looks like it. Trouble is we aren't a lot closer to solving the Lloyd Swenson beating. No witnesses have stepped forward and Superman has left no evidence behind. We're still waiting for an analysis from the state crime lab. As for Lloyd, the poor bum is still a month away from getting back to work."

Again the room was quiet. About then I delivered his order. Before he cut into his stack he sighed and said, "Well, since Paradise is fifteen miles from Vang it means we'll widen the search. We had our eye on a couple guys in the Vang area. We didn't have much on them except past behavior and strength. Now we'll have a few more suspects."

. . . .

That night the entire Joseph clan gathered for Jumpy's birthday. Aunt Elaine and Allen picked up Marme, who arrived looking fit and cheery. One of Dad's cousins, Tom Joseph, a carpenter, came with his wife Lil and their two kids. He told everyone that he knew Kid Hill. "He worked on my crew for almost a year."

Tom's wife, Lil, a rotund woman who always wore dresses with bright flowers, had a habit of finishing her husband's sentences. "Kid was poison so Tom fired him. He was forever turning one man against another. He is a mean fellow, isn't he Tom?"

Tom nodded. "I can't imagine many people, except his wife, feeling too bad for him."

Lil continued, "Suzy. Her name is Suzy. Maybe she'll have a few nights of peace, too. He is a bear to live with, and that's God's own truth. Isn't that true, Tom?"

Tom nodded.

"It would seem," Dad began.

After an appropriate time my mother prompted, "It would seem ..."

"That Superman," he sighed, "is picking the riff raff to pummel."

"To pummel?" Jumpy laughed. "I hate it when a man is pummeled. How many times a year do I read about a serious pummeling in the paper." Everyone laughed with Jumpy, including Dad.

After we ate I pulled cousin Tom aside and asked a few more questions about Kid. "He's worked for nearly every carpenter in the county," Tom said. "No one keeps him for any length of time. He's a good craftsman; it is just that he can't work with other men, and no one can supervise him. He always knows better than they do. He always knew better than me, and I was fifteen years in the business. I heard he's found a crew in La Crosse where he has been working for several months. Can you imagine driving all the way to La Crosse to work five to six days a week?"

When Lil saw that we were talking she came over to join us. "Were you talking about Kid?" she asked.

When we nodded she looked at Tom and asked, "Did you tell him about the time Kid brought his son to work?" Tom shook his head. "It was a disaster," she said vigorously. "For some reason the boy, about four at the time, had to be with his dad. Maybe the mother was sick. Anyway, Kid brought him to work and kept him in the car with the windows rolled down. Tom can tell you, he left the job every half hour and yelled at the boy. He looked like a scared little rabbit, didn't he Tom?"

As Tom nodded Mom came by and invited us to join Jumpy at the horseshoe pit. Jumpy loved to pitch horseshoes, so that was the way most parties at his house ended. Dad and Jumpy preferred to play as a team. Allen and I were the last team to challenge them. I don't know why we bothered, because they threw six or seven ringers in a row, while we didn't manage a single point.

Just before the party broke up I biked over to Candy's place. She was sitting in the back porch swing with a book on her lap. Her folks were in bed.

"I was hoping you'd come by," she said kissing me on the check.

"How was the party?"

"It was okay," I told her. Then noticing her red eyes I asked, "What's wrong?"

"When I went to the library I talked to Sharon, who works in the County Treasure Office. Her sister Suzy is married to the guy that got beat up."

"Kid Hill," I said.

"Right. She says that Suzy, who is a teacher's aide over at Harden, doesn't work in the summer. Now that Kid is banged the rest of the family will have to help her buy food and pay the rent. It will be weeks before Kid, who is a carpenter, will be able to earn a paycheck. When I first heard about the beating it seemed to be a long way away. Suddenly it feels very close."

I nodded and thought for a moment before I spoke, "I learned more about the beating at the party."

Candy wiped her eyes and signaled me to continue.

"Kid used to play ball with Duck Lake. He also worked for Dad's cousin Tom, who had to fire him. He thinks he has been working in La Crosse."

Candy added to our growing pile of information, "Dad says that Sheriff Silver thinks these are random beatings. He thinks the perpetrator may be some city kid who gets his kicks out of beating someone up. One night he is in Vang, the next he is in Paradise. Or it could be some big tough local guy who likes to fight. He is checking with the sheriff departments in the surrounding counties to see if there is someone who has a history of fighting. He is even doing some research on ex-boxers. Anyway, he thinks the whole thing is random."

"I don't buy it!" I said a bit too loud.

Candy quieted me by pointing at her parent's bedroom and reminding me they were already in bed. "Why not?"

"I think the two victims are too much alike for this to be a recreational beating. Both are bad asses. Both of them are mean, and they both have a hatful of enemies. If that isn't the thing that ties these together then there is baseball. They were both pretty good at it. Maybe there is a baseball connection. I don't know which one it is, but it seems that they have too much in common to be random."

"Here is what I'm wondering about," Candy said. "The last beating wasn't too far from the Paradise General Store, right?"

"Right."

"Well, that is where that Buck guy, the hot head who pitches for your team, lives. Right?"

"I can't imagine Buck beating two men senseless," I protested.

"Really? I watched him punch out a player from Harden a couple of years ago. He looked to me like he was perfectly capable of beating the tar out of two guys he doesn't like. Dad agrees."

"Your dad talked to you about Buck? Does that mean that Buck is a suspect?" I asked.

"Buck is one of the suspects," Candy said quietly, again pointing to her parent's bedroom window, which was slightly open. "As I said, they are looking for big strong men, men who have a history of fighting."

"Well," I said, "that's a pattern. They're looking for fighters. I can't believe they don't see other patterns. Even Dad says that Superman is beating up on the riff raff. That's seems to be the key pattern—men with a snarly background. Why don't you ask your dad if they are making a list of mean ex-baseball players?"

Instead of answering me she threw her arms around me and kissed me. "I wish we could do something to help. Keep your ears open at Little Oslo. It isn't just men who are being hurt by these beatings. They have wives and children who will suffer as well." She then pulled me close and gave me a wonderful kiss.

We had about an hour together on the back porch with absolutely no talking, until I tried to put my hand where she didn't want it. She spoke briefly, but emphatically, "No, Jake."

That brought the evening to a close. As I walked home I thought about Candy. She was kind. We always had fun, whether we were alone or with other people. I had mixed feelings about the limits she imposed, but maybe she was right to do so. All I knew is that I was frustrated.

By the time I reached home and climbed into bed my frustration was gone, and I was no longer thinking about Candy. I was thinking about something Candy said. I was thinking about the families who were losing their breadwinner. I also thought about Buck and wondered whether he knew either Lloyd or Kid. They all played ball. Did their relationship go beyond the ball field? Both Lloyd and Kid had a Paradise address. Did they shop at the Paradise General Store? Perhaps something had gone wrong at the store, or perhaps Buck had a score to settle from the past. Either way, Buck could be righting old wrongs. I would have to learn more about him.

· · · · · · ·

Smokey wasn't big on team meetings, but he pulled everyone together before the Duck Lake game. "Three weeks ago we were playing pretty good ball," he said. "We were taking an extra base. We were hitting our cutoffs. We were moving runners over with less than two outs. None of that has been happening lately. Although we've won the last two games we've gotten sloppy. Talk to each other out there. Keep your head in the game. When you leave first base and you can't see who is handling the ball, keep your eye on the third base coach. Finally, watch the bench for signals. We missed a couple steal signs last week and at least one hit and run. You've got to check every pitch.

"We've got a crucial two-game set. Tonight's game and the one on Wednesday will go a long way toward determining the league winner. Let's all play with our heads up."

What Smokey wanted and what happened were almost polar opposites. Against the Mallards we played with our heads down. Sherm Lewison singled to lead off the first, getting a rare hit on a pop fly that fell just out of the outreached hands of the second baseman. He promptly got picked off first base.

Two innings later our shortstop, Gene Thomas, scored when he tagged at third on a fly ball off the bat of LaVon Zitzner. The Mallards appealed the play and Gene was called out for leaving third base too soon.

In the seventh inning, with two outs, a ball was hit to third. Our third baseman fielded it clean on one hop and fired the ball to second for an easy force-out, but Sherm wasn't on the bag and the ball went all the way into right field where LaVon fielded it and tried to throw the runner out at third. The ball went over the third baseman's head and both runners scored.

I did nothing to help the team that night. I had a chance to throw out a runner trying to stretch a double into a triple and threw the ball wide of the bag. At the plate I popped up, struck out on a pitch out of the strike zone, and hit the ball weakly back to the pitcher. This was the first game of the summer where I didn't get on base at least once.

Smokey was livid and warned the team that, "We're going to have to make some changes on this team."

I rode home with Mom, Dad, and Candy nursing my wounds from the loss. Candy, who normally got involved with Dad in post-game analysis, didn't have a single thing to say about the game. Instead she talked quietly with me about her new assignment that started the next day at the court house. "I'm working in Judge Swiggum's office for the next three weeks," she said quietly.

"You don't expect to see much of the Judge, do you?" I asked.

"Last summer he talked to me several times during the first week I subbed in his office. During the next two weeks I hardly saw him. He arrived in the morning, asked me for a list of phone calls from the day before, and retired to his chambers. My phone lights up when he is on a line. During those ten days he never made or accepted a phone call. Not a single one. Every day, shortly after 11:30, he walked past my desk and announced that he was going for a long lunch. During the last seven days he never once returned in the afternoon."

"Was he at home?"

"I doubt it. The word around the courthouse is that he and his wife, Rose Marie, barely speak to each other, so I'm sure he didn't go home. Dad told me that he saw him driving north at midday on several occasions. I think dad looks carefully because he thinks the Judge is an accident waiting to happen. This isn't as big a problem in the middle of the day as it is at night, after he has been drinking. To add to the difficulties he is so short that without a pillow he can barely see out the window. Dad says there is often a passenger riding in the front seat with him. The scuttlebutt at the court house is that he goes all the way to La Crosse where he hangs out with a couple other judges at the country club. He may play a little golf, but most people think he travels up there to drink and play poker."

"Who was his traveling companion?"

Candy smiled, "Dad said it was Sam Casperson."

I had met Sam several times when I visited Marme. She had taught school with Sam's wife, Sarah. After Papa Dave's death, Sam, by then a widower, had asked Marme to go to dinner with him a few times. She turned him down each time. When we asked her about it she shook her head and said, "Oil and water."

Jumpy was sure the issue was Sam's lifestyle. "Sam lives the life of an adolescent. He comes and goes when he wants. He spends money as if it was water. Marme has raised her family. She'd have another kid to take care of if she dated Sam regularly."

"It would make sense that the Judge hung out with Sam," I said. "Sam loves to play golf and if the rumor I hear at Little Oslo is correct, he may be the only person in town who spends less time in his office than the Judge. Dad says Sam married money. Sarah's father had made some shrewd investments."

Candy spoke like she had given this a lot of thought, "Last summer I figure that the Judge needed Sam to drive him home. He could get by driving drunk in Wahissa, but I don't think the State Patrol would have cut him any slack up near La Crosse."

"What do you think your dad would do," I whispered, "if he saw him driving erratically down the road into Wahissa?"

"I don't think, I know what he would do," Candy whispered back. "Last summer he had orders to stop the Judge, take his keys, and drive him home. As far as I know he still has the same orders. Once he leaves the Judge at home he is to go to Sheriff Silver's house. The Sheriff will go with dad, no matter what time of the night, to get the car. Sheriff Silver will drive the car home, put it in the garage, and leave the keys on the front seat. The last I knew the other deputies had the same orders. They will do anything to keep the Judge out of the paper."

"Why do they go to such great lengths to coddle this guy?" I asked.

"Because they need the Judge to help them convict people. If they arrest him they develop an adversarial relationship, ultimately the Sheriff's department is the loser."

. . . .

We played better ball against Harden at home the following Wednesday, but not good enough to win. Lombardo brought his "A" game to Wahissa Stadium, striking out Sherm on three pitches to start the game. He had not allowed a ball out of the infield when I came to bat in the third inning. The first pitch was a bit high and as hard as I had ever seen it. I was still swinging when the ball was in the catcher's mitt. The next two pitches were changes. I nearly broke my back on the first, and I tapped a dribbler to short on the third.

In the fifth inning we scored two runs when Buck drove in the Zitzner brothers with a double. I struck out on a change-up to end the inning.

Lombardo led off the sixth with a home run, which put them ahead 4–2. He made that score stand up, retiring the last twelve hitters.

After the game, I looked up while changing my shoes to see the Eagles' pitcher standing right in front of me. "You pitched a whale of a game tonight," I told him.

"Did it go exactly as I told you?" he said with a sneer. "No more steals off me this year, kid. I'm just reminding you what I told you at home." As he started walking away he turned around and delivered one last insult. "I own you."

Smokey had overheard the entire conversation and now walked over and sat next to me. "He had your number tonight," the coach said. "You have to stay back on that change of his."

"Easier said than done," I replied. "I know what to do, I'm just having trouble doing it."

"You'll get him next time."

I decided to ask the coach the question that stumped me. "Can you tell me why he's needling me? I'm a nobody. I would have thought he would challenge Buck, or LaVon, or LaVern. They have the power. Instead, he picks on a 17-year-old left fielder who bats seventh. I don't get it."

"I do," Smokey said sticking a plug of tobacco in his cheek and nodding his head. "He knows that the way to beat us is to keep you off the bases. I'm not sure how we're going to help you face him with more confidence, but I know this, I've got to move you up in the order. One of these days I'm going to bat you leadoff. Lombardo just convinced me it was time to make the shift. It probably won't be against Camp Mc-Coy on Friday. Keep your mouth shut about this until I talk to Sherm. He isn't going to like hitting seventh."

The Prodigal Daughter

*N*o national holiday brought more joy to the people of Wahissa than Independence Day. At 9:00 on July 4 a huge parade began at the high school and proceeded west to Main Street before it turned south on Turner Street, which dead-ended at the fairgrounds where there was a big barbeque. Four or five marching bands headlined the parade each year, including bands from neighboring high schools. The visiting musicians were treated like royalty. In addition to the music, fifteen to twenty businesses sponsored floats. In between the floats was a series of convertibles featuring past winners of the Miss Wahissa contest. The last convertible was the current Miss Wahissa, usually a senior at the high school.

At the end of the day more than a thousand people assembled at Wahissa Park to watch the Jewelers play a ball game and another thousand arrived late and sat on the hill just outside the park to watch a gigantic fireworks display sponsored by a local service club.

Ted Towne, as was his custom, scheduled a team from Camp McCoy, which later changed its name to Fort McCoy, the U.S. army base near Sparta. Ted invited the Soldiers each year as a way of honoring our servicemen. Members of the VFW and American Legion marched around the park prior to the game and fired both their rifles and a cannon during the singing of the "Star Spangled Banner."

The only person who disliked the arrangement was Smokey, who could never figure out who we were playing. Since soldiers were forever coming and going from McCoy they fielded a different team nearly every week. Smokey drove up to Sparta twice to scout the Soldiers only to report that he saw two totally different teams. "How the hell can you play your best when you don't have any idea who you're playing against? This is like playing a phantom team," he muttered to anyone who would listen.

His major concern was deciding which pitcher to start. He wanted to save Buck, and he was concerned that his other pitchers couldn't come up with nine innings between them.

Smokey and Ted had lunch at Little Oslo on Tuesday, going over several of the administrative issues for the Jewelers. They deliberately moved to a table I didn't serve so I was out of hearing range. Still I was able to hear a bit of their conversation. At one point Ted suggested that Smokey pitch Sherm Lewison a few innings against the Soldiers, reminding Smokey that Sherm had been a fine pitcher five years ago.

"Hell," Smokey growled, "These days Sherm doesn't throw hard enough to break the big window in your store. I'm not sure he is playing well enough right now to stay on the field. I'm thinking of playing Cam at second."

. . . .

For some odd reason our family had decided years ago to use July 4 for the Joseph family reunion. That meant, of course, that none of us ever attended the big barbeque at the fair grounds.

I secretly wished that we could join our neighbors and friends at one of the city's biggest celebrations. Mom was torn. She wanted to be both places. Dad, Jumpy, and Marme looked forward for weeks to the reunion that began immediately after the parade. The men loved the gathering not only because they would see all of their cousins, but also because they had a fifteen-year winning streak at the horseshoe pit.

Marme wasn't a Joseph by birth, but she had married into the family and cared more for the relatives than anyone with Joseph blood. She always found a spot near the start of the parade so she could leave early and set up her lawn chair in Hans Nielson Hauge Park. There she served as the Joseph family's greeter and beloved elder. After her meltdown earlier in the week we all waited to see if she would approach the day with enough energy to last. Like an athlete who always gets up for the big games, Marme awoke early and was full of pep all day long.

She was waiting outside the door when Aunt Elaine and Allen arrived early to drive her to the parade. She didn't appear to be as frail as she was the past week, and, more important, she was determined to reign over the gathering. Though she lacked a tiara, she had the bearing of a queen.

Following the parade Aunt Elaine left immediately for the park. The moment they arrived she and Allen moved Marme's chair to the appropriate spot where she sat down. There she stayed all afternoon. Once people arrived they lined up to greet her the way they do a bride after a wedding. She didn't even leave to eat. Karen filled a plate and delivered it to her nibs.

Mom and I, who watched the parade in the heart of downtown where all the bands played their favorite Sousa marches, were nearly the last to arrive. By the time we got settled at the park a few of the games had already begun, and Dad and Jumpy were dominating the horseshoe pit. Tim, who was in charge of games for the younger children, saw us as we arrived and waved.

Allen and Elaine were in charge of the food setup. They had moved picnic tables to their proper places, made signs that told people where to put their various dishes, and made several gallons of lemonade with real lemons. Marme would never allow lemonade made with powder.

The last family to arrive caused quite a stir. Mom saw them get out of their cars and rushed over where Dad was pitching shoes to whisper, "Skip. Lucy Vangen and her entire family are here!"

Dad nearly dropped both horseshoes. He stopped, looked at Mom and asked, "Her entire family? Even Roger and Sherry?"

"The whole family," Mom repeated.

Everything I knew about Lucy and her family I learned from Marme, who loved Lucy like a daughter and remained close to her even when she was nearly alienated from the rest of the Joseph clan.

Lucy Joseph was Dad's cousin and closest female friend all the way through high school until she started to date Chet Vangen, a man she married one week after she graduated. Dad and Jumpy were both at her wedding, but that was the last time they had contact with her for several years. Neither Dad nor Jumpy were fond of Chet, and, according to Marme, Chet returned the feeling. The only person named Joseph that Chet cared for was Lucy. Dad and Jumpy both considered Chet arrogant and abrasive.

Chet was six years older than Lucy and owned a home about five miles west of Wahissa. He attended a Bible church a half mile from their home. After she was married Lucy joined the church and became the first member of the Joseph family to leave the Lutheran church.

Chet took over his father's printing business, Quality Press, and grew it until it became one of the most successful businesses in the county. He made a small fortune specializing in printing the glossy pages for fashion magazines based in New York. At its peak Quality Press employed three shifts a day, six days a week. You could see trucks arriving and leaving all week long.

Quality Printing was a family business in every sense. Lucy, who was quiet and retiring, was the company bookkeeper. Chet's brother and a cousin were printers, another cousin was in charge of the mailroom, and his son Roger served as a plant manager. Though Roger held the title, Chet was the acting plant manager because he was not one to delegate. He was in charge of nearly every detail, allowing Roger to make only the most mundane decisions.

Sherry, the Vangen's only daughter, was the golden child in the family. Chet sent Roger to technical school to learn another side of the printing business, but he believed that Sherry had the best business sense in the family. His goal for Sherry was for her to attend the University of Wisconsin, earn a business degree, and come home and eventually run the printing business.

According to Marme, Sherry, a carbon copy of her father, was stubborn and unwilling to have anyone tell her what to do. She insisted on attending a girl's school in the East. Her dad was adamant that she attend the University of Wisconsin, about 100 miles from home. She finally had her way.

While living in New Hampshire she became pregnant. Chet was furious. He ordered her to come home. She refused. He flew to New England vowing to bring her back "if I have to drag her all the way."

Though the details are sketchy, family lore suggests that Chet's eastern visit produced a monumental confrontation. Sherry refused to introduce Chet to the father of her baby or to return home with him. When Chet insisted that she follow him she called the cops. The police threatened to arrest him if he didn't leave immediately. Chet came home humiliated, hurt, and angry. He announced to his wife, "I have lost my daughter."

Lucy, of course, was torn between her husband and her daughter. She told Chet she was going east to spend time with Sherry, but Chet refused to let her go, insisting "Sherry has left our family."

Tim and I learned most of the details of the Vangen story when we went to visit Marme two years earlier and were startled to meet a beautiful young woman with a seven-month-old child. "Sherry," Marme said, "You remember my grandsons, Tim and Jake. Boys," she continued, "Sherry and her son, Thomas, are my house guests."

Sherry, with Marme's help, tried to arrange a meeting with Chet, but he refused to see her. Her brother Roger wouldn't even talk to her on the phone.

Shortly after Sherry's attempts at reconciliation were rejected, she moved from the east coast to Madison, where she lived as a single mother. She got a job and rented a two-bedroom apartment about a half mile from Camp Randal on the city's west side. The baby, a beautiful boy, was named Thomas Chester. Though she named the baby after her dad, he refused to acknowledge her or her son.

At one point Marme invited Chet to her home where she pleaded with him to visit his daughter. She urged him as a religious man to forgive Sherry and welcome his grandson. Chet listened politely and then walked to the door. "Mrs. Joseph," he said evenly, "I appreciate your advice. This, however, is a Vangen matter. It is of no concern to the Josephs."

Three weeks later Chet died of a heart attack while attending a basketball game. Tim and I saw the ambulance crew come into the gym and carry someone out. Only later did we find out it was Chet Vangen.

Lucy called Sherry and said, "I need to have you sit next to me at the funeral." Sherry arrived the next morning with Thomas. Her brother acted as if he didn't know her. Marme reported that after the funeral Lucy talked privately to Roger. Nobody knows exactly what was said, but it was clear that Lucy, who had lost a husband, tried to hold both of her children close.

After his father's death Roger assumed that he would take over Quality Printing. He knew that his mother didn't want to run the business and assumed she was not capable to do so. However, Lucy knew that if Roger were the president, Sherry would not have a job. Her solution was to assume the leadership, appoint Roger as Vice-President of Quality Printing, and hire Sherry to supervise work in the office.

Roger fought the arrangement from day one. Finally, in the spring, he and his mother collided. He told Lucy that he felt cheated. "I'm the one who stayed home and took care of the business," he shouted. "I worked overtime here while my sister whored around at some fancy school in the East. She may even be making as much as I am."

Lucy responded by reminding Roger that she loved him and wanted him to remain with the company, but she concluded, "As much as I want you to stay I must warn you that the next time you complain to anyone outside of this office about your job, you will be looking for work. Sherry is my only daughter and your only sister. She needs and deserves a second chance. She is going to work for this company."

Roger rejected his mother's words completely. In a voice that could be heard plainly through the walls he shouted, "Forget this second chance crap. This is about being fair. Sherry hasn't put in a day's work in this company in six years. If she's in, I'm out."

Roger had always been able to bully his mother. This time it didn't work.

"Then you are out," Lucy said firmly. "I want your keys. Lay them on my desk, now. Then leave the building. I'll clean out your desk and deliver all your personal items to your home tomorrow. You will be paid six months severance."

When Marme tells this story, jaws drop. Roger stood still looking like something had sucked all of the air out of his lungs. When Lucy put her hands on her hips, he took his keys out of his pocket and laid them silently on his mother's desk. He started to walk away when she interrupted him. "The car belongs to the company as well. Leave the car keys here. You can call your wife to pick you up."

He look dazed, but he removed the car keys from his ring and walked slowly out the door.

Lucy then walked through the building quietly assigning people to assume Roger's responsibility effective the next morning. When she concluded, she locked her office, said good night to Sherry, and drove home. She made herself a cup of hot chocolate, sat down in her recliner, and cried for an hour. Then she got in her car and drove to see Marme, asking her for advice.

Marme's word to Lucy was, "Wait. Allow Roger's wife, Myrna, to talk some sense into the boy's head." Marme reminded Lucy that she and Myrna had always been close. "Myrna is level-headed. Let her reason with Roger. I have a hunch that this story will have a happy ending."

Marme was right. Early the next morning before 7:00 a.m., when Lucy arrived at work, Roger and Myrna were sitting in their family car near the front door. Lucy waved and entered the building. A moment later there was a light tapping on her office door, which she had left ajar.

Roger stepped into the office with Myrna right behind him. "Do you believe in second chances for all your children?" he asked.

Lucy stepped from behind her desk and said, "With all my heart I do."

"Is it possible to get my job back?"

"It is, assuming you know that your sister will be working here as well."

He nodded.

"There will be no more acts of insubordination. Am I correct?"

"You are correct" he said, with his eyes fixed firmly on the floor.

Without a smile Lucy said, "You will find all of your keys sitting on your desk. Everything is as you left it."

The two stood a few feet apart for several seconds. "I need to make a phone call," Lucy said. "I told a couple of people you would not be in this morning. I'll let them know that has changed. No one knows that you were fired."

Roger started to cry. "I love you Mom. Myrna has helped me . . ."

He wanted to say more but Lucy hugged him and then told him, "Go! You have work to do."

According to Marme, the next few months went by smoothly. And now, at the invitation of my grandmother, they were about to become Josephs again. After I watched my dad greet his cousin. I said hello to Lucy, Sherry, and little Tommy. Then I found Roger and shook hands with him. Though he lived less than five miles from me I had never talked to him before that day. It felt like our family had just grown significantly.

· · · · · · ·

Smokey started Cam on the mound against the Soldiers of Camp McCoy. He threw well for three innings. In the fourth inning the Soldiers broke loose for five runs, including a home run with two on-board. Mo started the fifth and allowed two runs in each of the next two innings.

Camp McCoy threw a big left-hander whose first name was Duke. He stood six foot two inches and, though he had a good fastball, his bread and butter pitch was a sharp breaking curve. Later the Camp McCoy coach said Duke had only arrived three days earlier. He had signed with the Red Sox in 1950 directly after high school. He made it all the way to AAA until he blew out his elbow. On July 4 in Wahissa the big lefty was doing fine with his damaged elbow. Buck was the only Jeweler who could catch up with his fastball. Not only did we lose, we lost big. It was our third loss in a row. What had seemed to be a promising season was quickly going downhill.

· · · · · · ·

Following the game Candy and I found a dark spot along the left field line to watch the fireworks. We joined the crowd in applauding the various explosions that covered the sky like a magnificent kaleidoscope and cheered when the final rocket, a giant flag of the United States, concluded the display. We decided to walk home, rather than ride with either set of parents.

At the top of the hill Candy stopped and said, "Something struck me as very strange just now."

"What is it," I asked?

"This is the first day I haven't heard anyone mention the beatings since we first heard that Lloyd was hurt. Why do you suppose no one is talking about it today?"

"I have no idea," I said. "Perhaps it is because we are all too busy having a good time. We've got other things on our mind today."

"Most days Dad talks about the beatings the entire time he is home. Today he didn't have to work until he had duty tonight, and he didn't say a word. I was at the parade and no one said anything."

"Maybe this is a sign that the beatings are over," I said.

"I hope so," Candy said taking my hand. "I know that no woman has been beaten, and I know the beatings have taken place out in the country, but I think about them every time I leave the house at night."

"Do you worry when I'm with you?" I asked.

She laughed, kissed me, looked at me with all my baseball gear and said, "Not as long as you're carrying your bat."

The Phone Call

CHAPTER 11

On July 5 I went directly from Little Oslo to Ham's Standard Station to check in with the guys before I headed to the park for wind sprints. It was a 90-degree day, and I was dripping wet when I finished my third time of running the hill.

As soon as I parked my bike at the house, Mom met me at the door with a message. "Your Aunt Elaine called. She is worried about Allen. He received a phone call a couple of days ago, and according to her, "he has gone into a blue funk."

"Who called him?" I asked.

"Elaine doesn't know. She was outside when the phone rang. Allen ran in the house to answer it. When he came out ten minutes later, he was as white as a snowstorm. Elaine asked him what had happened and he said, 'Nothing.'" Mom shook her head and let out a deep sigh.

"Elaine wants to know if you and Tim will talk to him."

"I think Tim is planning to go to the game at Ft. Price tomorrow. Maybe he can take Allen with him. Tim can find out what is going on."

"Maybe you can go with Tim and the two of you can find out what is going on," Mom said. It sounded more like a command than a suggestion.

I was part way out the door when Mom said, "Jake, I think it is time that you know the whole story about Allen. Do you know that Joyce and Marvin are not his real parents?"

I stopped, turned around, and headed back into the kitchen. "What do you mean they are not his real parents?" I asked. "Allen is my cousin and friend. We've known each other for sixteen years, and suddenly I find out that he is not who I think he is. What's up?"

Mom sat down at the kitchen table while I sat across from her. She spoke gently, her blue eyes a pool of compassion, "Dad and I have hesitated talking to you about Allen. We have assumed that sooner or later he would tell you his story. We've been surprised that he chose to keep it a secret from most people. The circumstances are such that it is time that you know."

Mom took a deep breath and said, "Allen's birth mother is DeDe. She is also Joy's mother. DeDe is the only daughter of Ken and Marilyn Hayes; Marilyn is Marme's cousin. A month after Allen's third birthday, when Joy was six, DeDe, who had never been married, took the two of them to visit Crystal, a high school friend who lived in Sioux Falls, South Dakota. One of the first nights there DeDe met a guy by the name of Nick who said he would marry her, but didn't want her kids. DeDe, who was twenty-three at the time, impulsively jumped on the back of his motorcycle and headed west, leaving her two children behind with her friend. She left instructions for Crystal to call Marilyn, who lived in La Crosse."

I sat listening with my mouth wide open. "I can't believe it," I said.

"It's true," Mom said reaching across the table and laying her hand gently on my arm. "Marilyn, who was a widow, didn't drive. She called her niece, Joyce, who lived just a few blocks away with her husband Marvin. Marilyn told Joyce that she was in desperate need of help.

"Can you drive out to Sioux Falls and pick up the kids? Something has happened to DeDe. The kids are with DeDe's friend, Crystal, who is anxious for someone to come and get them. I expect DeDe will be back in a couple of days."

Joyce and Marvin left the next morning and brought two very confused children back to Wisconsin and delivered them to their grandmother. After a few days of trying to take care of two young kids, Marilyn was a nervous wreck. She called Joyce and Marvin again and asked if they could take care of the kids until DeDe returned. "I'm expecting her any day now," Marilyn said.

Joyce and Marvin picked up the two children that same day. Days passed and they didn't hear a word from DeDe. Days turned into weeks, and still they received not one word. Meanwhile, Joyce and Marvin were thrilled. This was a dream come true. They were unable to have their own children, and it was as if God had dropped off an entire family at their door. After two years, with Marilyn's permission, the court allowed them to adopt both children." Shortly after the adoption Trane Company, where Marvin worked, transferred him to the Milwaukee area.

Mom stopped and stared out the window thinking. Finally she spoke, "I'm not sure how much I should tell you. Allen ought to fill you in on most of this. Let me just say that when she graduated from high school Joy decided that she needed to find her birth mother. With Joyce and Marvin's blessing, she started a search. Marme says that after several months she made a connection."

"What about Allen?" I asked.

"Allen can answer for himself, but as I understand it, he wanted nothing to do with the mother who abandoned him. It has caused a huge rift between Allen and his sister." Mom paused and then said, "I think that is all I'm going to say. I'll let Allen finish the story."

"One more question," I said. "Joy made a connection. Where did she find DeDe?"

"Back in La Crosse," Mom answered quietly.

A bit later I met Tim at the Loft. I told him everything that Mom had told me, including the part about the phone calls earlier in the week. Several times I asked him, "Did you know?" Each time he assured me that he had no idea that Joyce and Marvin were not Allen's biological parents.

We both decided that I ought to ride with Smokey to Ft. Price the next day, in order to make it in time for batting practice. Tim and Allen would leave later, arriving in time for the start of the game. My plans were to return home with the two of them.

· · · · · · · ·

It took a three-game losing streak but Smokey finally moved me to the lead-off position. Rather than talk privately with Sherm before the game, he let him know along with the rest of the team by simply reading the batting order. Fifteen minutes before the game he addressed all of us, "Listen up. I've made a change in the batting order tonight." When he read my name for the lead-off position Sherm grunted. When he read Sherm's name in the seven hole, the second baseman muttered something profane, threw his glove at the screen, and walked toward third base. Once he was out of earshot the Zitzner brothers pulled me aside and told me they thought the move was way overdue. "You get on base and we'll get you home," LaVon assured me.

"This is good for the team," LaVern said nodding vigorously.

They were true to their word. Against the Mustangs I was on base five times and scored four runs. I got into scoring position twice by stealing a base. After the game several players told me I made Smokey look like a genius.

In the first inning I walked, stole second, and scored on a single to right field. I scored again in the third when LaVern doubled to deep left center field. In the fifth I scored a third time when LaVern again doubled to deep left center field. Late in the game I trotted home ahead of LaVon when he drove a fastball into a pine grove in dead center field for a home run.

Sherm went 0–4, with a walk. I was changing my shoes after the game when I overheard two players talking. "How long can Smokey keep Sherm in the line-up?" the first one asked. "He isn't even hitting his weight."

"To add to it," the second one said, "his play at second has gone to pot."

"My wife has a theory," the first one added. "She thinks there is big trouble at the Lewison household. She doesn't know anything for sure, but she teaches with Sherm's wife, Helen, and she says something isn't right. She thinks Sherm's playing is a reflection of a bigger problem."

Tim and Allen were a part of the tiny Jewelers' cheering section. At first people booed every time the two guys cheered. As the game progressed and we widened the margin, the Ft. Price crowd got quiet. Toward the end of the game the locals took an early exit, and all we could hear was Tim, Allen, and a handful of Wahissa fans.

We stopped at a restaurant before we left town so I could get something to eat. I didn't like to eat heavy before a game and was always famished when the game was over. As we were waiting for our order, Tim spoke directly to Allen. "Aunt Elaine says that you got pretty shook up over a phone call. What's going on?"

Allen looked at the table and tears filled his eyes. "I'm so confused," he said, his voice cracking. "Do you guys know that Joyce is not my birth mom?"

We both shook our heads.

"She is my real mom, no question about that," Allen said emphatically. "She is the best mom a guy could ever ask for." Then he wiped his eyes with a napkin.

"To this day I have not met my birth mother since she abandoned me on a whim when I was three. Her name is DeDe. We were in South Dakota, so the story goes, visiting one of her friends. Some guy told her that she was beautiful and that he loved her. He evidently told her he wanted to spend the rest of his life with her, but he didn't want children. The next day DeDe decided to leave with him for parts unknown. By motorcycle for God's sake! Can you imagine a mother dumping her kids with a friend and leaving on the back of a motorcycle?" Allen shook his head and wiped his eyes.

Tim said, "And that's the last time you ever saw her?"

"I don't remember ever seeing her in person, though we have a couple of pictures of her," he said shaking his head. He paused for a moment before he added, "But I have thought about her every day of my life. I have studied those pictures and wondered what she is like. When I was little I asked myself what I did that was so terrible that she would leave me. As I got older I tried to understand what made her do what she did. I asked myself, 'Did something happen to her when she was a girl?' How, why, did she get pregnant, twice? Joy and I have two different fathers. Why did neither one of them marry DeDe? Why have neither one of them ever tried to find us? Why did DeDe not come back after a week or a month or, for God's sake, a year?"

"I can't believe that you have never met her," Tim said.

"It's true. Not only have I not met her, I have virtually heard nothing about her," Allen said. He paused and then added, "Until two years ago."

"What happened two years ago?" I said.

"That is when Joy decided to find her," Allen responded.

"How did that turn out?" Tim asked.

"After several months Joy was successful. I'm not sure what exactly took place because Joy was working in Madison at the time, living with a girlfriend. DeDe was back in La Crosse, living alone, or so I assume. After Joy made contact by phone the two of them got together. After they met a second time Joy drove to Wauwatosa and told me that DeDe wanted to see me. I told her DeDe could stick it. I told her that I had a mother and that I would be true to my mother, whose name was Joyce."

"Didn't you want to meet DeDe?" I asked. "Didn't you want to know what she looked like and what she was doing? Didn't you want to know why she left you in South Dakota and why she didn't come back for you?"

"Of course I did," Allen said angrily. "I had thought about DeDe every day of my life. I told myself a thousand stories about why she left and why she didn't come back. But when I was offered an opportunity to meet her it seemed wrong. It seemed disloyal."

"That was what the phone call was about the other day?" Tim asked.

"It was," Allen said, "and it caught me totally off guard."

"Who was calling?" I asked.

"I don't know," Allen responded. "Here is what happened. I had been mowing the lawn and was heading into the house to get a drink of water when I heard the phone ring. I ran inside and answered. A woman spoke to me in a near whisper and asked, 'Were you born May 19, 1933?'"

"That sounds spooky," I said.

"It was," Allen replied. "I managed to say, 'Who is this, and why do you ask?'"

"The voice said, 'If you were born May 19, 1933, I can tell you where your mother lives.'

"I got upset and said, 'My mother Joyce lives at 4420 Parmenter in Wauwatosa.'"The other voice said, 'I am talking about your birth mother, Delores.'

"I answered, 'The only mother I have is named Joyce. She is the mother who raised me and the only mother who has loved me.'

"'If you are who I think you are there is another mother who loves you,' the voice said. 'I can give you her address and phone number.'

"I don't want either," I shouted and hung up.

"About this time Elaine came walking in the door. Evidently she heard me yell. "What was that all about?" she asked.

"I had no idea what I ought to say so I said the first thing that came into my mind, 'It was just someone who had the wrong number and insisted that they had the right number. I'm sorry I got so irritated, but I found them to be very impolite.' Elaine looked unconvinced, but smiled and walked into the kitchen with the spinach she had just picked from her garden."

About that time the waitress brought our food and we sat quietly for a few minutes and ate. Finally Tim broke the silence, "Are you glad you said what you did?"

Allen, looking pale, said, "I don't know. I think the answer is yes and no. First, the woman who called didn't identify herself. It may have been DeDe. Then again, it could have been someone who was playing a trick on me."

"What is your best guess," I said. "Do you think the person who called was sincere?"

Allen thought for a moment and said, "Yes. Yes, I think she was sincere." Then after more silence he said, "What do I do next?"

Tim, ever upbeat said, "I'd go talk to Marme. She makes more sense than anyone I've ever known."

I agreed.

As we rode home to Wahissa little was said. When we reached Elaine's farm Allen thanked us both for listening and then said, "I'm going to visit Marme tomorrow."

The Big Dispute

*U*nfortunately Allen was not able to visit Marme on Wednesday. Mark and Karen had gone by bike to spend the afternoon with her and found the house totally empty. They spent an hour riding around the neighborhood searching for her until Mark suggested that they look in Nielson Park.

His instincts were perfect. They found her just off the path in a heavily wooded section where she had fallen. It wasn't clear to Karen and Mark if she had sprained an ankle or broken a leg. Karen gave Mark orders to ask one of the park neighbors to use their phone to call the oil and gas office, while she stayed with Marme.

When the kids arrived Marme was frightened. She had begun to wonder if anyone would find her before dark. She later confessed to Dr. Quincy that she couldn't remember the last time when she felt that much fear. "I'm ashamed," she told the doctor. "Scripture advises us, 'Do not fear what they fear, nor be in dread.' But I was full of fear."

The longer she sat with Karen the calmer she became.

Mark was able to find someone home so he could make a call. Mom, who was working that afternoon, tried to call Jumpy, but when she couldn't reach him she managed to find Dad on the CB. Dad finished what he was doing and arrived at the park thirty minutes later. He drove his truck across the lawn to the edge of the forest and ran to the place where Karen was keeping watch.

Dad scooped his mother into his arms and carried her to his truck, where he lifted her up, placing her gently on the front seat of his cab. By this time Marme was chirping like a bird. "Oh, thou noble knight," she sang, "carry me home in your beautiful chariot."

Dad, who drove far too fast coming in from the country, managed a wary smile. He was certain that his worst fears for his mother's safety had taken place. He was finding it difficult to shift gears and began to laugh. "I'm taking you to the Quincy Clinic," he told his mother.

"You are doing no such thing," she said emphatically. "You will take me home and call Dr. David on the phone. When he has time he will come and see me. I'm sure that all I have is a sprain."

"And . . ." Dad got stuck for a moment while Marme waited patiently for her son to continue. "And if it is more than a sprain," Dad argued, "it will be too late to have x-rays. You'll have to wait until tomorrow."

"Then wait I shall, oh noble knight," Marme said. "Take me home."

Dad, who never won an argument with Marme did as his mother directed.

In the meantime Mom walked from the office to the house and left a message for me. When I came home I peddled down to see her, and she told me what had happened. She had been unable to reach Elaine, so we tried again. This time she was home. Before she hung up I asked for Allen, suggesting that he not visit Marme that afternoon, then I rode over and relieved Dad. I stayed until Elaine arrived.

Later, Mom filled me in on the details. About 5:30 Dr. Quincy arrived with his little black bag. He checked her knee and her ankle and determined that she had indeed sprained both. He instructed Elaine to wrap both in ice and keep the leg elevated. "Tomorrow morning start putting heat on it," he instructed. Today doctors direct people to continue to ice it for several days, but back then it was ice and then heat. Marme followed instructions to the last detail.

I visited Marme on Tuesday. I was planning to visit on Wednesday as well when I received a call from Mom. "Jake, Marme has had enough company. She let us all know that she needs some time to herself. I'm calling in case you were planning to go after work."

. . . .

Relieved of that responsibility, I headed home and hung out with Tim until it was time for me to go to the ballpark. When I arrived it was like being in a different world, a world where I didn't have to worry about anything happening to my grandmother. My only concern was the game against Browntown.

Early in the game most of the action took place off the field. Ted Towne was always talkative, but that night he was hyperactive. His normal M.O. was to talk incessantly to the members of our team. "Way to go, Buck." "Hang in there, LaVon." "You'll get 'em next time, Gene." He was seldom negative though people in all parts of the park could hear every word he spoke. Only occasionally did he direct his words to the other team or the umpires.

On this particular night he was yapping at someone from the time the opening pitch was thrown. He had words of advice for the Browntown hitters and the pitcher, and he was quite upset with the way the umpire was calling balls and strikes. All of this changed on a single play in the bottom of the fifth when the home plate umpire called Gene, our shortstop, out at the plate. From my vantage point on the bench it looked like Gene's hook slide took him around the catcher. He appeared to catch home plate with his left foot as he slid by and should have been called safe.

The umpire saw it and called it differently. His right hand went up and Ted erupted. Initially our entire bench joined him, but Ted protested so vociferously that we all just turned and watched him. He was standing on his seat shaking his fist and screaming. Finally the home plate umpire walked close to his box, put his hands on his hips, and warned him to quiet down. "If you persist in being a disruption I will be forced to take stern methods," the man in blue said.

Ted yelled, "You have no right to tell me what I can do. You are in charge of the baseball field. I have my rights. Behind this screen it is a free country and I can yell all day long."

The umpire raised both hands, interrupting Ted's tirade and spoke in a deep bass, "Mr. Towne, your rights are extremely limited within the confines of this ballpark." He then quoted the number and section in the rulebook that punished disruptive behavior from the stands. From that point on we didn't hear a peep out of our fearless leader.

For a moment the Jewelers' bench sat in total silence until Cam began, in a voice heard only by the players, to mimic the umpire. Looking at our first baseman he said in a false deep voice, "Mr. Zitzner, if you persist in being a disruption I'm going to look up some words in my dictionary and threaten you. You realize your rights are extremely limited as long as you don't read every section in the rule book?" Then turning toward the rest of the team he asked, "Since when have we hired English teachers to umpire games? In the old days the ump would tell a blowhard, 'I'm coming over there to kick your ass.' Now that we have a more learned ump he's going to take stern measures."

Initially, Smokey tried to stop the bench from laughing out loud, but it only encouraged Cam. The coach's attempts didn't last long, because with the umpire's warning came an explosion of power from the Jewelers' bats. As the score mounted each inning even Smokey was caught smiling at Cam's antics, which led the infielder to recite a little verse, "What is so rare as a day in June? Then if ever comes perfect days. And your manager manages a smile or two, to destroy the foggy haze." Either Smokey didn't hear him or decided not to comment.

When our catcher popped up to end the eighth inning, Cam turned his hat around backwards and threatened stern measures on the big man. We laughed all the way through the ninth inning and took home our eighth win of the season.

Tom Knight

CHAPTER 13

mokey warned us that we were going to have our hands full against an improving Chiefs team. Baaken, the lefty from Madison, had settled into being one of the best pitchers in the league, and the big first baseman from Boscobel had a home run in each of the last three games. That night, however, the Jewelers played great baseball starting with our first at bat. I walked to lead off and advanced to second when the ball bounced away from the catcher. After Gene bunted me to third, LaVon hit a ball in the hole, and I crossed home plate without a throw. We scored a run in each of the next three innings.

Buck, who had only pitched two innings on Wednesday against Browntown, seemed rested. He threw as hard as he had all year long, and he managed to keep their power hitters off balance with a bunch of slow stuff. I caught two balls while standing ten feet from the fence.

In the seventh inning, when they replaced the starting

pitcher, the Zitzners greeted the new hurler with back-to-back home runs. We finished off the game with a three-run eighth inning and won by seven runs.

. . . .

Taverns or no taverns was a question placed before the citizens of Wahissa on a regular basis. For a period of ten years the anti-tavern folks kept the city "dry," which meant it eliminated all liquor stores and taverns.

A strange coalition comprised of conservative church people and members of the VFW, American Legion, and the Caribou Club came to the polls year after year to vote against demon rum. Support from the VFW and others developed because the same ordinance that prohibited taverns and liquor stores allowed booze to be sold at private clubs. Members of the clubs voted to stay dry because it boosted revenue for their organizations, which were open every day except Sunday.

In the late 1940s some enterprising men formed the Caribou Club, an organization formed solely to provide alcoholic beverages for citizens of the city. Dues for the Caribou Club were one dollar a year. When membership grew to several hundred in 1950 the dry coalition folded. A new election was held, and Wahissa overwhelmingly voted to go "wet."

Within a matter of months three taverns opened up. Two were on the edge of the city and one, the Minuteman, was downtown just two blocks from Little Oslo. The Minuteman had a full dinner menu consisting primarily of deep-fried foods.

Dad and Jumpy, who were known to have a bottle of beer on social occasions, took no public stand on the tavern issue. However, Mom said privately that Dad usually voted dry because, "We just don't need taverns in Wahissa."

When bars arrived none of the Joseph family set foot in either the Minuteman or the other two taverns, although, as Tim observed, "Our folks don't mind driving fifteen miles to have supper at a restaurant outside Wahissa that serves liquor." Since our parents didn't eat at the Minuteman, Tim and I had never been in the restaurant.

My route to work took me past the Minuteman both early morning and mid-afternoon. On Monday, July 14, I heard the clock at the bank strike the quarter hour, 5:45, as I turned the corner near the bar. I quickly pulled up when I saw three police vehicles parked in front of the bar. The chief of police was outside talking to Sheriff Silver. Phil Paulson, Candy's dad was standing next to his squad car about thirty feet from the entrance to the bar.

I pedaled to him and said, "What's up?"

"Another beating," he said matter-of-fact. "Tom Knight. It's gotta be Superman. Same M.O. Broken fingers, broken arm, face busted up. Terrible."

"Tom Knight?" I said a bit confused. "He doesn't fit the profile of the other victims."

"That's what got Wahissa's two top cops talking. By the way, when is the last time you've seen those two having a friendly gab fest on a Wahissa street? They aren't exactly buddies, you know."

Just then I heard the clock strike 6:00, so I waved good-bye and pedaled to the alley behind Little Oslo where I left my bike. I dashed into the restaurant, slipped on my apron, and grabbed a coffee pot.

I wasn't two feet out of the kitchen when Moose grabbed me by the arm. I was sure he was going to blast me for being late. I was about to explain when he said, "Another beating. This time it's in Wahissa. Can you believe it? It took place just outside of the Minuteman.

I nodded. "I just talked to Phil Paulson." Moose and Cookie dropped everything and listened as I shared the valued news.

"Who's the victim?" Cookie asked.

"Tom Knight," I said.

Moose gasped, "Tom Knight? Can you believe it?" He took off his sailor cap, waved it in the air, and announced for all to hear, "Tom Knight's our plumber. He was here last Saturday and cleared out a line that was plugged. Now we find out that he got the crap beat out of him. Superman's moving a bit closer."

Everyone in the room was shaking their head and muttering, "Tom Knight." Moose filled in for all of us, "He isn't anything like Lloyd or Kid Hill. What in tarnation is going on in this county?"

Slowly the tables began to fill. First the Silver Table, sans the Sheriff, and then the painters, without Sherm and Woody. I assumed the two of them were late, but Swish told me to serve the table. "We're going to be short two this morning," he said cheerfully. "It must have been a doozy of a party last night."

I wasn't sure what kind of a party he could be talking about because Sherm was at Wahissa Park until nearly 10:00. Then again, there was plenty of time to party after that.

About the time most of the regular breakfast crowd was ready to leave Sheriff Silver entered. He answered a chorus of questions and then waved his hands. "Let me do this one time. Last night, about midnight, someone beat the living daylights out of Tom Knight. Most of you know Tom. He's a hardworking plumber who was probably minding his own business. Now here's the answer to your questions: Yes, it appears to be a companion to the other two beatings. Yes, we are surprised that this one took place in Wahissa. No, we have no one who saw anything happen. Yes, we are hopeful that someone at the Minuteman will be able to identify the perpetrator."

He started to sit down and then stood again. "If anyone here saw Tom last night at anytime we would like to hear from you."

Before the morning was over reports about Tom began to circulate. One person saw him about 11:15 in the Minuteman and reported, "He was well on his way to a serious shine."

My dad was not the only man in town who had ridiculed a woman's fear following the beatings. Men everywhere had pointed out the obvious: All of the victims lived in the country. All of them had been hanging out at taverns and all had been men. With the Tom Knight case two out of three of those points were still true, but now that violence had taken place in the city of Wahissa the fear level went off the charts. No matter how often someone reminded people that all of the victims were men and all were drunk at the time, women everywhere were afraid to go out at night. Hardware stores ran out of locks, and men were grounded. Women wanted their husbands to stay home.

My mother returned from church circle a few days after Superman struck close to home to tell us that she and her friends were all frightened. "We are going to demand that Buster and Sheriff Silver make the capture of this bandit a high priority. We're not sure that it is even safe to walk the streets. And," she concluded, "we will no longer meet in the evening until this whole mess is settled."

Dad couldn't believe it. "Not a single woman has been injured," he said slowly. "Not a single person has been harmed in or near their house."

"True," my mother answered testily, "but last week you said that all of the beatings took place in the country. Last night one of them took place here in Wahissa. If the violence can spread from Vang and Paradise to Wahissa, what is to stop it from moving from the Minuteman to our street?"

Dad's only answer was, "This is the most ridiculous thing I've ever heard. Fear is taking control of this entire town."

A Surprise in the Night

On Wednesday, July 16, Smokey unveiled his plan to beat the two teams that were ahead of us in the standings. "To win the championship we need to beat both Duck Lake and Harden. If we lose to either one we are probably out of the race. That's the reason I'm giving the ball to Chris tonight." He looked directly at the young southpaw, "I need you to give me seven solid innings. I'm relying on you. Mo, Cam, I'm planning on you fellows finishing the game. On Sunday, I'm throwing Buck against Harden. I figure he will go a full nine innings. I don't see another way to make this work."

The whole team rallied around Chris, patting him on the back and telling him he could go seven innings. "You're our guy, you can do it," we all said over and over. Much to the surprise of most of us, that night he was our guy. He pitched out of a jam in the first inning and then allowed single runs in the second, third, fourth, and sixth. Meanwhile, the Jewelers' bats were exploding. Most of the power came from Buck who was playing first base and batting in the three spot ahead of the Zitzners for the first time all year. Smokey must have figured that since he was moving his chess pieces around he'd make some other changes in the batting order. The big man had two home runs and a double and drove in six runs. Cam, playing second base in place of Sherm, had two singles and a double, his first multi-hit night of the season.

With a four-run lead after seven innings Smokey moved Cam to the mound. He followed up his solid play at second base with two strong innings, allowing only one single in the ninth inning. The win set up our game on the road against Harden.

Since the Duck Lake game started nearly an hour later than any of the other games, Moose had told me that I didn't have to come in until 7:00. Still, I was awake at the same time and arrived only fifteen minutes later than normal, at 6:15. I was feeling pretty good about being forty-five minutes earlier than expected, until I got the evil eye from Moose. It was clear that though he gave me permission to be late, he expected me to be there by 6:00.

The café was unusually quite until 10:00 a.m. when the "guess the number crowd arrived." Cookie explained that the whole place was in mourning over the beating of Tom Knight. Moose had a different theory. "When the Sheriff is gone, the whole place is like a morgue." It was true that the presence of Sheriff Silver did raise the spirits of the entire establishment. I wondered why he was absent and asked Ken Brown if he knew what was happening.

"He's doing some detective work," was all the big man would say.

Later Candy told me that they thought they had a lead. A salesman from La Crosse thought he knew the identity of Superman and offered to meet the Sheriff in Harden. The hot lead, like all of the hot leads, turned out to be bogus. The entire sheriff's department was wearing thin.

Dad and Mom normally attended all out-of-town games, taking Candy with them. On Sunday, July 20, they decided to attend an anniversary for one of the Joseph cousins, in Richland Center, some thirty-five miles away. Since they were driving to the anniversary celebration with Jumpy and Melinda, they let me take the family car to the game in Harden. I seized the chance to have time alone with Candy.

. . . .

Lombardo started his mind games with me before the game began. He walked past me when I was taking batting practice and said, "I own you. Tonight, you are mine." Every time I looked toward the bench he was looking my way.

The big Harden pitcher had just finished his warm-ups, and I was about to head toward the plate when Buck walked up to me, took me by the shoulder, and pointed toward left field. He then whispered in my ear, "This doesn't mean a damn thing. But it is time to start seeing whether Dick is as confident as he is putting on. I figure that anyone who is spending as much time as he is trying to psych you out is afraid of you." Then he turned and looked toward third again. Finally, he said, "Make him throw a strike before you swing. He knows you are the guy that sets our table."

I walked to the plate and saw Lombardo peeking toward third. I wasn't sure if Buck had got into his head, but he at least had diverted his attention. Lombardo's first pitch was high and outside. The second pitch was low and inside. On the third pitch I put my bat on my shoulder and never moved. Ball three. Then I stepped out and looked toward third. Twice more I stepped out of the batter's box. When he finally threw, the pitch was wide again. I walked on four pitches.

I checked the signs. The steal was off. I took a big lead and leaned toward first. Lombardo threw to first, and I got back easily. I took a larger lead, and he threw again. The third time he fired to first the ball got away from the first baseman, and I coasted into second.

Still Smokey didn't give me a steal sign, so I danced off second taking a huge lead. That brought the second baseman to the bag and another throw from the pitcher. When he finally threw to home it was wide. The cat and mouse game continued, until Gene walked on a 3–1 count. Now we had two on and no outs.

On a 1–1 pitch LaVon Zitzner hit a towering fly ball to right center, which the center fielder caught backing up. I tagged and headed toward third. Terry Ekern was coaching third, and as I was about to slide I saw him frantically waving me past the bag. Without looking over my shoulder I put on a burst of speed, hit third base with my left foot, pivoted, and headed for home. LaVern, the next hitter, was where he was suppose to be, standing behind the umpire, coaching me on the play at the plate. He put his palms down flat, telling me to slide, and pointed to his left. He wanted me to hook. I did and beat the throw by a foot. We were up 1–0 and Lombardo was steaming.

Later I found out that the center fielder had thrown softly into second. He figured I'd tag, and he knew he had no play at third, but he never dreamed I'd take two bases. Instead of a hard throw to second he threw a balloon. The second baseman went fifteen feet out on the outfield grass to meet the throw. When Terry saw how far out the second baseman had wandered, and knowing that he had a weak arm, he made the decision to test him. It worked like a charm.

Lombardo walked LaVern and Buck drove him in with a scorching double to left center field. Buck took the mound in the bottom of the first with a two-run lead.

Not a single Eagles' runner reached base until the fourth inning when their shortstop singled. He was immediately erased on a beautiful double play, short, to second to first, with Cy, our first baseman, digging Cam's throw out of the dirt.

In the top of the fifth I came up for the third time. On a 2–2 pitch Lombardo fooled me badly with his palm ball. I was way out front but somehow managed to chop at the ball. It bounced over the first baseman's head and dribbled into right field. Chris was coaching first and waved me to second. As I headed to second I glanced to third and saw Terry waving me to third. I went into third standing. Later Smokey said, "It's been a long time since I've seen a 115-foot triple." The ball had landed on a spot just out of the reach of the first baseman, the second baseman, and the right fielder, and I had a three-bagger.

Gene came to bat with one out. I checked and saw no sign from Smokey. I took a small lead and watched as the count went to 2–0. I looked again and this time Smokey flashed the bunt. Later he explained that he didn't intend that it be a suicide squeeze, but we only had one sign for a bunt.

Lombardo went to a stretch and when he lifted his leg I took off for home. I was fifteen feet down the baseline when I realized he had pitched out. Though Gene tried to get the bat on the ball it was an unreachable pitch, high and outside. I put on my breaks and headed back to third. The catcher fired to third and I headed to home. Rather than running me down, the third baseman immediately fired to the catcher. I headed to third. When I saw the catcher throw again I took off for home and decided it was now or never. The throw from third base reached home just as I did. The catcher was standing in the base path, and I hit him as hard as I could. We both fell to the ground, and as I put my hand on home plate I saw the ball rolling toward the screen. I was safe.

Buck hit a home run to lead off the sixth and pitched a full nine innings, allowing a single run in the eighth. We were going home with a 4–1 win and a share of the league lead.

I put my shoes on quickly and deliberately walked past the Eagles' bench. Lombardo was talking to the coach and sponsor, Keith Bridges. "You pitched well," I said to him as I walked by.

"You were lucky," he growled at me.

I flashed him a big smile, "You're right. Some nights you win on skill, some nights you win on luck. Tonight we had luck. See you in Wahissa."

As I walked down right field toward the parking lot where Candy was waiting, I saw Buck trotting across the field. A tall man with a baseball hat and field glasses around his neck stepped out of the stands and shook Buck's hand. The man looked very familiar, but at that distance I couldn't figure out who he was.

. . . .

Candy and I stopped at the A&W Root Beer stand on the edge of town for a burger and a cold drink and then visited a dark corner of the golf course for a few minutes of kissing before we headed to Wahissa. We were only a few miles out of town when I remembered a different route that Dad used, County Road ZZ. It had a lot of twists and turns, and for a stretch followed the Kickapoo River, which with the help of a full moon, could be seen through the trees most of the time. She slid over and cuddled as we wove our way slowly back home. I was probably traveling no more than thirty-five miles an hour and was only ten miles from the Wahissa city limits when Candy let out a shout, "Turn around. I think I saw a car. It looked like it ran off the road."

I did a U-turn and drove back slowly to the spot she identified. A large dark car, that turned out to be a Cadillac, had gone part way down an embankment. Had we been traveling fast and had the taillights of the Cadillac not been on, there was no way that Candy would have spotted it. I parked off the road, and we carefully made our way down to the vehicle. When we were five feet away she stopped and whispered. "That is Judge Swiggum's car. I'm absolutely positive."

We moved closer and could hear a couple of voices inside the car. One was a female voice and she was crying. The other was the Judge's deep base, which sounded confused. "Mrs. Swiggum can be a handful," Candy whispered. "Let's talk to them from a distance before we get to the car."

Heeding her advice, "I called. Hello there. Are you okay?"

The female voice immediately shouted, "Oh, thank God. Thank God someone has found us." Then she stuck her head through the window and shouted, "Help. I can't get the door open."

I moved next to the car and saw that the door was wedged against a small sapling. I yanked on it and after twisting and pulling was able to pull it up by its roots. "I think you can open the door now," I shouted.

Slowly the door opened and a frightened woman peered out. It was dark, but as we looked into the unlit car we could see that the woman was a lot younger than the Judge. I offered her my hand to help her get out of the seat and could now see that she was not Rose Marie Swiggum. It was still pitch black and though I didn't know who she was, she immediately identified me, "Oh, my god, Jake," she cried, "get us out of here."

As I pulled her out of the car she began to cry uncontrollably. "Oh, sweet Jesus, I thought I was going to die," she wailed. She threw her arms around me and sobbed. Finally, she composed herself enough to add, "I am so glad to see you," she cried. "I am so glad to see anyone."

Quickly I untangled myself from her embrace and with Candy at my side moved to the other side of the car where I tugged on the door. Candy, who was standing next to the door pointed inside. I looked and nodded. "Sir," I shouted. "The reason you can't open your door is that it is locked."

The Judge fumbled with the lock and finally pulled the tab up. I opened his door and let him out. He stumbled and would have fallen had I not caught him as he tried to get out of the front seat. Clearly he was drunk.

Circling the car I could see that the tires had sunk into several inches of mud. There was no way we could get it out without help. I turned to Candy, handing her my car keys. "Drive immediately to Ken Brown's house," I said in a soft voice. "Tell him we need his wrecker right now. Tell him we need him to drive it, not one of his employees. Finally, tell him to follow you back. I'll hold down the fort here and see if I can calm down the woman."

"Should I tell him whose car is stuck?" she asked.

"Certainly," I responded

Then she nodded toward the woman who was leaning against a tree. "Who is she?" Candy whispered.

"Helen Lewison," I answered. "She's a third-grade teacher in Wahissa."

"Sherm's wife?" Candy asked incredulously.

"You got it," I responded. "Are you clear?"

"I've got it covered," Candy said walking toward our parked car.

The woman weaved her way over to me, throwing her arms around me. "What am I going to do?" she cried. "What is going to happen to me?"

I looked over to the car and saw that the Judge was standing with his hands on the front window of his Cadillac and his head bowed to the ground. "Mrs. Lewison, let me take a look at you," I said.

"Please, call me Helen," she said.

I gently took her head in my hands and tilted it toward the

moonlight. There was no cut or obvious bruise. "Does your head hurt?"

"No, but my leg does."

Kneeling on the ground I ran my hands over the leg she extended, her right one. I could feel a small knob. "No blood," I announced. "You probably ought to see a doctor when you get home."

She started crying. "How can I keep this from Sherman?"

I was about to respond when the Judge started moving in our direction and fell over a tree, his glasses flying in the air. Quickly I retrieved his glasses, moved to his side, and helped him to his feet. "This is treacherous ground, sir. It would be best if you don't move around too much. Perhaps you can go back to the car and sit in the front seat."

He nodded and, with my help, moved back to the car. Though the car wasn't running I could see that the ignition was on. I reached in, turned it off, and also turned off the lights, which were beginning to dim. Then I helped him sit down sideways on the seat, with his feet facing the open door.

Mrs. Lewison, Helen, walked over to the door and held his hand. "We are in a heap of trouble," she said to the Judge." Then looking at me she asked, "Do you need to report this?"

Shaking my head I said, "If this works the way I've planned, we can get you back into town with only one man knowing anything about it."

Lifting his head up the Judge spoke rather plainly, "Who's that."

"Your friend, Ken Brown. He's coming with a tow truck. My plan is for him to take your car to his garage. You can figure out the rest later."

"What will Rose Marie do?" Helen asked.

The Judge looked to me as if I had the answer. "You'll be feeling better in an hour or so," I assured him. "We'll take you home then."

A big smile came over the Judge's face. "Hell, she'll be asleep by then. There are a few advantages of having separate bedrooms." Then he leaned forward and spoke in a stage whisper, "Don't I know the girl who was with you?"

Nodding I said, "That was Candy Paulson, sir. She is the one filling in while your secretary is on vacation."

He looked confused for a moment before a spark of recognition lit up his face. "I thought I knew her. How long has she been working for me?"

"This is only her first week," I said, being careful not to remind him that she had worked for him three weeks the previous summer.

"No wonder I didn't know her name," he said triumphantly. "Her name again?"

"Candy. Candy Paulson."

"Fine young lady. Doing a hell of a job for me." Suddenly he became quite pale, and Helen moved away. The Judge put his head between his legs and coughed up some terrible stuff. He wiped his mouth on the sleeve of his suit coat and leaned back into the car, putting his head back.

Helen took me by the hand and limped toward the road. "How bad is your leg?" I asked.

"There isn't much pain. I can handle it," she said with a grimace.

We walked up close to the road where she sat on a stump. Not a single car had passed us the entire time we were there. "I'm still concerned about Sherman finding out," she said.

I thought for a moment. "He doesn't always go straight home from the game, does he?" I asked. "I think he and some of the guys often go out for a drink, particularly after a win."

Her face lit up. "You won?"

I nodded.

"Terrific. A win for everyone," she said in her most cheery voice to date. "Normally I'm in bed when he comes back from out of town." She sighed deeply. "Maybe there is hope." Then she got up and walked to the road and looked toward Wahissa. "When do you expect them?"

"Assuming Ken is at home, they could be here in another fifteen minutes," I observed.

She came back and sat on the stump again. "My marriage is a mess," she said with a catch in her voice. "Sherman has a girlfriend somewhere. I've never met her, but I know she's out there. She wears a cheap lilac perfume. The aroma is all over his shirts. It makes me gag to smell it. Can you imagine smelling another woman on your husband's shirts? He doesn't know that I know. Of course I don't know much. I don't know when he sees her. I don't know where he sees her, and I don't know who she is, but I know she's out there somewhere. I also know she has terrible taste in fragrances." She laughed until she began coughing. Helen wasn't drunk, but she spoke and laughed a bit louder than necessary.

Again she walked up to the road, looked toward Wahissa and then came back.

"One night this winter when Sherman's basketball team went out of town, I went to a bar for a drink. I had never gone to a bar alone in my life, not even when I was in college. The Judge was there. He told me I looked pretty and asked if he could sit down with me. It had been ages since anyone told me I was pretty." She wiped her eyes and continued, "We had a couple of drinks and he asked me for my phone number. I don't know what got into me, but I told him he could call after school because I was always home alone. Sherman had basketball practice every night after school."

She became silent. I thought she was embarrassed that she had talked so much and told me the details of her life. Suddenly she continued, "I only see him the nights that Sherman plays ball. We've only spent one night together. It was a night that Sherman went to the state tournament."

She looked up at me, sighed again, and looked toward the Judge, "I shouldn't have let him drive. He's been drinking since late afternoon. When he goes to La Crosse he has a friend who drives. I think it's a guy thing. If I were a man he would have asked me to drive, and we wouldn't have missed the turn."

I looked up. At the place where the car had left the road it was as straight as a plumb line.

While I had my eyes in that direction I could see the lights of two vehicles coming from the direction of Wahissa. A moment later Candy parked on the side the road, got out of the car, and pointed in our direction. The truck pulled up next to us and Ken Brown jumped out of the cab.

"Hey, Scout, you've had quite a night. Heard you beat the socks off the Kicapoogens." He saw Helen, smiled and extended his hand. "We're going to take care of you just fine. You'll be home in just a few minutes. Let me see the black Caddy."

"I think you'll see better if you turn the lights of the tow truck on the car," I suggested.

"Right you are, Scout," he said and went back to the truck, started it, and pointed it toward the car. Then he got out and walked around it. "We'll have it out of here in no time," he announced.

He went to the front door and tapped the Judge on the shoulder. "Buzzy, it is time to get moving."

I turned to Helen and said, "Buzzy?"

"It's what all his friends call him," she said with a shrug.

The Judge stood up and got his bearings. Ken walked him to the cab and helped him climb up into the passenger's seat. "Give me just a minute," Ken said to the Judge.

He pulled out some chains, made some connections, made certain the car was in the correct gear, and got into the cab. He pushed a couple handles and suddenly the rear end of the car came straight up. He backed up and the Cadillac followed the wrecker like an obedient soldier.

When he got to the road he jumped out and addressed Helen, "Can you make it through the night without seeing a doctor?"

She nodded.

"Fine." Then he addressed Candy and me. "The two of you take Helen home. If her husband's there she'll have to deal with it. I'll take Buzzy with me. He'll be fine by the time I leave him at his front door."

Helen went with Candy to our car. I started to follow, but Ken took me by the arm. "You have done a hell of a job tonight. I won't forget this." He patted me on the back and headed toward his truck.

When I got back to the car Helen was waiting by the door. She put her arms around me and kissed me gently on the cheek. "I'm forever in you debt. Some day I'll find a way to repay your kindness," she said before she climbed into the back seat.

With Candy beside me, we headed for Wahissa. Less than fifteen minutes later we reached the city limits. I traveled the back streets until I reached the Lewison house. "Go around to the back, please," Helen said.

She didn't speak again as she got out of the car and limped into the dark house. At first not a single light was turned on. Finally, we saw a dim light coming from a side room, which we figured was a bedroom. The car clock read 12:16.

"Let's take a swing through downtown," I said to Candy. We drove down Main Street and turned right on Branch. I slowed down when we came to the Minuteman Bar where the front door was wide open. We looked and both saw several Jewelers, Steve, Cy, and Terry. Over in a corner Sherm sat by himself. Candy smiled, squeezed my hand, and we drove away.

I pulled up in the front of her house and was about to turn off the engine when she shook her head. "Park in the back. I need a little time with my hero."

We parked under a big oak that blocked her house. We kissed for a few minutes before I moved my hand to her breast. Immediately her hand squeezed my wrist and she said, "Your wake-up call comes quite early. Time to go home."

I walked her to the door and kissed her good night. Then I climbed back in the car and said to myself, "So much for being a hero."

The Appeal

I planned to cheat a bit and sleep an extra fifteen minutes on Monday. I set my alarm a quarter hour later, but a summertime of disciplined rising had me up at the usual time, 5:15. After a shower I ran Dad's Norelco across my face and headed downstairs.

Mom was preparing Dad's breakfast when I walked through the kitchen. "You got home terribly late last night," she said with a raised eyebrow. "I hope nothing went wrong."

"No," I assured her. "Everything went fine. A bunch of us stayed afterward to celebrate the victory. We won 4–1."

"I know," she smiled. "I just heard it on the radio. The announcer said that you scored two runs, and Buck pitched great ball." She walked over and hugged me. "I am so proud of you," she said. "How is Candy?"

"She's fine," I said shortly. "Tell me about the anniversary."

Mom's attention quickly shifted to their trip to Richland Center. "It was amazing," she gushed. "All their wedding attendants were present. They came from all over the country. It wasn't a small wedding. Eight men and eight women stood up with them, and they were all there," she said repeating herself. "Just think, thirty years later and all your friends are not only alive and healthy, but able to come to your party." She sighed. "That would be so special."

Mom went to the window, which faced south, and stared, as if she could see Richland Center. I walked over, put my arms around her waist, kissed her and told her I'd see her late that afternoon. As I rode toward Little Oslo I thought about the differences between my mother and my father. The anniversary celebrated a wedding on Dad's side of the family, and he would have preferred to be at the ball game in Harden. For Mom family reunions and wedding anniversaries were the world series of human events. These were the places where you heard stories about people you hadn't seen in years and found out what was happening to children and grandchildren. In twenty years Mom had become so attached to the Joseph family that she adored the relatives more than Dad and Jumpy.

· · · · · · · ·

Shortly after I arrived at Little Oslo I noted that three people were seated at the Silver Table, which was at least forty-five minutes early. By 6:30 every member of the Silver group, except the Sheriff, had arrived and were huddled together, talking as to not let anyone else hear. When I went over to take their orders everyone became quiet.

"Something strange is happening at the Silver Table," I told Moose. "It's as if a group of junior high girls were trading secrets."

Moose took off the sailor cap, scratched his head, and agreed, "It is way too quiet in here."

About that time Ken Brown got up and headed to the men's room. Before he could return, Moose cut him off and began to interrogate him. Ken responded by speaking in total animation, arms waving and head thrown back. Moose, who was not the world's finest listener, stood stock still in rapt attention. From a distance I tried to read lips, without success. I finally gave up and cleaned up one of the back tables. When I returned to the kitchen Moose was smiling.

"They've got a suspect in the beatings," he said. "Sid and two deputies have left this morning for Paradise to interrogate and possibly arrest the thug."

"When did this break?"

"Last night. Late. Ken said he was out on a call close to midnight and ran into Sid. The Sheriff told him that one of his deputies had been called to handle a fight outside the Paradise Dance Hall. A big man from over near Kickapoo City beat up one of the locals. Evidently he dropped a fellow by the name of Swede with three or four punches. Swede swung, but never laid a hand on the big guy. When Swede tried to get up, with blood running down his face, the big fella said, 'If you make it to your feet I'll do to you what I did to Lloyd Swenson.' Several witnesses heard him say it. The deputy arrived after the confession and decided he didn't have enough evidence to arrest the guy. Sid's a bit miffed that his man didn't cuff him on the spot. Evidently he did manage to get the man's address. As I said, Sid's on his way right now."

"Why is the Silver Table so hush-hush?" I asked.

"Evidently Sid asked Ken not to broadcast it this morning."

"He probably wants to announce the arrest himself," I speculated.

"Or it might be that he is being cautious. Anyway, he told Ken it was okay to tell the guys at the table, but not to go beyond that. Ken said it sounds like a sure thing."

By the time the 10:00 group arrived everyone was talking about the imminent arrest of Superman.

At noon Candy and one of the women she was working with at the courthouse came to lunch. The woman was taking Candy out to celebrate her time in their office. I pulled Candy aside and told her what I knew. Immediately tears filled her eyes.

"What's wrong?" I asked.

"Dad was the deputy on the scene in Paradise last night. He says that in his judgment the confession wasn't believable, but the Sheriff blistered him something terrible. Silver told him he had blown their chance to solve the case, and that he was sick of Dad's inability to act decisively. Dad told Sid that hearsay evidence wouldn't hold up in court, and Silver blew him away. This morning he selected two other deputies to accompany him and left dad at the jail. Dad is feeling pretty blue."

"Did your dad tell you the man's name?"

"Casey Skogen. Says he drives truck for a firm in Harden, though he lives outside of Kickapoo City. Jake, something needs to be done about all these beatings. It is causing problems for people everywhere. You and I need to see if we can do something. Let's talk about this tonight."

I couldn't spend more time with Candy because August Bolstad, who ate with his three unmarried sisters, was waving at me. The Bolstads were a cranky group who demanded speedy service. When I waited on him, I'd ask if he'd like to hear what the specials were and he'd say, "What can we get quickly? We're in a hurry."

Once, when I told Cookie that they wanted their meal quickly, he growled, "He's eighty-two years old and retired. All he does is sit on his ass all day and read books. What's the hurry?"

The four Bolstads came to Little Oslo once a week and for some reason always picked my table. August marched in ahead of his three sisters, also named after the months of the year. The oldest was April, and the younger ones, who were in their early 60s, were May and June.

· · · · · · ·

At supper Mom would frequently ask me who I had met or waited on that day. One night I told her that the Bolstads had been in and then said, "I find the entire family very peculiar."

Mom, who seldom said anything negative about anyone said, "That is because they are peculiar. There was a period of about four years when they only talked to each other through their lawyers."

"What was all of that about?" I asked.

"August was the only one of the siblings who married," Mom explained. When his wife died in childbirth he was left alone to raise a little boy, August, Jr. or Auggie. June, the youngest of the sisters, moved out of the home she shared with her two sisters and her mother and became a mother to little Auggie. She was warm and compassionate, and a very good mother. She was quite different than August, who tended to be a bit stiff. August was a CPA and appeared to me to be far more comfortable with numbers than with people.

"It looked to me that April and May resented their brother selecting June to live with him and the family quickly divided into two camps—August and June on one side and April and May on the other. Someone once said it was summer against spring in the Bolstad household. One day Mother Bolstad passed away. It was assumed that she had failed to leave a will. Following the funeral when the family gathered at the house, the sisters pointed out that nearly everything in the house was marked with a piece of tape on the back or underside. The finest and most valuable pictures and antiques had a tag that read, 'This is for April,' or 'This is for May.' Initially August and June thought nothing of it, assuming that their mother was rewarding the two children who lived with her until her death.

"One day the family attorney called and asked the four siblings to come to his office for a reading of the will. They all were surprised, and April and May were clearly upset. They responded by suggesting that there was no will, since their mother had never mentioned one. The lawyer told the sisters that their mother had written the will ten years earlier and had visited him once a year to update it. The last time she had met with him was only three weeks before her death.

"The lawyer showed the family the signatures that witnessed the will and then began to read a detailed list of what each child was to receive, right down to knives and forks. The longer the lawyer read the colder the room became. The list differed dramatically from the tags found on the backside of the pictures and antiques. It was very obvious that April and May, not Mother Bolstad, had tagged the valuables in the house. August and June were incensed.

"When the reading was finished, August and June stood and stared with contempt at the two women who sat with heads hanging in shame. Then August and June left the room and didn't speak to their sisters for months. They hired a moving company to pick up the items listed in the will. In the past they had eaten together three to four times a week. Now they didn't speak or see each other.

"They all belonged to our church, and they all continued to worship every Sunday, though they sat as far apart as they were able. August, who taught the adult Bible class, let it be known that his errant sisters were not welcome. This went on for several months."

"How long ago did this take place?" I asked.

"I'm not quite sure," Mom said thoughtfully. "Perhaps eight to ten years ago."

"Obviously it got solved," I observed. "What happened?"

"One day Marme went to visit the pastor. She had been reading her Bible and told Pastor Hauge that there was a passage that addressed the Bolstad situation. "It is Matthew 18:15-20," she told him.

The pastor nodded and summarized the passage, "If a brother or sister sins against you, go to them and show them their fault. Do it privately. If they listen you have won your brother or sister back."

"Marme said something to the effect that both sides were in the wrong. Pastor Hauge asked her to explain. Marme said that April and May had deliberately attempted to deceive their siblings and to gain goods by dishonest means. 'In a sense they were attempting to steal things from their brother and sister."

"And what have August and June done?" the pastor asked Marme.

"They have refused to forgive their sisters. Forgiveness, according to the Lord's Prayer is a command, not a suggestion. 'Forgive us our trespasses as we forgive those who trespass against us.'"

"What did Pastor Hauge say to that?" I asked.

"He smiled and agreed with Marme. I don't quite remember what happened next," Mom said looking off into space. "I know Marme went to visit the two sisters while Pastor visited August and June. Pastor suggested that the man who taught the Bible class had the burden of doing the word and not just teaching it. Marme convinced the two sisters to confess their sin and ask for forgiveness. It wasn't long after that when we saw them all back together again."

"You wouldn't know that there was anything in their past that divided them from the way they come to Little Oslo," I observed.

"I think that this is one time when forgiveness brought a family back together again." Mom observed.

· · · · · · ·

Until I met the Bolstads I had never paid much attention to names. Suddenly I realized that Wahissa had some rather colorful handles. Tim worked for Crash Johnson, who ran a body shop. I had always assumed that Crash was his name. One day I asked Moose if Crash had another name.

Moose screwed up his face, "Of course he has another name. You don't think his mama baptized him Crash, do you? His real name is Tillman." Moose thought for a moment. "When he was growing up, kids would tease him by calling him Tilly. With a name like that you probably prefer being called Crash."

One day I overheard someone ask our fire chief, "Who gave you your nickname?" Until that moment I assumed Blaze Ellison was his real name. No one called him anything else.

"His real name is Reid," Moose said when I asked.

When I told Dad about my discovery he asked if I knew how Wolf Paulson got his name.

I shook my head and said, "I don't have a clue." Again, I had always thought Wolf was his real name, perhaps a shortened name for Wolfgang.

"When he was a boy," Dad reported, "he called the police to report that he had seen a wolf running wild in the neighborhood. They called ten or so men armed with rifles to patrol the neighborhood. It turned out he had seen a cat and it wasn't even a large cat. The name Wolf stuck."

As the summer wore on I found out how Tinker Munson, a repair man was named, but I never did find out who came up with Pookie Bailey, Scum Harris or, for that matter, Moose Mellem.

By the time I finished waiting on the Bolstads and my other customers, Candy was on her way back to work. I knew I'd have to talk to her about her dad after the game.

It was a confident group of Jewelers that arrived at the ballpark on the night of the twenty-third. The sound of ball meeting bat in batting practice seemed sharp and the infield play was crisp. Smokey announced that Cam would open on the mound and Buck would be on first.

For the second game in a row I opened the game by walking on four pitches. One pitch later I scored on a triple in the gap in right center. LaVern drove in that runner giving Cam a two-run lead when he went to the mound for the first time.

We expanded our lead to 6–0 and Cam kept Ft. Price off the scoreboard until the sixth inning when the Mustangs loaded the bases with one out. Kim Hornung, their first baseman, hit a line drive that soared over LaVern's head. Hornung ended up on third with a stand-up triple. The score was 6–3.

As the next hitter came to bat I saw Buck call time out, walk to the mound, and point to first. It looked like he was instructing Cam. Buck stepped on the mound and then he stepped off pointing back to first. Finally, he ran back to first. Cam mimicked the big guy by stepping on the mound and then stepping off. He then threw the ball to first where Buck stepped on the bag. The field umpire raised his right hand in the air and pointed to Hornung on third base. It appeared from where I stood that he had just called the Ft. Price first baseman out.

As soon as the umpire's arm went up, Hornung ran across the diamond screaming. The manager for the Mustangs, a short man who must have weighed 250 pounds, waddled to first screaming expletives that I could hear plainly in the outfield. I trotted slowly toward the infield and joined the Zitzners, who were standing behind second base trying to figure out what had just taken place.

The home-plate umpire joined the field umpire near the pitcher's mound. They huddled briefly and the home-plate umpire pointed at the manager before pointing to the parking lot. The three of us were amazed. I had never seen a manager ejected prior to that moment. Seconds later the field umpire ejected Hornung. The two men in black stood back to back as the Mustang players swarmed the field shouting and cursing.

Suddenly, there was a piercing whistle. It was the home-plate umpire. He had reached in his pocket and produced a silver whistle, the kind that football referees normally carried. With the sound of the whistle all activity ceased. He then walked to the screen behind home plate and requested use of the public address microphone.

As soon as the microphone reached his hand he spoke in a booming voice: "Ladies and gentleman. Mr. Conrad, the field umpire accepted the appeal of Wahissa and called number 21 for Ft. Price out for failing to touch first base before touching second. There is no doubt in Mr. Conrad's mind that number 21 missed the bag. I then ejected Mr. Hanson, the Ft. Price manager for cursing, and Mr. Conrad ejected Mr. Hornung, number 21, for cursing. If Ft. Price insists on further displays of unsportsmanlike conduct we will declare that Ft. Price forfeits to Wahissa. If they are willing to go back to their dugout the game will proceed as follows. Since the batter missed first base he is out, and all the runners must return to the base they were on prior to the play. No runs count. There are two outs. The score is 6–0."

There were a few boos from the Ft. Price fans, but they were amazingly quiet. We figured later that they were mostly confused.

As we retreated to our positions something was happening over at Ted Towne's box, behind the Jewelers' bench. A heated conversation was taking place between Ted, someone I didn't recognize, and Smokey. A moment later Smokey waved for Buck to join them.

Meanwhile, the umpires stood near the mound watching as Hornung and the manager moved slowly toward the parking lot. When they disappeared from view the umpire bellowed, "Play ball."

As the next Ft. Price player approached the plate, Smokey waved his hand and walked slowly to home plate where he began a conversation with the home-plate umpire. People in the stands began to clap rhythmically, to urge the umpires to start the game. Smokey appeared to have a book in his hands, which he handed to the umpire. The two men began to read from the book. Finally, the umpire walked back to the screen and the public address announcer handed him the microphone again.

"There has been a mistake made. According to the rules, runs scored by the men on base count and the batter is out. The score is 6–3. Play ball."

The announcement was met by a chorus of boos from our fans and utter confusion from both benches. None of us were sure what just took place, but before we were clear, Cam stepped on the mound and threw a fastball, which the Ft. Price batter hit toward center field. LaVern caught it and the inning was over. We raced in from the field to find out what just happened.

Smokey had Buck explain the process of an appeal. "An appeal is quite complicated," he said slowly. "The pitcher must first step on the rubber, before stepping off and throwing to the base that they say was missed. If we don't do it correctly, the appeal is disallowed. Since he didn't know the procedure, I tried to walk Cam through step-by-step."

"After the play was over we learned that the umpire had made a mistake. He disallowed the runs, when by rule they actually counted. A friend of mine brought the rule to Smokey's attention. We decided that we should read the proper rule to the umpire. Smokey conferred with the umpire and allowed him to read the section that pertained. After he read the rule, the umpire reversed his decision. It was the right thing to do."

I was impressed. Smokey put three runs on the board by pointing out a mistake. I was proud of him.

Later, I found out that the stranger and Buck convinced Smokey that if they didn't correct the mistake immediately Ft. Price could protest. If they won the protest it would be possible that we'd have to play the game over.

· · · · · · ·

At the end of the game I was looking for Mom and Dad, hoping to ride home with them, when Candy ran up to me, hugged me and said, "Walk me home, Jake. This is a beautiful night."

Bat and glove in hand I walked up the hill toward home, struggling to keep up with Candy who was moving at a torrid pace. When we reached a grove of pine trees she pulled me in and kissed me. "Jake, this is a wonderful night."

I figured you never questioned a girl who wanted to make out, but after she repeated herself several times I asked, "What's up?"

"Everything worked out. Dad's in the clear. Sheriff Silver came back in the office and thanked him for saving the department a major embarrassment."

"Great. How did it all happen?"

"Well, the Sheriff and the other two deputies drove to Kickapoo City early this morning to interrogate Casey Skogen. They left at 5:30 and didn't get to his place a minute too soon. Casey had his rig loaded and was headed for a location in Illinois. Sheriff Silver was carrying a warrant for his arrest. Seems they made an early morning visit to the Judge's home and had him sign the warrant. By the way, Dad said the Judge was in a foul mood, can you imagine that?

"Casey convinced them that rather than take him to the county jail they should question him at his kitchen table. He answered all their questions and in essence told them that what he said during the fight was just a bunch of bull. He said he wasn't within three hundred miles of where Lloyd or Kid were mauled. When they didn't believe him he went to his semi and pulled out a detailed log that he kept for tax purposes. The log had him on the road the nights that Lloyd, Kid, and Tom were mugged. They concluded that the man was telling the truth."

"Did they just take his word that the log was accurate?"

"No. They called the company he works for and asked if they knew where Casey was on such and such nights. They also had records, which matched the log. The deputies then visited a couple of neighbors who said that Casey is an okay guy when he isn't drinking, and that he doesn't drink very often."

"Then what happened?" I asked.

Candy hugged me and continued, "The Sheriff drove back to the jail and told dad that he was right. There wasn't enough evidence. He said, 'If you would have brought that man in based on that one statement we would look like a bunch of asses.' He apologized to Dad for his intemperate remarks."

"Good for Silver," I exclaimed. "It takes a big man to admit he made a mistake."

"Dad is floating on cloud nine," Candy said, and she kissed me again.

When I went home that night I thought it was amazing how often we both suffer and benefit from the mistakes of others.

Reconciliation

CHAPTER 16

On Friday, July 25, I went directly from work to see Marme. When I reached her house I saw Aunt Elaine's car in the driveway. The two of them were sitting on the porch drinking ice tea and eating chocolate chip cookies. I quickly raided the freezer, chose lemonade rather than tea, and joined them.

As I sat down I asked, "How is Allen?"

"I'm not sure," Elaine answered. "He talked briefly with Marme, but then walked over to see you. He expected that you'd go home after work."

"Has he had any more phone calls?" I asked.

"None that I know of, but he may have made a call of his own. I'm not sure. He did speak with Marme alone for a few minutes."

I turned and waited for her to tell me what was happening. She sat quietly looking at the floor until she said gently, "Why don't you find Allen. I think he can fill you in on what is happening better than anyone."

As usual, Marme made perfect sense. Why should she tell me what is happening in Allen's life when Allen was perfectly capable of telling me himself. I finished the cookies, drank the rest of the lemonade, bid my aunt and grandmother good-bye, and began to ride toward home.

About a block from our house I saw Allen walking slowly, his hands in his pockets. I coasted up to him, dismounted, and began to walk beside him. "Great day for a walk," he said cheerfully.

I agreed and we walked in silence until we arrived at the back of our place. "Let me park my bike," I suggested. "I'll get some Cokes and we'll head for the Loft. Tim will be there shortly."

By the time we reached the Loft, Tim had already arrived. "Crash closed a bit early," he explained. "I think he is going to a stock car race in La Crosse."

It was only moments after we popped open the Cokes and settled in the lounge chairs that Tim asked, "Have you had any more phone calls?"

"No," Allen said smiling, "but I made a couple."

We both leaned forward waiting for the next sentence, but he just looked at us. Again, Tim broke the silence. "Who did you call?"

"Can I tell you the whole story?"

Tim leaned forward, "Only if you put it in gear."

Allen thought for a moment and then began, "I went to see Marme a couple of days after her fall. Elaine said she was doing well, so I dropped in. I planned not to say anything if she didn't seem to be strong, but she was the old Marme. I ended up telling her everything. Of course, she knew most of it. When I finished I asked her for whatever insight she had. She said, 'Come over here and sit next to me.' I did.

"'Have you ever heard of St. Francis of Assisi?' she asked me.

"I told her I had.

"'What do you know about him?' she said sweetly.

"I know he loved all of nature. I know that he loved birds and animals. I know that thousands of people have his statue in their gardens.

"'Anything else?' she asked.

"Not much," I said. "Oh yeah, I have heard a prayer of his in church, something about becoming an instrument of God's peace.

"Marme nodded and began to recite it from memory.

Lord, make me an instrument of Thy peace;
Where there is hatred, let me sow love;
where there is injury, pardon;
where there is error, the truth;
where there is doubt, the faith;
where there is despair, hope;
where there is darkness, light;
And where there is sadness, joy.

"She stopped and said, 'There is more. It is a beautiful poem. Here is what I know about St. Francis. He was kind, gentle, loving, and caring. And yet, he made one terrible mistake. He had a rift with his father and it never healed. As far as I know his father did nothing to reconcile, and neither did Francis. He was one of the most wonderful people who ever lived and yet he had a fight with his father in his twenties and they remained separated forever. Do you know why?'

"I shook my head. 'I have no idea.'

"Marme looked at me and said, 'Because each person thought it was the task of the other to make the first move.' We sat for several minutes before she spoke again. 'There is another father and son story with a different ending. You can find it in the second half of the fifteenth chapter of St. Lukes gospel. Most people call it the Parable of the Prodigal Son. Once again a father and son are separated. When you have time, read it.'

"That was all she said. Nothing more. I waited, but she just smiled at me and held my hand.

"Finally, I got up, thanked her, and went outside where I got in the car and drove back to Elaine's farm. A strange idea came to me. Until that moment I had assumed that the responsibility for contact between DeDe and me was all hers. Now I realize that was no longer true. If we were to meet, I bore equal responsibility. When I reached Elaine's house another idea struck me. I had thought about her every day for years, but I had never prayed for her. I went to my room, sat on my bed, and asked God to help DeDe. When I finished praying I realized that she might be hurting just as much as I was. Up to that moment I always thought about how she had wronged me. When I finished praying I realized she also must be carrying a heavy burden. Before I left my room I read the story Marme had suggested, the story of the father and his separated son.

"When Elaine came in the house I said, 'What do you think Joyce would say if I called DeDe on the phone?'

"Elaine looked surprised. Then she walked over, hugged me and said, 'I think she would say, "It is about time."'

"I said, 'Tonight, I would like to call her. May I use the phone?'

"She smiled and said, 'Please do. And talk for as long as you find it necessary. When you make that call you will make a lot of people happy.'

"I said, 'I will feel better if I call Joyce and Marvin first.' Elaine just nodded.

"Now, to finally answer your question. That night I called my mom and dad. Mom told me Dad was not home. I said, 'Mom, I am calling to ask your permission to call DeDe on the phone.'

"There was silence on the other end and then she said, 'Allen, for years I have prayed that you would want to talk with DeDe. I know that the two of you need to make a connection before you put your life together.'

"I told her that I planned to call her that night.

"She said, 'Allen, do you have her number?'

"I said, 'I don't think so.'

"'Get a piece of paper and something to write with,' she said, 'and I will give it to you.'

"'You have her number?' I was surprised.

"'I have talked to her several times in the last two years. We pray for each other. Joy helped us make the connection.'

"She gave me the number, and I told her I loved her. That night I made the second phone call. The voice on the other end of the line simply answered by saying, 'Hello, this is Delores.' The woman sounded much older than I imagined DeDe to be.

"I said, 'My name is Allen. I was born on May 19, 1933.'

"After a moment the voice said, 'I have been waiting to hear your voice. Will you please forgive me for what I did?'

"I said, 'Yes. I forgive you.' Then I thought for a moment and said, 'Will you forgive me for waiting so long to call you?'

"It sounded like she was crying, but eventually she said, 'After all that I did I'm not sure I have the right to forgive you, but if it helps, I do. Oh my, how I forgive you.'

"We talked for a short time before I asked, 'May I visit you?'

"She answered immediately. 'Yes. I hope it is soon.'

"After some more talking I arranged to drive up to La Crosse on Sunday to see her. I'm wondering if one of you is able to go with me. I would like to have company and someone to talk to on the way home. I'm quite sure Elaine will go with me, but I thought it might be best if I went with a guy."

I explained that it would be difficult to travel on Sundays since I played ball. "If you could go on a Saturday I could get some time off in the afternoon and go."

Allen explained that DeDe, or Delores, as she now was known, worked on Saturdays.

Tim said he could go most Sundays, and they immediately began to make plans. Tim offered to drive his car. They set the date for Sunday, August 17.

The next Sunday the three of us sat together in church when Pastor Hauge preached about Esau and Jacob reconciling near the Jabbok River. I was amazed at how often the lessons on Sunday fit what was happening during the week. It often seemed as if Pastor Hauge had been listening to what was happening in our family before he prepared his sermon.

That night we played Brownstown on their diamond. We blew them out. Leading 8–0 after we batted in the fourth inning, Smokey told Buck he was going to move him to first and have Mo pitch. "I could put you back in if I need you, but this would be a good night for me to give you a rest. We have a lot of innings next week," he said.

I was ready to head to left field when he waved me over. "Put on the catching gear," he told me. I was surprised and delighted. As I was putting on the shin guards he said, "I'll call pitches from the dugout. Don't be too obvious when you look my way. One finger on my chin is a fastball. You won't get that very often. If I cup my chin with my entire hand, it's a curve. My hand in my lap means you'll call the knuckler. He's only got three pitches. Let's see how you handle it."

Brownstown didn't have a very good team, but they had a first baseman by the name of Metzger who could knock the cover off the ball. We normally pitched very carefully to Metzger. He led off the bottom of the fourth. After going curve ball, curve ball, Mo waved off a third breaking ball and tried to slip a fastball by him. Metzger hit the ball out of the park, about 365 feet to left center field.

As Metzger rounded third I looked over and saw Smokey standing with his hands on his hips glaring at Mo. From that point on Mo didn't shake off a single sign. Also from that pitch Mo went primarily to the knuckle ball. The first two didn't do anything, but were thankfully out of the strike zone. Then, with the third pitch, the knuckle ball came alive. It danced through the air, dipping and hopping, like a humming-bird with hiccups.

I tried to catch the hummingbird in my bare hands, or in this case, with a stiff catcher's mitt. The mitt was stiff because it had a lot of padding that was added to protect the catcher from the pitcher's fastball. The problem was Mo wasn't throwing any fastballs. During the fourth inning I caught three out of every five balls thrown to me. I knocked down a couple and only one ball got entirely past me.

The pitch that totally eluded my glove was a third strike with two outs. By the time I caught up with the ball the runner was on first base. After one pitch to the next batter, a strike, the runner was on second base. He had such a good jump, and the ball took so long to get to me, that I didn't even make a throw to second.

I called time out and went to the mound to talk with Mo. He said, "Can you handle the next three, Jake?"

"For sure," I responded. Then a plan came to me. "We'll throw a knuckler on the first pitch. I don't think he'll try to steal on the first pitch. Then we'll pitch out on the second, and I'll try to nail him at third. Give me your fastball up and out of the strike zone."

Mo nodded and I headed back to the plate. The next pitch was a dandy. It bobbed and weaved and the batter swung and missed it by a foot. The next pitch was high and outside, just as we had planned. I jumped up, caught the ball, and was ready to throw to third when the player, who was running with his head up, saw the pitchout and headed back to second. I turned and threw the ball right at the bag at second, but Sherm Lewison, who played second base, was ten feet away from the bag standing and watching. Just about the time I thought the ball would roll into center field, the shortstop came running, caught the ball, and made a swipe with his glove, all in one motion. The runner was out and our bench exploded.

We got two more runs in the top of the fifth and when I went out to catch at the end of the inning I had made a major adjustment. I borrowed a first basemen's glove. It was the biggest glove around and it enabled me to trap a few more of the get-away knucklers.

Metzger drove in a run in the eighth inning, but Mo shut them down until the ninth, when Cam came in to relieve. I switched back to a catcher's mitt, and Cam set them down 1–2–3. We went home with a 12–2 victory, and I got an atta-boy from Smokey. Cam, who had only pitched in two games all summer, was thrilled and patted me on the back. "And how about that throw to second," he grinned.

"Not bad for a guy with a weak arm," I offered.

Cam was the driver that night. The two of us got into his car and laughed all the way back to Wahissa. Winning is sure a lot more fun than losing.

The New Orleans Stars

The night of our first game Smokey had pulled the team together and said, "Ted has an announcement to make."

Our owner strutted into the dugout and said, "Men, this afternoon I signed a contract with the New Orleans Stars. They're a colored team whose season usually ends in late July. They barnstorm the month of August. I called a team owner in Rockford who hosted them last year. He plans to have them back. That was good enough for me, so I signed them. We'll play them at Wahissa Stadium on August 15, a Friday."

"What they got, Ted?" Buck asked.

"They've got lots of power, and they've got a lot of speed. Remember, this is a pro team. Every man on the team is paid. They feature a woman, Toni Rock, at second base. They say she once got a hit off Satchel Page. My friend in Rockford said she is one of the weak links on the team, but she draws a crowd."

Smokey spoke up. "We'll face pitching that will be as good as you'll find in AA or AAA. You'll see a couple of guys who could follow Jackie Robinson to the majors now that the color barrier is broken. Colored ball in the south is good baseball. This will be our chance to see how we match up with the big boys."

. . . .

Posters for the game between the Stars and the Jewelers went up shortly after July 4. Ted expected that the crowd would be as large as the one that saw the Monarchs play three years earlier and bigger than the one they drew when the team played the House of David the year before.

There was always a lot of baseball talk at Little Oslo, but I didn't hear anyone talk about the Stars coming to town until a day in late July when Moose asked Ted a question in his usual bombastic voice. "Where will these colored ballplayers stay when they come to town?"

"I'm not in charge of getting them rooms, but I assume that they're staying with Bud over at the Lincoln," Ted responded.

The Hotel Lincoln was a three-story building in the heart of the business district. Bud Fortune, who took over from his dad, had what appeared to be a thriving business. His rates were reasonable and, people said, the rooms were clean, which helped him pick up business from people traveling through Wahissa on their way to either La Crosse or Madison.

Max Fisher, who owned a store near the hotel seemed a bit upset, "Do you think that is wise? I can't imagine anyone staying there with a bunch of coloreds."

"What's the problem?" Ted asked.

"Are you a simpleton?" Max Fisher responded. "Colored guys in a hotel will create a major headache."

"What kind of a headache?" Ted insisted.

"You know. All kinds of things. Smell, for openers."

"Smell? What do you know? How many colored people have you met?"

"I know what I know," Max countered. "I've talked to people who have told me the smell can be just awful."

"Personally, I think you are full of shit," Ted countered. "Anyway, we don't know where they're going to stay, do we? They might stay in La Crosse and come in the day of the game and go back that night. They can be back in La Crosse in under an hour."

This conversation continued over the next week. Some argued that the team was staying at the Lincoln and others argued that it would be smart to stay in La Crosse, since that is where they would be playing the next night. "It doesn't make sense to drive down here the day before the game when you can come on game day and go back to your rooms." Someone else argued that the prices were better at the Lincoln and therefore "it only stands to reason that they're staying right here in Wahissa."

Finally, Cookie did what no one else seemed to think of; he walked over and asked Bud if he was housing a baseball team in August. When he returned, Cookie, who could go a week without talking, was the center of attention. "They're staying at the Lincoln. Bud told me so himself. I don't want to suggest that Bud isn't tuned into the same station as the rest of us, but he didn't know they're colored. He booked them over the phone. You know what he said to me? He said, 'They didn't sound colored.'" Cookie slapped his knee and repeated himself, "They didn't sound colored! How's that?"

Peals of laughter followed each time Cookie told it. Like a great storyteller, who he normally wasn't, the story got better with each telling. Before long he had Bud slapping his head when Cookie told him what was happening.

A couple of days later someone wrote, in chalk, on the sidewalk in front of the hotel: Home of the Colored Stars.

The last week in July, Mom came home from church circle and announced that she had been in the midst of an argument that afternoon. "Elizabeth Monson started things off by saying she thought Bud ought to help those boys find a better place to stay. Several women seemed to agree that Wahissa is not the right place for a bunch of colored ballplayers to sleep. Agnes Einerson said that many people believe Bud will never rent a room in the hotel again. It just won't be the same place. I tried to keep quiet, but it made me mad. I ended up saying, 'What kind of town do we have that would consider pulling the welcome mat back from a bunch of men who are over a thousand miles away from home? If they can play in this town they should stay in this town.'"

Dad, who was one of the least demonstrative people I've ever met in my life got up out of his chair, walked over to Mom, and kissed her. "Lou," he said holding her head in his hands, "every day you make me proud to be your husband."

Mom blushed, smiled at me, and then kissed him back.

If housing the New Orleans Stars was a settled issue in the Skip and Lou Joseph home, it sure wasn't at Little Oslo. Every day loud discussions broke out. The first week in August we heard that many people planned to fill the street the day of the game. One day we almost had a fight when someone said loud enough for Ted to hear, "If the Lincoln goes out of business you can thank Ted Towne." Ted got up and started moving in the direction of the loudmouth, but Woody Carlson was faster. He stood between the two men and then said to Ted in a voice loud enough for everyone to hear, "There is no accounting for pure ignorance." With that he turned and faced the man who had now turned away. No one would be stupid enough to pick a fight with Woody.

One week before the game, Pastor Hauge came into Little Oslo and asked, "Is Maynard here?" He had me stumped until Cookie answered from the back, "Maynard, that is Moose, will be back in a few minutes." Until that moment I didn't even know Moose had another name.

I asked if he would like anything while he was waiting. "Coffee black," he said with a smile, "and while I'm at it I'll have a donut. Are they fresh?"

I assured them they were fresh that morning, direct from City Bakery.

"How is your summer, Jake?" he asked me.

"I'm having a terrific time," I told him. "I love working here, and it is great playing with the Jewelers."

"I saw your game on Wednesday," he told me. He must have seen the surprise spread across my face. "I've seen four games this summer, and all of your home games this spring." He then laughed. "I often sit down the foul line in left. I moved there a few years ago when I found people looking to see how I responded to what you might call, coarse language, coming from the field. I've been around that kind of language most of my life, but people don't know it and get uncomfortable when I'm near. Now I can see the entire game and people don't worry about what I'm thinking. You're a fine ballplayer, Jake. I know the team values you for your bat and speed, but I think you are their best outfielder. It is obvious that you've studied the hitters. Without direction from the bench you play each batter a bit different. Either you've taken notes or you've got a natural instinct."

It then dawned on me that I had seen him sitting there, but didn't recognize him. He wore a hat and he often had binoculars. He was the guy I saw shaking hands with Buck after a recent game and the one who helped us avoid a nasty situation following the appeal in the Ft. Price game. I was also amazed and impressed that he watched close enough to see how I played each hitter. No one, not even Smokey, had ever commented on that part of my defense.

He bit into his donut and then said matter-of-factly, "For what it's worth, I think Lombardo tips his palm ball by wiping his hand on his pant leg before he throws it."

Just then Moose, or Maynard, walked in. Pastor Hauge went over, talked quietly with him, and the two men went into Moose's office.

When they came out both were smiling. They shook hands and the pastor waved at me and left.

That night at supper I told my parents about my conversation with Pastor Hauge earlier in the day. "I had no idea he was a baseball fan," I said approvingly. "He commented about the way I shade different hitters."

Dad, who had been the church council president for several years, always called the pastor by his first name. "David," he began slowly before stopping.

My mother prompted, "David . . ."

"David played a lot of baseball growing up. When he first came to town he was going to play with the Jewelers, but in those days most of the games started early Sunday afternoon and he was afraid he'd be late coming from church. He was a catcher, I believe. I'm almost positive that he once caught Buck."

About half an hour after supper Dad excused himself saying he had a meeting at church. It seemed strange that Dad, who hardly ever left the house after dark, was leaving for a meeting at church. I looked at my mother and she just shrugged. I thought that meant, "I don't know what this is about." He got home after nine and went right to his bedroom. I was out on the porch listening to the Cardinals game on KMOX (the voice of St. Louis), which we couldn't get during the day, but came in loud and clear at night, particularly if I turned the antenna a certain direction. Before I went upstairs I looked at his bedroom and thought, "There is something strange about his silence. Normally, he talks to me before he turns in for the night."

Operation Hospitality

CHAPTER 18

efore I jumped on my bike to go to work on Thursday morning, I saw a suitcase sitting outside my parents' bedroom. I looked for my mother to ask about it, but I couldn't find her. I looked out back and saw Dad cleaning the inside of the car. The suitcase puzzled me, but I thought, "I'll check with them when I get home.

Midway through the morning, before the 10:00 crowd arrived, Moose pulled Cookie and me aside and said, "The next couple days we're going to expand our hours. We're going to be open for supper. We'll serve our Saturday noon menu. I did an inventory and we should have enough for both Thursday and Friday nights. I don't expect to be open on Saturday night."

I listened quietly but Cookie was agitated. "What the hell is this all about?" he demanded.

Moose spoke slowly and deliberately, hoping, no doubt, that he could get Cookie to lower his volume and his anxiety. "I'm expecting more business. We'll probably have twenty-five or so folks tonight and tomorrow night. Can I count on you to work some overtime? Jake, I know you've got a ballgame tomorrow night, so just let me know when you need to go and I'll get some help."

I told Moose, "I can work tonight and tomorrow, and it would be great if I could get out of here by 5:30. Batting practice starts at 6:00."

"I forgot about batting practice," Moose said, "Why don't you plan to leave at 5:00. I'll go with plan B." Then he looked at Cookie.

"You can always count on me," the cook grumbled, "even when I don't have a damn clue as to what is happening."

Moose patted him on the back and said, "You'll need to order extra bread from Farley when the Sunbeam truck comes by. And double-check the chicken. We need enough to serve thirty."

When the buzz was over, about 2:15, Moose told me that I could leave. "I won't need you until 4:15," he said.

Just then a customer walked in and announced, "A bus just arrived in front of the Lincoln. About fifteen colored guys got off. A couple of them are the size of a small mountain. There must be twenty, thirty people gathering across the street. I don't know what's going to happen."

I told Moose that I was going to go over and take a look. Moose smiled and said, "Everything is going to be fine, Jake. It is all under control."

I ran the two blocks and arrived just in time to see the last of the ballplayers walking up the steps into the hotel. The customer had given a pretty accurate account. There were at least twenty-five people, mostly men, standing in small groups looking in the direction of the hotel.

One of the men on the corner saw me and said, "It ain't a good idea to have them colored stay in town, Jake. I don't mind 'em playing ball at night, but this isn't good for the city."

Remembering my mother's line I said, "If they're going to play in town they ought to stay in town." I walked to a spot where I could see what was happening without talking to people.

A few minutes later a couple of the Stars walked down the steps of the hotel and looked around. Both of them were dressed in suits. I quickly walked across the street, extended my hand and said, "Hi, I'm Jake Joseph. I play left field for the Jewelers. Welcome to Wahissa."

One of the men, who must have been six foot three, shook my hand and said politely, "I'm Jerry Johnson. I play first base." He then nodded to his companion, "He's Charlie Johnson, my brother. He catches."

We shook hands and talked briefly about their trip. "We were in Rochester last night, and we'll be in La Crosse Saturday night," Jerry said. "Some weeks we play six or seven games. We're enjoying a night off."

Charlie was looking around. "Quite a crowd," he noted. Then he dropped his voice and said, "Are they friendly?"

Turning my back to the street I said, "Most of them are curious. Their ancestors came from Sweden and Norway. We don't have a lot of people visiting us who have dark skin.

Just then I saw our family car pull up in front of the hotel. My mother was driving. She turned off the ignition and Dad got out of the door on the passenger's side, while Pastor Hauge exited from the back. They opened the trunk and pulled out two suitcases. Both of them greeted me. I must have been staring because Pastor Hauge smiled at me and said, "It's okay, Jake. Everything will become clear in a few minutes. Can you introduce us to your friends?"

"Yes," I stammered. "This is Charlie Johnson and Jerry Johnson. They're brothers. Jerry plays first base for the Stars and Charlie catches." I must have neglected to tell the Johnson brothers the names of the two men with suitcases, because Pastor Hauge extended his hand and said, "I'm David Hauge. I'm a pastor here in Wahissa."

Dad who was grinning ear to ear said, "Even though he may not admit it, I'm Skip, Jake's dad. We're staying the night with you fellows."

Pastor Hauge picked up his suitcase and said, "We're going to check in now. We'll see you both at supper."

No sooner had the two of them walked up the steps than a car driven by Mrs. Carlson stopped. Woody and Swish, my high school baseball coach, got out and retrieved their suitcases from the trunk. Moments later a car driven by Dani Brown carrying Ted Towne and

Ken Brown showed up. The last to arrive was the president of First National, Karl Schmidt, who walked across the street from the bank, suitcase in hand. To say I was astonished is a gross understatement. Later, Dad dubbed the adventure, "Operation Hospitality."

I now understood what was happening back at Little Oslo. I asked Jerry and Charlie to excuse me. I then ran back the two blocks and tied on my apron. I tried to look ticked off at Moose for not letting me in on the secret, but the truth was I was ready to burst with pride at what they were doing. "So this is what you and Pastor Hauge were planning," I said to Moose, slapping him on the back. "How come you didn't tell me?"

"You can't get into trouble for what you don't know," Moose said, slapping me back. "Now, help me get the tables arranged. A couple of minutes later Pastor Hauge entered the door and started putting name tags in front of every plate. The arrangement had each table seating four Stars and either one or two men from Wahissa. The Stars' manager, Eddy Casperson, the traveling secretary, and the Johnson brothers sat at one table with Dad and pastor.

Around 5:00 the room began to fill. It was a glorious sight. Black men and white men were shaking hands and laughing. It had to be a first in Wahissa. Just before Pastor Hauge attempted to quiet the room for an announcement, Max Fisher and the Sheriff entered timidly. They waved at the pastor who walked over to greet them. They huddled and whispered. Later I found out that they told him that even though they hadn't been in on the planning, they would like to have supper with the team. Dad who was standing next to the pastor said the exact quote from Max went something like this, "I know I expressed my doubts about this entire venture but I'm behind you 100 percent. If I wasn't Jewish I'd join your church tomorrow morning."

Pastor welcomed them and slid two additional chairs around the tables. The Sheriff walked around and shook the hand of every one of the Stars. He looked like a man campaigning for votes in the next election.

When it appeared that everyone had arrived, Pastor Hauge asked for people's attention and welcomed the Stars to Wahissa. "We're proud to have you in town. We hope you like Wahissa as much as we do. Here in my hand are free tickets for the movie now playing at The Strand, entitled, "Blackbeard the Pirate," staring Robert Newton, William Bendix, Irene Ryan and . . ." he acted as if he had forgotten, "Oh, yes, Linda Darnell." The Stars all applauded vigorously, and I'm sure it wasn't for William Bendix.

He then asked the men to bow their heads as he gave thanks. He thanked God for a whole lot of things, including the game of baseball and Swedish pancakes. His *Amen* was greeted with a rousing *AMEN* from the Stars. He was about to tell us to start serving when one of the Stars, Jonah Harris, the third baseman, stood and got everyone's attention.

"First of all I want to thank y'all for this wonderful greeting. Several nights we had to eat take out on the bus when we couldn't get a restaurant to serve us. This is one of the warmest welcomes we've received. We're most grateful. Now don't get me wrong, we still plan to beat your ball club tomorrow night, but we are grateful."

The room exploded in laughter and Ted Towne announced that the Jewelers would show no mercy. More laughter.

Then Jonah finished. "I'm a believer and one of the problems we face on the road is that we're normally traveling on Sunday. I'm wondering if the pastor would be so kind as to open the church tomorrow for some hymns and prayers. It would be much appreciated. We'd also like a sermon. We haven't heard the Word for nearly a month." Shouts of approval came from around the room.

Pastor Hauge stood and told them that he would plan a service for the next morning. "Let's hold it at 11:00, the normal time for Sunday morning worship. I'm not sure our organist is available, but we'll come up with something."

Jonah smiled and said, "If it okay with you, Isaiah, our center fielder, plays a fine gospel piano."

"I think we have our service almost planned," Pastor announced. "Now, let the serving begin."

Mona, Moose, and I brought hot plates of chicken, potatoes, and corn on the cob to each of the tables. Swedish pancakes followed, heaping plates of them. At first there was an explosion of noise as the Stars experienced Scandinavian food for the first time. One of the men shouted, "This is good. Where do you sign up to be Swedish?"

Then, as they settled in to eat, the room got quiet. Moose pulled his serving crew together and said, "When you hear the buzz again you know they are pretty well done with the main course. Then it's time for dessert." Desert was apple pie and ice cream.

As the meal was being eaten I noted several cars driving slowly on the street outside, people straining to see what was going on.

On one of my trips to the tables near the bay windows, Woody touched me on the arm. "I'd like you to meet the men at our table," he said to me with a big smile. "The man to my left is Isaiah Black who plays center field and piano for the Stars."

The entire table laughed at Woody's clever introduction.

"Across the table is Benjamin Green their left fielder." He then looked at the men and said, "This is Jake Joseph who has made a terrific contribution to the Jewelers this summer. He plays left field. We are very proud of Jake. Not only is he a fine ballplayer and a good student, he sings in our church choir."

I nodded to each of the men and told them as much as I'd like to stay and chat, I had to deliver more food to hungry people. Both Isaiah and Benjamin stood and shook my hand. As I went back to the kitchen I had a terrific feeling. I had received a wonderful compliment from a man I greatly admired.

On my next trip out of the kitchen my eyes fell on a person who appeared to be sitting alone, even though she was at a table with five other persons. Toni Rock, the second baseman, was the lone female seated at a table. Mona must have noticed it too, because when she served her last plate she pulled a chair up and began to talk to "the only woman playing a major men's game" or so the publicity led us to believe.

Toni Rock was about five foot nine and had a rough complexion. She was dark and appeared to be shy. Later, Candy said that a woman traveling solo with that many men had every right to be shy. Toni smiled broadly as Mona listened to her.

After the meal, which was paid for by the Hospitality Committee, most of the men walked over to the Strand to see Linda Darnell. I stayed to clean up.

When I got home shortly after eight, Mom, Tim, Karen, and Candy were waiting on the porch. They were dying to have the details. I told the story as best I could and then turned to my mother, "When did you know about this?"

"I think it started the day after I told you and your father about my circle meeting," Mom said. "Skip went to see Pastor Hauge and they laid out a plan. Skip agreed to visit a handful of men and ask them to stay at the Lincoln. He talked to six, but two turned him down. Ken Brown offered to pay for the meals, and Karl Schmidt arranged to purchase the theatre tickets. Woody and Swish not only agreed to stay, but made a financial donation as well. Pastor Hauge recruited the rest of the folks. He visited Moose and convened the meeting at church last Friday."

"It sure took people by surprise today," I said with a lump in my throat. "Dad said you make him proud every day. Well, both of you make me proud."

"This isn't over with yet," Mom warned. "We've got tomorrow and Saturday morning ahead of us."

Game Day

CHAPTER 19

I was wide-awake by 4:30 a.m. on Friday, August 15. I showered, shaved what beard I had, left for Little Oslo before 5:30, and arrived nearly twenty minutes early. As usual, Moose glared at me as if I was late. "This is going to be a wild day," he said by way of greeting. "Mona's coming in this morning to give us a hand."

By 6:30 the restaurant was full, and people were waiting for a table. The word had reached people that Little Oslo was the center of activity. What was interesting was that we had three tables of women, something normally unheard-of early in the morning.

About 9:00 the Stars started drifting in, dressed in suits and ties. Right behind them arrived the men who had stayed overnight at the Lincoln, also in their Sunday best. The only time I had ever seen Dad with a tie was for weddings, funerals, and worship. When he walked into Little Oslo I realized that he was one of the best-looking men I had ever seen.

Most of the Stars ordered the combo and insisted on paying for their meals, even though Moose told us not to charge them. I had more tips that Friday than any other day during the summer.

About 10:00 the coffee crowd began to appear, and Eddy, the traveling secretary, went to each table where members of the Stars were sitting and suggested that the men go back to the hotel to make room for the regulars. Dad and Woody left with them, and after a brief stop at the hotel walked ten ballplayers to Maple Street Lutheran, which was about four blocks east of the Lincoln.

As they left Moose put his hand on my shoulder and said, "I know you'd love to go to that service this morning, Jake, but I need you. I think we're going to have a full house at noon."

I assured him it was okay, though I would have given anything to be a part of the singing. Later Mom said that the church was nearly packed. Not only did we have a lot of people from our church, but a bunch from the Methodist and Congregational churches also came. Max Fisher showed up and told everyone who would listen that for at least one day he was a Jewish-Lutheran. The pastor from the Methodist church stood at the door and greeted all the people from his church who came.

You may wonder why other churches weren't represented. The simple answer is that in 1952 there were only six churches in Wahissa. The Catholic Church was quite small and shared a priest with a parish fifteen miles away. The remaining two churches were also Lutheran, though their pastors turned down Pastor Hauge's invitation to participate.

About fifteen minutes before the singing was to begin, a group of ten men came marching down Maple Street with signs protesting just about everything that was taking place. One of the signs said, "Boycott Little Oslo, home of Nigger Ballplayers." Another sign said something about the Lincoln being the "Home of Niggers," and another said, "Be Ye Separate."

I wasn't there, but later, Dad, who was standing outside gave me all the details. He said he recognized one of the men as the pastor of a fundamentalist church near Duck Lake and another as the leader of a tiny Bible church with a Vang address. Dad who knew more people than nearly anyone else in the county said he had never seen the rest of them. About a half dozen people from Wahissa stood on the sidewalks applauding the protesters.

When the protesters reached the outside steps in the front of the church, Pastor Hauge walked out into the street and and told them they were totally within their rights to carry signs and offer their opinions. He then said, "We live in a great country where we are guaranteed the right to freely assemble and the right to express our opinions. You men may think that we are quite different, but that isn't true. We have more in common than most people realize. For example, do you believe that Christ died for all?"

Each of the men looked at the leader who nodded and said that he did.

"That's wonderful," Pastor Hauge exclaimed. "So do I. So do the people who have gathered inside. So do the colored men who came to sing hymns and pray."

Then he smiled again and said, "Do you believe that the blood of Christ has been poured out for the forgiveness of all sin?"

Again, they looked at their leader who was nodding his head.

"Isn't that great! So do I. We are about to sing a song in praise to God called, 'There Is Power in the Blood.' Do you sing that song in your churches?" They all nodded.

"Isn't it amazing how much we have in common," the pastor said in a voice that just got a bit louder. "Do you believe that Jesus Christ is your personal Lord and Savior?"

This time all ten, without looking elsewhere said, "Praise the Lord," and things like that.

Pastor Hauge shouted triumphantly, "That means we are brothers in the faith."

"We are here," the small man with a goatee who seemed to be the leader said, "to declare that the races should be separate." He pointed to the sign that read, "Be Ye Separate."

Pastor Hauge, with a huge smile on his face, addressed the group, "You have chosen to be companions with a significant group who lived during the time of Jesus. They, too, believed that they should separate themselves from everyone else who was different. In fact, their name meant *to separate*. They were called *Pharisees*. You must be modern-day Pharisees. Jesus disagreed with them, but he loved them. He ate with them. He prayed for them. That is what I want to do. I want to pray for each of you."

With that he started praying, thanking God for "these strong men of faith who believe in the Savior, Jesus." Then he moved to one of them and put his hands on the man's shoulder and prayed, "I pray for this man. Make him both a disciple and an ambassador for your love. Let your love pour through him to everyone for whom you gave your precious blood, all the people on this street, and all the people in the church."

One by one he put his hands on the shoulders of the men, praying for each of them. When he came to the leader he prayed, "I thank you Lord for this man of courage who is willing to stand up for what he believes to be right. Show him your truth, O Lord. If it is good for him to be separate, give him a sign. If you want him to love his neighbors as he loves himself, give him a different sign."

When he finished he announced. "I am sorry that I can't stay with you and talk longer. I need to go inside where we are going to sing praises to God. Go in peace, my brothers."

With that, he walked in the church. The protesters looked confused, talked briefly to one another, and then slowly drifted away, as did the dozen people lined up across the street from the church.

· · · · · · ·

Candy and Tim took time off work to attend the service and reported late that night there was some powerful singing that took place. Isaiah pounded the piano, and for the first time in memory, Lutherans actually clapped their hands and joined the Stars in shouting "Alleluia." The next day Dad told me, "It is not easy for Norwegians to clap their hands and sing at the same time."

Dad and Jumpy sang a duet, "Ride the Chariot," and received thunderous applause. Dad said it was the first time he and Jumpy had ever heard clapping after they sang in church.

Pastor Hauge, speaking without notes, but repeating some of his sermon from the previous Sunday, used Galatians 3:28 as his text: "There is neither Jew nor Greek, there is neither bond nor free, there is neither male nor female: for ye are all one in Christ Jesus." Tim said it wasn't his best sermon but that was okay because most people didn't come for the sermon anyway. They came for the singing. The players in attendance applauded everything that was said and sang with great gusto. And then the praying started.

Candy told me she had never heard such praying. At least eight of the Stars prayed. In voices that filled the church they praised God for just about everything you can imagine. One of the prayers was greeted with applause, something that has never happened before or since in that church.

Later one of the players explained to Pastor Hauge that the prayers were rather long because he hadn't left time for testifying. "We used the prayer time to testify," he explained.

Pastor Hauge asked him what would have happened if he had invited testimonies. The man thought for a moment and then said, "The service would have lasted another forty-five minutes. Perhaps it was better that we testified through prayer."

· · · · · · · ·

If the town was upset about the Stars' staying at the Lincoln, you couldn't prove it at Little Oslo. It was a circus-like atmosphere all day long.

I was planning to stay until 5:00, but at 3:00 Mrs. Hauge and three women from church came in to assist with the serving. I guess this was plan B. Moose asked me to help find them aprons and to show them where to locate the silverware and dishes. "When you've finished helping the women, go home. It would be great if you could get a short nap this afternoon. This is going to be the biggest game in Wahissa history."

I lay down about 3:30, but I was too excited to sleep. I went downstairs shortly after 4:00 and Mom made me an omelet. I left for the ballpark at 4:30.

I was the first to take batting practice a little after 5:00. By the time I finished there must have been 200 people in the stadium. By 6:00 when the Stars took their batting practice there were 1,000.

Later, people who were in attendance for the Stars' batting practice said it was one of the highlights of the night. Jerry Johnson, the big first baseman must have hit seven or eight balls over the fence. The kids who retrieved them for a nickel apiece loved it and the crowd oohed and aahed like it was a fireworks display.

Fifteen minutes before the game was to begin Smokey pulled us together in the dugout. "They're going to start with their lefty, Jones," he said. "I watched him pitch in Rockford. He has a nasty screwball. Jake, stay close to first if you get on. I watched him pick off two runners in the first four innings. I doubt if he'll pitch the entire game because he pitched four innings on Wednesday. Their backup is the shortstop who goes by the name *Double Duty Dandridge*. He's basically a curve ball pitcher."

He turned to Buck. "You're going to have to use off-speed stuff on the Johnson brothers. They sit on the fastball and can both hit it into the next county as you witnessed in batting practice. Jerry, the first baseman, is the better hitter of the two. The woman, Toni Rock, will try to work you for a walk. She chokes up and fouls off everything that is high or on the outside of the plate." Looking at the Zitzners he said, "She is a Punch-and-Judy hitter. She slaps at the ball and usually hits it to right field. Buck, you can probably overpower her with your fastball, especially if you keep it inside. Harris, the third baseman is probably the fastest man on the field. No disrespect to Jake, but he has at least one more gear than Jake does. He'll bunt his way on if you let him. Infielders, you don't dare play him too deep because he'll beat a long throw every time. We need to keep him off the bases, because as Jonah Harris goes, so goes the Stars."

Smokey looked at the field and then gave his final thoughts. "Don't let all this peace and goodwill crap that has been happening the last two days take your minds off winning. Our goal is to beat their ass. To win we have to play good defense and prevent the big inning. On offense I'll be surprised if we're able to blast off. We have to think about singles, rather than a fence buster. We'll go for one run at a time. That means we need base runners. Work the count; pick up a walk here and there. Advance the runner. Don't help the pitcher out."

Then he read the batting order. He had me leading off and playing left field. There was one change. He moved Sherm back in the lineup and had him batting in the nine spot. You might have thought that would cheer him up, but it actually put him in a worse mood than he had been in the last few games.

In the first inning Buck retired the first two batters with some serious heat and then went sidearm and threw curve balls out of the strike zone to Jerry Johnson. The big guy tried to pull the 2–0 pitch and ended up hitting a lazy fly to right center. The side was retired 1–2–3.

As the pitcher was warming up I looked around the stadium. I saw Mom and Dad and the Hauges sitting behind our bench in Ted Towne's box. There were more people in the park than I had ever seen. They filled the bleachers and sat all the way out to deep left and right fields. Later I heard that 2,100 had paid their way into the game. Add that to the kids who snuck in and we had pretty close to 2,200 people.

All 2,200 were cheering when I stepped up to the plate. The first pitch was a fastball across the letters. I was so far behind it that I heard it pop in the catcher's mitt before my bat crossed the plate. I had never seen a ball thrown that fast before.

I stepped out and tried to clear my head. The next pitch was outside and was equally fast. The count was 1–1. On 2–2 I fouled the ball back into the screen and felt like it was a moral victory. I swung and missed at the next pitch, which was in the dirt. The cheering of the crowd told me that the ball had got past the catcher and rolled to the screen. I took off for first and beat the throw by a step.

On the way to first I felt a pull in my right leg. When I reached first I called time out. Smokey came running and rubbed my calf. "You okay?" he asked.

"I think so," I said and walked a few steps. "I don't think it is serious." Then I stretched and told him I was fine.

Both the first baseman and the pitcher watched me carefully. I took no more than a two-foot lead off first base as the pitcher delivered.

Ball one. I stayed close to the bag as the count got to 2–2. I peered at Smokey, who gave our signs. Green light. He wanted me to steal second.

I stayed close to the bag but as Jones lifted his leg I took off. He seemed to hesitate for just a second before delivering a fastball high. The catcher double clutched, and then threw the ball right on the bag. The second baseman tagged me sliding in, but the moment's hesitation was enough, and I beat the throw by a whisker. Later the pitcher told Smokey that we had suckered him with the limp. He was so convinced that I couldn't run that he never even looked at first.

The next hitter laid a bunt down the third base line, forcing the third baseman to throw to first and sending me to third. LaVern Zitzner flied out to medium center field, and I scored easily. LaVon struck out, but we led 1–0, without a hit.

The Stars got hits in the second, third, and fourth innings, but Buck pitched his way out of trouble. In the fifth Jerry Johnson came up for the third time. Buck had teased him with slow curves the first times up. On a 2–2 pitch, with the bases empty, he decided to challenge him. He threw a fastball slightly above the waist on the outside of the plate. When Jerry hit that ball it sounded like a rocket was being launched. The Zitzner boys in center and right field turned and watched it as it soared over the fence and hit the tower halfway up. At first there was total silence. Then 2,200 people stood up and applauded. All the players in the infield applauded, and Buck bowed to the big first baseman as he rounded third. This was the first time in the history of the park that anyone had hit the tower.

The only person not clapping was Smokey, who told Mo Johnson to go warm up. Smokey wasn't a happy manager when his pitchers departed from a working strategy.

When we came up in the bottom of the sixth a new pitcher, Double Duty Dandridge, was on the mound for the Stars. Smokey went up and down the bench reminding everyone that he was a curve ball pitcher. After Sherm Lewison fouled out I singled to right field. Smokey gave me the steal sign on the first pitch. I wished he had waited until I had a chance to see his motion to home at least once, but knowing that he benched Buck for missing a sign I decided to do as I was ordered.

When Double Duty lifted his left leg I took off for second. He saw me go and pivoted and threw to first. Both umpires threw up their hands and yelled balk, and I was awarded second base. Dandridge was upset, but his manager just nodded. Clearly he was guilty.

When the next hitter flied out to right, I decided to test the right fielder's arm. I tagged and headed for third. The throw was down the line about five feet, and I was safe.

LaVon worked the pitcher for a walk and on the first pitch LaVern lined a curve ball to left. It was the first hit of the night for the Jewelers, and we led 2–1.

When Buck hit a towering fly ball, which the center fielder caught at the fence, I was headed to the outfield. I heard Smokey's voice. "Jake, put on the shin guards. I want you to catch Mo."

Later Smokey would tell us that he felt a soft breeze coming from the west and decided to see what Mo could do. Buck moved to first, and I borrowed the first baseman's mitt called the "Trapper" and headed to the plate.

The butterfly was dipping for the first two batters, who weakly flied out. The third hitter in the seventh was Jonah Harris, who hit a looping line drive to center. I headed to the mound to have a chat with Mo. "Can you keep him close and give me a shot at him when he steals?" I asked.

Mo told me he would try, but Harris was running on the first pitch and made it to second without a throw from me. Two pitches later he was on third base, beating my throw easily. He was clearly as fast as advertised.

When the count was 2–2 Mo threw a beautiful butterfly that fell to the ground as the batter swung and missed. I managed to block the ball, which squirted toward the third base line. As I ran to retrieve it I saw the batter take off for first and Harris take off for home. I grabbed the ball a fraction of a second before Harris arrived. He lowered his shoulder and decided to try to jar the ball loose. I held on and touched him with the ball. We had survived the seventh inning, though I was seeing more stars than the team from New Orleans.

No one scored until the ninth, when Jerry Johnson doubled and Charlie Johnson brought him home with a single. The score was 2–2 as we came to bat in the bottom of the ninth.

I led off and flied out to right. The next hitter struck out. As the Zitzner boys came to the plate I knew what Smokey was thinking, "Don't make me go another inning with Mo. His charmed life is almost up."

LaVon doubled just inside the left field line. On a 3–2 pitch his brother LaVern hit a ball that cleared the fence on one hop, a ground rule double. As LaVern crossed the plate we mobbed both of the Zitzners. Once again 2,200 people stood and cheered, only this time it was for their home team. As we began to shake hands with the Stars we were told that this was their first defeat in fifteen games.

The Johnson brothers both hugged me as if they were glad we had beaten them. Jonah Harris sought out Ted Towne and told him that if he ever decided to pay a position player he would love to spend time in Wahissa. All of the men who had stayed at the Lincoln came on the field and talked to the players. It was a love fest.

Dad, Mom, and the Hauges met me at the fence. "Your best game ever," Dad crowed. Pastor Hauge agreed. Mom just hugged me. I thanked them and looked for Candy. She was standing by the dugout, holding my bag. Before I reached her she started running toward left field. When I caught her, she turned, dropped the bag and kissed me. "I have never been prouder of you than I was tonight," she told me. In a dark corner of left field I was amply rewarded for "my best game ever."

Visiting Delores

CHAPTER 20

During July and August, nearly every church choir in our area took a vacation. When the pastors ran out of sixteen-year-old trumpet players and screechy sopranos from their own church, the phone rang off the hook at Joseph Brothers Oil and Gas asking if the Two Tenors, Jumpy and Skip, were available to sing. Whenever possible they said yes. In one four-week period they sang at First United Methodist Church in Wahissa, St. John Lutheran in Vang, First Congregational in Wahissa, and St. Peter's Lutheran in Harden.

On occasion Mom would accompany them on the piano, but most of the time Jumpy carried a pitch pipe and they sang a cappella. On Sunday, August 17, the Two Tenors sang at our church, Maple Street Lutheran, for the third time that summer. It was their first time in public since their triumphant duet when the Stars were in town. Early in the service we heard "I'm Going to Ride the Chariot" with

Mom playing a rousing piano. Over the years "Chariot" became their signature song. It certainly was a great favorite of most congregations. During the offering they sang "My Hope Is Built on Nothing Less" without accompaniment, just their silky voices in two-part harmony.

In our church people did not applaud for duets any more than they applauded for sermons. Both were deemed offerings to God. The congregation was expected to sit quietly following an anthem or duet and ponder the musical offering. That Sunday the people took a cue from the New Orleans ballplayers and did something most uncharacteristic for a bunch of Lutherans, they stood and clapped after the second duet. Dad and Jumpy who had looked embarrassed when it happened on Friday, August 15, smiled broadly. I think they enjoyed the recognition. Pastor Hague was clearly pleased, and Marme jumped to her feet and let the whole congregation know how proud she was of her sons.

Tim and I talked about this strange turn of events as we were leaving the service that day. Until a week ago we had never heard an "Amen," "Alleluia," or Praise the Lord" in church. When we shared our observations with Dad he responded by saying, "Blame it on the Stars." He was right. Many of the Maple Street members had been present for the prayer meeting/hymn sing when the Stars were in town and found that a little emotion was rather enjoyable. If they could clap for strangers, they could clap for their favorite locals.

As soon as worship was finished we all walked Tim and Allen to the car to wish them well on their trip to La Crosse. For some reason Karen was all teary and hugged Allen at least three or four times. Elaine, who would have jumped in the back seat in a moment if the boys had asked her to go, was equally emotional, though she tried not to show it.

When Karen, Elaine, and the women were finished hugging, the men stepped up, shook Allen's hand, and slapped him on the back. I thanked Tim for being the driver and asked him to check in when they got home that night.

After lunch I rode over to Candy's house and joined in a card game called "500." The best I can explain it is that 500 is euchre with enough cards for ten tricks. We played several games, men against women before Mr. and Mrs. Paulson got in a verbal skirmish, each accusing the other of sending signs to help their partner bid.

An early end to the game allowed me to leave for home where Dad and Mom were waiting to drive me to the game in Duck Lake. Dad liked to be early. Jumpy claimed that about fifty percent of the time when they were to sing at an out of town church, they arrived before the church was even open. The game in Duck Lake was starting an hour earlier than the regular starting time of 7:00 to accommodate "Corn Fest," which took place the third weekend each August.

We were about five miles away from our destination when a red convertible with the top down passed us at a blazing speed. Mom asked, "Isn't that Cam Taylor's car? Who is the man in the front seat?"

Dad announced that he was driving fifty-five miles per hour and that the red car passed him like he was standing still. Only then did he answer Mom's question, "I think it was Sherm Lewison riding with him."

We arrived not knowing who would pitch for the Jewelers. It was Smokey's stated policy to pitch Buck against the big three, Harden, Duck Lake, and Kickapoo City whenever possible, but Buck had pitched five innings on Friday and was therefore a no-go. Mo, the man with the rubber arm, could pitch a few innings in relief, but he, too, had pitched two days earlier. The moment the team finished batting practice Smokey announced that Cam would start and that Mo would pitch against Kickapoo City on Wednesday. He reminded us that if we won the next two games and Harden won their contests, we would play them for the championship the following Sunday in Wahissa.

After the first inning the outcome of the game was never in doubt. We batted around in the first inning scoring seven runs, including four on Buck's grand slam. We added to that total by scoring a run in each of the next three innings, and Cam pitched his best game as a Jeweler. When he struck out the side in the ninth inning we went home with a 12–4 victory.

. . . .

It was 9:30 when I opened the kitchen door and found the note on the table. "If you get home before 10:00 come down and talk. Tim."

Tim and Jumpy were listening to the radio in the living room when I rapped lightly on the kitchen door. They waved me in and the three of us gathered around the kitchen table.

I came for news about Allen, but first Jumpy, who had already heard about the reunion in La Crosse, asked for a first hand report on the game. I gave him the score, told about our big first inning, and the fine pitching from Cam. He wanted to know what I did each time I came to bat and pounded me on the back when I told him that I had three singles and a double.

Before he headed to bed he put his hand on Tim's shoulders, smiled broadly and said, "This has been a great season, but I'm really looking forward to next summer when there will be two Josephs on the Jewelers."

Tim tried to lower his dad's expectations saying, "We're a long way away, Dad. It might not happen."

Jumpy, however, was convinced that 1953 would be a repeat of earlier years when he and his brother Skip had played for the Wahissa city team. He waved at both of us and turned in for the night.

That made us ready for the business at hand. "How'd it go?"

"It was an amazing day," he answered. "Allen was so nervous we had to stop just outside of Coon Valley where he tossed his cookies."

"What made him so nervous?" I asked.

"He wasn't sure how the day was going to play out. He was afraid that either DeDe wouldn't like him or he wouldn't like her. He was afraid that he wouldn't know what to say. Should he ask about her motorcycle boyfriend? Should he ask her why she didn't come back sooner? And then there was the question of his real father. Should he ask about him? Why did he and his sister have different dads? He told me he had barely slept the last several nights. I think the entire turmoil just made him sick to his stomach. It was a good thing that I rode with him."

"Once he lost his lunch, then what?" I asked.

"Then he was hungry again. There is a little burger joint as you come into La Crosse, called the *Hut*. He told me he'd like to stop there.

I asked him if it was wise to try to eat again, but he insisted that he didn't want to meet DeDe on an empty stomach."

"Did you have any trouble finding the house?"

Tim shook his head. "No," he said. "Allen had good directions and it was only a block off Fifth Avenue, which is one of the main streets. I parked the car and asked if he wanted me to go in with him. He grabbed me and nearly shouted 'Yes! That's why I had you come along.'

"We walked up the steps onto a porch, but before the bell rang the door opened. A small woman stood in the doorway. She's rather heavy and she looked a lot older than I imagined. She greeted us with a wry smile, 'I'm Delores. Perhaps you know me as DeDe.'

"Allen shook her hand. She then said, 'Would you give me a hug?' And that was when the tears began to flow. They both cried, and from that moment on it couldn't have gone better.

"Delores invited us into the house and answered nearly every one of Allen's questions without him even asking. She started out by telling him that she regretted nearly everything that happened from that day in Sioux Falls until the moment Joy first called her. She said that she had believed that Mick, the guy on the cycle, would change his mind and come back to be a father to her kids. The longer she was with him, she said, the more she realized that Mick would not be a good father. By the time she had it all figured out she felt trapped.

"She and Mick did a lot of drinking together. Nearly every morning she woke up with a terrible headache. She was working as a waitress at the time. At some point her best friend said, 'DeDe, you've got a serious drinking problem. You need help. If you keep drinking you'll never get your kids back.'

"Like most drinkers she refused to believe her friend and continued living the same lifestyle for several more years. But the words of her friend were planted deeply in her mind, and she slowly could see that she was in real trouble. She didn't feel worthy to return home and be a mother when she was drinking, and she didn't know how to stop. She continued to live with Mick, though she says she never really loved him. She was afraid if she left him she would be a three-time loser. They never got married.

"For the first couple years Mick took all of the money that DeDe made as a waitress. After awhile she began to hide some of it, planning for a day when she could escape. They were living in Oklahoma at the time. Finally, she began to attend AA. The stories at AA gave her hope that she not only could quit drinking, but she could put her life back together again.

"One morning, after she had been sober for six months, one of the people from AA picked her up in the dead of night while Mick slept and drove her, with a single suitcase, to a bus station forty miles away. She had saved enough money to get back to La Crosse and start her life all over.

"Marilyn, her mother, was waiting for her, but she was quite sick. DeDe, Delores, provided care for her mother for the last days of her life. In her will Marilyn left her the house.

"Delores, who has a good job at Trane Company, started attending the church where she was baptized and confirmed. Equally important she continued to attend AA meetings and to put her life in order, hoping that she could make some connection with Joy and Allen. One day Joy called her on the phone. Delores drove to Madison to see her daughter, and they began to meet every other month.

"Meanwhile she met a widower, Shane, at church. He's six or seven years older than her and has two children in their late twenties. Shane and Delores were married a year ago. He sold his house on the north side of La Crosse and moved in with her. It was Shane who convinced her that she needed to make contact with Allen. Too nervous to phone herself, she asked a friend to call him. It was that friend that reached Allen a few weeks ago.

"When she finished she apologized to Allen for abandoning him and told him, 'I think about you and pray for you every day.' Tim thought for a moment and then shook his head. There was this sweet moment not long before we left when Delores said, 'I know that you have a mother. I have forfeited that title. I would like to be your friend. I'm hoping that you will give me a chance to show you that I really do love you.'"

"And," I began, "how did Allen respond?"

"He was beautiful," Tim said holding back the tears. "He hugged Delores and said, I am a very lucky guy. I now have two mothers who love me."

As he brushed back the tears I could tell he was exhausted. "You look beat. Was this whole thing tiring?" I asked.

"I have worked a ten-hour day at the shop and not felt as worn out," he confessed. "I wouldn't be a very good counselor. I never said a word and yet I feel drained."

"How is Allen doing?" I asked.

"He's okay. There were a lot of tears. He told her that she was wonderful, that he really liked her, and that he was glad he had come. Before he left he asked if she would be willing to visit him at Elaine's house.

"Delores said, 'You name the day and I will be there.'"

"What is with the name change?" I asked.

"Evidently, when she sobered up she decided to change her name. DeDe was the woman who drank and partied. Delores is the woman who is sober, who goes to work each day, and who wants to get to know her children."

We sat in silence for a few minutes, and then I stood to go home. "I wish I could have gone with you," I said. "I think you were a part of something pretty special. Not many guys meet their mom at age nineteen. You were there to see it."

I punched him on the shoulder to tell him I loved him and headed up the hill. Five in the morning came early.

Fuzzy Kvamme

CHAPTER 21

When I reported to work on Monday I expected that everyone would be talking about the red-hot Jewelers. I also expected a number of pats on the back and a few atta-boys from customers. Instead, Little Oslo was as quiet as a morgue, even though it was almost full by 6:00.

"What's up?" I asked Cookie in a whisper.

"Round four," he mumbled.

I obviously looked confused so he put down his spatula, looked at me and said, "Some poor bastard got his brains beat in over at Paradise last night."

I looked at the Silver Table where the Sheriff was sitting alone. I put on my apron, grabbed a coffee pot, and filled his cup. "Combo?" I asked.

"Sure," he said weakly.

As I walked away he said, "Double up on the bacon this morning, okay?"

By the time I completed his order his table was full and the men were talking quietly. They knew the Sheriff was taking this very personal. "Caught us off guard," I heard him say. "We weren't expecting anything on a Sunday. Changed his M.O. I've had deputies in unmarked cars down there every Friday and Saturday for three weeks."

"Different night, but everything else fits the pattern?" Ken Brown asked.

"Pretty much. Face busted up, fingers broken, right arm smashed. It was his power arm, the right one. Always the power arm. Superman has done his homework. Fuzzy was a righty."

"Fuzzy?" someone asked.

"Fuzzy Kvamme," the Sheriff said sipping his coffee. "His dad was a pretty good farmer, but he is a lazy S.O.B. He has a couple of acres of tobacco and milks ten-twelve cows. Who in hell is going to harvest that crop? Who is going to milk those cows? Not a one armed man, I can tell you that."

"I know Fuzzy," Karl Schmidt added. "At least I know his wife. She teaches school here in Wahissa. Sweet woman. He looks hung over most of the time. With that beard he could play for the House of David."

"Used to play for Duck Lake," Ted Towne added. "Faster than lightning. He once walked and then stole second, third, and home on us. Thank God he was a lousy hitter. If he could have swiped first he would have scored every time up."

"Weren't three of these victims ballplayers?" another fellow asked.

"All but Tom Knight," the Sheriff said. "Up to now I thought this was a coincidence. We might have something here." He thought for a moment and then turned to Ted. "He's young enough, why isn't he still playing?"

Ted was emphatic, "Booze. He came drunk one time too many. They couldn't depend on him."

"There is one very strange thing about this victim," Sid told the group. "We can't find anyone who saw Fuzzy at the bar or the dance hall. All the other victims had been drinking earlier in the evening. His car was sitting in his driveway fifteen miles away. How did he get to Paradise? We got the call around midnight when someone found the poor bastard half a mile from the dance hall."

"Maybe he was with a bunch of buddies who picked him up at home," someone suggested.

"If so, we haven't been able to locate anyone who will admit to being with him last night," the Sheriff observed.

"Where does that leave you?" Ken asked.

"It suggests that he was riding with whoever beat the snot out of him," Silver said.

Ted whistled. "That means Superman is making house calls. He's picking people up at home before he beats them senseless. Was he drunk?"

"We assume he was drunk. All we can say for sure is that he'd been drinking. There are a lot of missing pieces to this puzzle."

By that time the painters had arrived and I was out of earshot, collecting thermos bottles. I noticed that Sherm and Woody had bandaged right hands. "What happened to the two of you?" I asked.

Sherm, who seemed rather defensive, answered quickly. "We got into a wasp nest on the job Friday and got bit up." Woody nodded sadly.

As I completed their orders and their silver thermoses I was thinking of the bandages. Something didn't make sense to me.

After I delivered the coffee I began to collect for their bill. Each man had left his money and a small tip, either a half dollar or a quarter next to his place, except Sherm. I caught him at the door talking to Woody. "I think you forgot to pay," I said quietly.

"You're full of shit," he snarled at me. "You've been on me all summer. I left my money under my plate."

I apologized and went back to look, but found nothing. I counted again and found only four had paid.

This was the first time all summer someone had shorted me. I considered my options. I could tell Moose, or I could confront Sherm again the next day. When I finished cleaning off the table I reached into my pocket where I kept my tips and counted out the exact amount of Sherm's bill and rang it up. There was no use bothering Moose with this kind of thing.

· · · · · · ·

After work, smarting from Sherm's failure to pay and curious about the wrapped hands, I rode my bike across town where Cam lived. Cam's family was wealthy, freeing him from the necessity of finding a summer job. He lived a block from Sherm. I knew Cam had given Sherm a ride to the game in his red convertible.

When I arrived his mom told me he was in his room. She walked to the stairs and shouted to him, "Cam, Jake's here."

Cam stood on the top step and motioned for me to join him. His room occupied two thirds of the entire upstairs of the Taylor's massive home. When his sister, who was five years older than Cam, got married, his parents tore out the wall that separated their bedrooms and made one big room with a cathedral ceiling. His phonograph was playing "Heart and Soul" by the Four Aces.

"Hey," he said, "that was a blast last night."

"You had a two-hit night," I observed.

He laughed, "My second one of the season."

"I was glad that Smokey put Sherm in at first toward the end of the game. And he had a hit, a double in the seventh inning. Not bad for a guy with a bandaged hand."

"What are you talking about? Cam asked. "He didn't have a bandaged hand."

"He had a bandage on his hand when he ate breakfast today."

"Then something happened to him after I let him off downtown at the Minuteman last night. He rode both ways with me and I never saw a bandage." He thought for a moment, "You must have him mixed up with someone else."

"You're sure he didn't have a bandage?"

Cam nearly spit the words out, "I'm positive."

I was too, but I was seeking confirmation.

That evening, on Candy's back porch, I told her what had happened.

She squinted at me and said, "Sherm has a bogus bandage, fails to pay his bill, and cusses you out. What does this add up to?"

I shook my head. "I have no idea. I know he is ticked off about his lack of playing time and being moved down the order, but that doesn't lead me anywhere."

The next morning, as the painters were leaving, Woody stayed behind. "Jake, Sherm asked me to pick up his tab yesterday and I forgot. I hope it didn't cause any big problems," he said as he handed me a wad of bills.

"I'll get your change," I said.

"No change needed," he said as he walked out of the restaurant.

· · · · · · ·

Late that afternoon Tim and I talked while we played ping-pong. "There is no way that Sherm asked Woody to pay his bill," I said. "Woody overheard me talking to Sherm the day before. If Sherm had asked him he would have paid me on the spot, or Sherm would have told me Woody was paying."

"Right," Tim said. "When you confronted him he told you he left the money under his plate."

"And nothing was there when I went back to search. This is strange," I said. "I have a hunch this has something to do with Superman."

"Now I think you are full of it," Tim growled. "There is no logical connection between a painter not paying his bill and four guys getting the crap beat out of them all over the country."

"Explain why Sherm's hand is bandaged on Monday morning, but not Sunday night," I said, "particularly when he was 'hurt' on Friday."

"Are you standing there telling me that Sherm is Superman?" Tim said. "While you're at it you might as well say that Woody is Batman and Moose is Robin. How you can link either of them with the beatings is beyond me."

Soon we finished our set, which Tim won 3–2. "Do it again?" he asked.

"No. I'm going over to see Candy. Maybe she can figure this thing out."

"If she can you ought to marry her on the spot," Tim said.

"What has figuring this puzzle out got to do with getting married?"

"Because," Tim said, "if she can find Superman from the clues you have, she will make you the richest man in the world. She can also make plasma out of beets and find oil with a crooked stick.

A Visit to Paradise

CHAPTER 22

We arrived at Kickapoo City on August 20, ready to face the red-hot Chiefs. They had started the season slowly, but were now playing excellent baseball, winning four games in a row, including back-to-back victories over Duck Lake and Harden. Their victory at Harden created a two-way tie for first place. Curt Baaken, their Madison import, had out dueled Lombardo 3–2, the previous Wednesday.

We also were on fire. We had now won ten games in a row, beating not only our conference opponents, but also the Stars, a fine traveling team. We were playing our best ball of the season, and we knew that a win over the Chiefs would give us a chance to reach our goal of a conference championship.

Shortly after we arrived at the Kickapoo City field we discovered that Curt Baaken, their ace pitcher, was back in Madison. When he failed to show for pre-game workouts the manager called him at home and talked to his mother who said he had gone to a movie with a bunch of friends. She didn't know where he was. "He didn't mention anything about playing baseball tonight," she said. No one knew what had gone wrong, but they couldn't just drive over and find out. Madison was over two hours away. I guess that is one of the disadvantages of importing a player who lives a long way away.

The Baaken news allowed us to relax. Perhaps we relaxed too much. Even Smokey began to talk as if this game was in the bag.

A lot depended on Cam who, as usual, started strong. He had great stuff for the first few innings and then quickly lost steam. Smokey announced before the game that his intention was to make it without Buck, even though the big guy said he was ready if we needed him.

We had taken an early lead against the Chiefs, before we went cold. The score was tied 4–4 in the fifth when they filled the bases with no outs. Smokey went to the mound with no one warming up. He took the ball out of Cam's hand and waved to me in left field. As I ran in I figured he wanted me to catch Mo. I headed for the dugout to get a different glove, but Smokey waved me to the mound. "You're my pitcher," is all he said. I was stunned. I hadn't thrown an inning all summer.

Steve, our catcher, looked as confused as I felt. Smokey patted me on the back and said, "The next two hitters pull off the ball on curves. Throw your first pitch hard and inside. Then go to your slow stuff. Keep it down and away. Get us out of this inning and I'll pitch Mo the rest of the way. I hate to have him come in with a runner on third. We never know if his butterfly will end up back by the screen."

When Smokey went back to the dugout, Steve, mask in hand, said, "What do you throw?"

I shrugged and said, "Not much. I've got a fastball and I throw my curve overhand, three quarters, and side arm. It is all slow stuff. I don't think I'll cross you up."

He laughed, "You give me the signals. I'll flash a bunch of stuff because the runners will be trying to steal the sign. Shake off my signs once for a fastball and twice for one of your curves. It won't make any difference to me which one you throw. Let's hope you only face three hitters." He started back and then stopped, turned around, and said, "The ump will probably only give you eight pitches to warm up. If you don't have to show them your best stuff, save it."

Steve turned and took a couple steps toward the plate before he turned around and approached me again. "The hitter is Severson, the catcher. He has a great swing, but he is slower than the wrath of God. Keep it low and we've got a chance to double him." Then he trotted back to his spot behind the plate.

To warm up I started with a two-seam fastball and then tried my curve ball going a couple of different ways. My best pitch was the curve that I threw three quarters. It usually broke down and away. When I was throwing it proper it was almost to the ground by the time it crossed the plate. Soon the umpire raised two fingers to indicate that I was allowed only two more warm-ups.

I took my last two pitches and then stepped on the rubber. I checked the runners and peered in for a sign. Steve was flashing three fingers and a fist. I shook him off once and went to a full wind-up. My fastball was high and tight. Actually, it was a bit too tight and the batter fell down getting out of the way. The umpire bellowed, "Balllll one." I peeked at Smokey and saw him staring at the tobacco juice he had just spit on the ground.

The next pitch was a side-armed curve that did exactly what I hoped, breaking so that it never quite crossed the plate. The hitter went after it and fouled it off. The umpire, who was a bit of a show-off, cried "Stee-rike one."

Next I went to my prize three quarters curve. Instead of landing ankle high, as I planned, the ball crossed the plate about waist high, nice and slow. The batter hit it hard, a line drive between third and short. Gene dove, knocked it down, picked it up, and threw a perfect strike to home. Steve caught it like a first basemen, with his right foot on home plate, took one step and fired to first, beating the slow-moving catcher. Three pitches, two outs. I had benefited from a combination of luck and great fielding.

The next hitter stepped in with a huge smile on his face. I think he was actually smacking his lips in anticipation. The pitch that turned into a double play was, in Jewelers' lingo, a giant lollypop. It was big and sweet. The hitter probably hadn't seen anything that slow since grade school. My first pitch, a curve, was wide and he let it go. The second curve, the best I had was, unfortunately, waist high, down the middle. He was waiting for it and swung so hard he lifted himself off the ground. The ball soared to center field where LaVern caught it against the wall. Two more feet and it would have been a home run.

I ran to the dugout where a relieved Smokey said, "Well, that's an experiment we won't try again." He waved at Buck. I guess I'm going to need you after all."

Buck put the team down in order in the eighth.

In the eighth inning our bats woke up. The Zitzner boys doubled back to back, and Buck drove a fastball over the fence in left field just left of the sign that read 340 feet. We walked away with a 7–5 victory. We had squeaked by beating Kickapoo City's second best pitcher. At this time in the season we had to breathe deeply and say, "A win is a win, however you get it."

. . . .

That night, rather than think about the game, I thought about the beatings. About midnight, lying in bed, I made a decision to visit the Paradise Dance Hall on Saturday night. Even though one of the two Paradise beatings took place on a Friday and the other on a Sunday, I knew by listening to the men at the Silver Table and the guys at Ham's Station that most of the action at PDH took place on Saturday nights.

The next day I shared my idea with Tim and asked him to go with me. "Here is what I have in mind," I told him. "We go to the dance and make friends with people who go there all the time. That will allow us to ask some questions. Who knows what information we might uncover."

Tim was skeptical. "You ought to keep your nose out of it," he told me. "That is why we have police. Who do you think you are, Sam Spade?"

"I'm just curious," I responded. "I'm not trying to do the work of the Sheriff's department. I just want to see some things for myself, and I'd like you to go with me."

"Why are you so interested in four bums who have been beat up? What are they to you?" he asked.

I tried to explain that I listened to men talk about these beatings day after day at Little Oslo. I told him about the families who were living hand-to-mouth while their breadwinner was healing. I tried to tell him that all the conversation at the café and all of the talks with Candy created a concern. I tried to tell him that I had a hunch about things, and that I might be able to help.

Tim was unconvinced, and the more I talked the more I realized that I didn't have much of a reason for being interested. I could tell by Tim's face that he was baffled by my interest and quite frankly, so was I.

Still, good reason or not, I was determined to go, which I did about 7:00 Saturday night. I had been told that nothing significant began until 8:30, so I stopped at Ham's to check in with the gang. About ten guys were all hanging around the back bays trading yarns. I listened for a few minutes and then decided to head toward Paradise while it was still light.

The village itself had a small, white frame Lutheran Church and a large, red brick Catholic church, two bars, a gas station, Paradise General Store, a grade school, and the Paradise Dance Hall. Everything except the churches and the school was open. I slowed down when I passed Buck's and through the front window could see the big guy behind the counter talking to a couple of older men.

I parked the car behind one of the churches and since there were no sidewalks, walked a block in the street to the dance hall. There were more cars than I expected. I went around the backside of the hall and saw a little walking trail that ran along Paradise Creek. I followed the trail and could see that it passed behind the general store. It would be simple for someone to walk out the back door of the store, walk down the path, beat up someone, get back to the store via the same path, and never be seen. Trees with low hanging branches were on either side of the path.

"The sheriff was looking for car tracks," I thought. "But if Buck did it there wouldn't be any car tracks."

I walked behind the store and saw that a house was connected to the store by an enclosed walkway. "Even better," I thought. "Buck can move from store to house and never be seen."

By this time I could hear music coming from the dance hall and I walked back. I paid a buck at the door and got stamped. "There are two kinds of stamps," the woman who took my money said with a crooked smile. "Yours is a 'No Beer' stamp."

I nodded and went into the hall. I hadn't planned to drink so I didn't care what kind of stamp she gave me. Though there were perhaps fifty people in the hall only three couples were dancing. I recognized several guys who played basketball for one of the river towns standing on the other side of the room. Their school was in a different league and wasn't as big as Wahissa, but we scrimmaged them at Christmas time. They waved for me to join them.

"Hey Jake," a small guy by the name of Tony said holding out his hand. "What you doing so far from home?"

"I wanted to see the famous Paradise Dance Hall for myself," I told him.

I couldn't remember the name of the big guy standing next to him, but I knew he guarded me in the scrimmage. "I'm Rich," he said with a huge smile. "I'm the guy you humiliated last Christmas. I've never had anyone blow by me so fast and so often in my life."

"Good to see you, Rich," I countered. "We must have caught you on an off day, because you guys won your conference championship. The second half of the season was awesome for you." It was true. Their team, led by Tony, was undefeated in conference play after Christmas.

We talked sports for quite awhile before I ventured into the reason for my trip. "This place has developed quite a reputation," I observed. "Two beatings in a month."

"This didn't turn out to be paradise for Kid and Fuzzy. Someone knocked them out cold," Tony said.

"Did you know either of them?" I asked.

"I kinda know Kid," he said hesitatingly. "I don't think anyone really knows him. He's an asshole. Must have been a good ballplayer at one time. I have a cousin who played against him several years ago. Said he was a terrific hitter. By the way, Buck played on that same team."

"With your cousin?" I asked.

"No, with Kid. They were buddies, according to my cousin."

"What about Fuzzy?" I asked.

"He's not from around here, though they found him a half mile away. I don't know him at all. Lloyd is a different case. I see him plenty. His milk truck is parked everywhere, mostly in front of taverns. I have no idea when he works. When I see him he looks like he's got half a shine on."

When we ran out of things to say about the victims the conversation turned to females. Rich asked me, "Do you know any of the girls?"

"Not a one," I responded.

"Do you want to?" he smiled.

"Either that or I'll have to dance with you."

Rich's smile got even larger, "In that case, to protect myself, let me offer you a complete analysis of the girls in the hall." By this time there were well over 200 people, though most of them were older. A group of girls had clustered about thirty feet from us. Rich, without pointing, described each of them.

When he finished I said, "You said nothing about the two blondes standing at the right edge of the group."

Tony laughed, "And for good reason. We've got our eye on them."

"If you weren't hustling the blondes, who would you . . . ?"

"Courtney, the . . ."

"I remember," I said heading in that direction. She was the cute redhead standing in the middle of the group. I walked over to her and said, "Would you like to dance?"

She responded enthusiastically, "I'd love to dance."

When the song was over we moved away from her friends and continued to talk. "If you didn't ask me I was planning to ask you," she said with a grin.

"Glad I saved you the trouble."

In two minutes before the next dance I found out that she lived just a few miles away and that she would be a junior in high school the following year. She had a younger sister and a younger brother and she worked as a waitress in a resort about fifteen miles away. "I make good money on tips," she assured me.

We danced two more times before she said to me, "Want to take a ride?"

As we headed to my car behind the church I told her, "I don't know my way around this area."

"I do," she assured me. Quickly she gave me directions and we headed up a hill driving a couple miles on a ridge before she said, "Turn right here." It was a cemetery. "Park behind that building," she said sweetly. I was certain that this wasn't her first time at this location.

I parked the car and turned off the ignition. She wasted no time, slipping over next to me and putting her hand on mine. "This will be the easiest first kiss I've ever had," I thought.

We kissed for several minutes before she startled me with a question, "Do you want me to take off my blouse?"

I must have said yes because she immediately unbuttoned her blouse and slid out of it. She put her arms around me and whispered, "You can unsnap my bra."

As often as I had wanted to accomplish the same thing with Candy I had never had my hands on a bra strap. I fumbled with it several times until she laughed. "I'll do it for you." Immediately the bra fell into her lap and I looked at her with total amazement.

As we kissed for what seemed like a wonderfully long time, I fondled her right breast and then her left. It was my first time, and I was so aroused that I couldn't change positions. Then she whispered, "Do you want to do anything else?"

We had already gone further than I had thought possible. A thousand pictures flashed through my mind, including a picture of Candy. I'm not sure how long it took me to respond to her offer before I heard myself say, "I don't think so. I think this is far enough until we get to know each other better."

Courtney looked surprised and then hugged me so hard the air almost went out of my lungs. "You are one in a million," she cooed. "Most guys are begging for more. You're right. This is far enough for the first night. We need to save something for later, right?"

"Right," I responded. But what I was thinking was, "I don't think there will be a later."

She turned sideways and slid under my arms so that we sat in an embrace. "Do you live far from here?" I whispered.

She giggled. "Our farm is just half a mile down this road. If you kicked me out I could walk from here. She sat up and pointed, "You see that little house over there?"

I nodded.

"That's where Lloyd Swenson lives, the guy who got beat up not long ago."

I felt like I had just struck pay dirt. "What is he like?"

"He's mean. Mean to his kids, terrible mean to Sonia, his wife. He beat her many times. He's threatened many people. This past spring he beat her, but she never made a charge against him. She could have. I saw the social worker, Mrs. Carlson, at their place several times. In fact, one time her husband, who I think coaches in Wahissa, came with her. Mom said she was sure Mrs. Carlson was frightened and brought her husband along for protection."

Coach Carlson's wife was a social worker! That was news to me. I had seen them both in church, but never thought to ask what she did. Most women stayed home in 1952. I assumed that Mrs. Carlson did too.

Courtney didn't have much more to say, and we were done making out, so she put her bra and blouse back on and I drove back into Paradise. The lights in the general store and the gas station were off. I parked the car and walked her back toward the dance hall. A couple of doors away she pulled me into the shadows and threw her arms around me. "When will I see you again?" she asked as she kissed me lightly.

"Now that I've found Paradise I'll have to come back soon," I lied.

After a long and somewhat awkward pause she asked, "Do you have a girl in Wahissa?"

I stammered briefly before I said, "Kinda. Yeah, I do."

She looked sad, "I thought so. Most of the polite guys are usually tied up." She kissed me again. "I really had a great time. You're a gentleman. If she dumps you, look me up, okay?"

"You are a treat," I said. This time I initiated the kiss. "I had a great time. I mean it." I hugged her one more time.

She started to walk away before she turned and came back. "I figure you're a virgin. That's sweet. Just know this, as far as anyone is concerned nothing happened tonight. I don't kiss and tell." Then she stopped and whispered, "But I'd love another chance." Then she was gone.

I stood still for a minute wondering what I had missed. Then I walked to the long porch in front of the hall and showed the woman at the door my stamp. She smiled her crooked smile at me and waved me in. I stepped in the now smoke-filled room and looked around. The floor was full of dancers. I saw Rich and Tony with the two blondes. Tony spotted me and gave me a thumbs-up. He must have seen me leave with Courtney. I looked at my watch and saw that it was a few minutes after 11:00. It was time for me to go home.

Just then I felt a heavy hand on my shoulder. "Hey buddy, what you doin' down here in the boonies?" It was Buck.

"Everybody wants to visit Paradise," I said grinning.

"Step outside. I can't hear myself think with this noise."

"Not a country fan?" I inquired.

"Strictly Bing Crosby and Perry Como," he said. He looked hard at me and said, "You've done a hell of a job for us this year. Before the season Smokey told me that I may have to pitch outside so we have fewer shots to left, but you've made a liar out of him. That catch you had on Wednesday was one of the finest I've seen, and I've been playing for quite some time."

"Someone tonight said that you played with one of the fellows that got beat up," I ventured.

"Actually played with two of them. Lloyd and I were teammates two different times, and Kid and I grew up together. We raised some serious hell right after high school. We played ball together a couple of summers, but then parted company when I signed with the Reds.

When I moved back he was drinking every night. Pearl, my wife, wouldn't have any of that, so I didn't see Kid any more. A good woman will get a man on the straight and narrow faster than any preacher." He laughed.

"A good woman and a good preacher are an amazing combination," I said, with a touch of regret.

"True." He thought for a while. "Sheriff Silver came visiting this past week. Some people were speculating that I was the man who beat up those four guys. I told him I was at the store the night Kid got blasted, but Pearl and I drove to La Crosse after the game on Sunday for a wedding dance. And I wasn't within miles of Vang when Lloyd got hurt. Hell, Vang's nearly twenty miles away. Why would a non-drinker be in Vang in the first place?"

"For revenge?" I ventured.

"Except I have nothing against Kid or Lloyd. We're still friends. Both of them know it wasn't me. I can see why the Sheriff came. I played ball against Fuzzy. He stole on me every time he got on base, but he did me no harm. If anything, Lloyd would be mad at me, not the other way around. I've turned him down several times lately when he wanted credit. I've told him I like him, but he's a poor risk. Silver said that he knew I was strong enough to whip those guys, and I told him that was a compliment I didn't need. I have a temper, but I haven't been in a fight outside of a ball game since I got married. It is the God's honest truth."

There was one more thing I needed to check out. "Did you ever play ball with a guy by the name of David Hauge?" I asked.

"Sure did," Buck said enthusiastically. "Davy Hauge and I played American Legion ball. He was a catcher and a damn good one. We all thought he ought to go pro, but seems he got recruited by a different team."

"He's my pastor," I told him.

"That's what he told me," Buck responded.

"Then, you've seen him recently."

"I talk to him after most games. He knows more about the game of baseball than anyone in this part of the country, and he sees more sitting in left field than most guys do who are on the field. He's the one who knew the appeal rule and may have saved us serious problems. Twice this year he has spotted a flaw in my delivery and shared it with me. If he gives you any advise on baseball, pay attention. Hell, pay attention to anything he says on any subject. Gotta go. Pearl's waiting." Then he paused before he concluded, "I think the Sheriff believed me. I hope he did."

I did. Going home that night I wondered if Buck and Pastor Hauge talked about anything other than baseball. Finally, I scratched Buck off my mental list of possible aggressors and added a new name.

Heeding Advice

CHAPTER 23

*I*t was late when I got home. I turned the ignition off and coasted the last fifty feet of the driveway into an open garage. I closed the car door as quietly as I could, lowered the garage door, and tiptoed into the house. Anyone watching from a distance would take me for an errant husband sneaking home after a night out.

To get to the second floor I had to climb the squeaky steps just outside of Mom and Dad's bedroom. I was certain they designed the house that way and deliberately made certain that the boards in the stairway were old and dry. I was at the top of the first flight when I heard Mom's voice. "Is everything okay, Jake?"

I came down three steps and said quietly, in case Dad hadn't heard. "Everything is fine. I'm later than I planned, but there was no trouble. The car is fine."

The next voice was considerably lower. "Sleep well, son," my father said.

"Good night," I replied and went the rest of the steps two at a time. It was a cinch that I would never get by with anything in that household. Semper Fidelis, the motto that drove the Marine Corps, could have been posted over the bedroom of Skip and Lou Joseph.

Quickly I dressed for bed and then spent a few moments thinking about Paradise. I found that I had covered everything on the way home and was about to turn out the lights when I saw my baseball uniform, washed, ironed, hanging in my open closet. Mom always took good care of me. I wore the cleanest pants and shirt on the team. Some of the fellows went two or three games without cleaning their uniforms. Not me. Not as long as I lived under Lou Joseph's roof. She washed everything, hand scrubbing the stains, after every game. Cleanliness was not just next to godliness, it was a companion.

Tomorrow would be the sixteenth and final game of the season. I thought about the joy of playing. I loved everything about the game—running, hitting, catching the ball—it was all a thrill, and I got to do it in front of 1,000 people twice a week.

I lay down and tried to say my prayers, but it was no use. Praying while prone was a fruitless pursuit. Prayer worked best when I was standing or on my knees. I slid over and knelt. I gave thanks for my parents, Marme, and the ability to play baseball. Then I asked for forgiveness. I was sure I had violated some commandment that night, and I certainly hadn't been fair to Candy. I was totally confused about what was a sin and what wasn't when it came to girls. I found myself dozing, which I often did when I was praying. I slid back into bed and decided it was time to get some sleep.

Before I closed my eyes I thought about Ted Towne, Smokey, and all the guys who had played for years without winning a championship. I thought about my parents and my friends, who came to every game and supported the Jewelers. How long had it been since any of them had cheered for a winner? I thought about Dad and Jumpy and how, win or lose, they were always my biggest supporters. For a moment I imagined carrying Buck off the field and pounding Smokey on the back 'til he nearly swallowed his chaw. I thought about my part. In one picture I was leaping high into the air and snaring a line drive off

Lombardo's bat at the fence. I imagined him shaking his fist toward me in left field. Then I saw myself hitting a line drive and running to first, on to second, past third, and crossing the plate while the catcher shook his head in amazement. I looked to the mound and Lombardo was throwing his hands in the air and saying, "He's too fast for us."

It got fuzzy after that. I fell asleep and dreamed about baseball most of the night. My dreams were almost totally opposite of what I imagined when I was still awake. All my fears were realized. I dropped fly balls, threw to the wrong base, and struck out, things I had avoided most of the summer. I heard the downstairs clock strike two, three, and four. After that I was somewhere between sleep and no sleep, in a kind of a fog. Finally, I woke, sat up in bed, and looked at my clock. It was 8:12. We usually left to pick up Marme at 10:30, to make certain we would be on time for 11:00 worship. I had plenty of time to shower, dress, and eat breakfast.

The wonderful aroma of waffles and maple syrup was drifting upstairs. Waffles were a Sunday morning custom not only at our house, but at every Joseph family dwelling. The men always prepared the meal. In the summer we had fresh berries and whipped cream. In the winter we had raspberry and strawberry preserves. I'm not sure where the others bought their maple syrup, but Dad purchased ours from a farmer on his gas route. Mom always heated the maple syrup, otherwise, she said, it cooled off the waffles. Thirty-six years later, living in Kansas, we have the same Sunday morning menu. We still have warm maple syrup and eat fresh fruit on our waffles as often as possible. The only difference is that now I am the chef.

When I came down to eat, Mom was alone in the kitchen. "Did Dad eat already?" I asked.

Mom had her back to me, but she nodded and said, "He went over to Marme's house. Jumpy stayed the night with her."

"What happened?" I demanded. "Is something wrong?"

When Mom turned around her eyes were red. "They're taking her to Calvary Home this afternoon." She wiped her eyes on her apron. "This is hard Jake. Dad and Jumpy have been struggling with this for weeks. The decision got easier yesterday when she fell again. The neighbors called and Jumpy picked her up. This time when she fell she hit her head. She was terribly confused. She didn't know Jumpy or Dad. She really can't stay at home any longer. They have put off this decision as long as they could. Both of them feel it is time to act. I agree."

I wanted to shout, "You can't put Marme in a home. It will kill her." The problem was, I knew Dad and Jumpy were right. If they didn't put her in a home it would probably kill her.

As I sat at the table I remembered the big family council that we held about three years earlier. We were at Jumpy's place to talk about Marme's future. Jumpy proposed that he and Melinda build an apartment off the south side of their house that would be Marme's place. She would have independence and yet the family could keep an eye on her.

Dad thought that was too big a burden for Melinda and Jumpy to handle and countered by suggesting that Marme stay in her home until Tim and I went off to college. "We'll move upstairs to Jake's room and Marme can have our bedroom on the ground floor," Dad suggested. She can stay with us six months of the year and then stay with you six months of the year. If you want to build an apartment, fine, but remember you'll have an extra room when Tim leaves."

Tim and I didn't mind Marme living with us but we didn't want to lose our rooms, even when we left for school. "What if I go to La Crosse?" Tim said. "I'll be home a lot of weekends. I don't want to sleep with Mark when I come home."

My argument didn't make quite as much sense, but the essence of it was that I wanted to keep my room. My Mom felt the same way.

We all knew that Elaine couldn't take care of Marme, unless she sold the farm and moved into town. To leave the place where she and her husband worked together would break her heart.

None of the discussion counted anyway. When Marme got wind of the plans she torpedoed all suggestions. "I am not moving in with either of my sons, and I don't want to share my house with Elaine. I'm not worried about either of my boys. They deserve me. If I could take care of them for eighteen years they can take care of me for three or four. If they find me a burden, tough luck!

"The reason I'm not about to move is for the sake of the women. It isn't fair to Melinda and Lou. I know this first hand. When Dave and I first got married his mother moved in with us. There is not room for two women in one house. Not even if it is my daughter. I survived, but barely. So, thanks, but no thanks. When I can't take care of myself, I want to go to Calvary Home. I'll know people there, and the pastor comes to visit regularly. That is my final word on that subject!"

That is why Jumpy and Dad were headed to Calvary. Evidently Dad and Elaine had visited the home and made arrangements earlier in the week. They thought they were several weeks away, but when she fell they called and the director told them he had a room available immediately. Dad took it.

Jumpy had stayed overnight with Marme. Dad ate early and had left a half hour ago to spell his brother. Just before I sat down to eat, I saw Jumpy's truck pull up in front of our house. Mom met him at the door.

"She wants to go to church. Skip wants me to bring his suit over to the house. I'll change and meet him in forty-five minutes. Marme and Elaine will have lunch with us. Melinda said I should invite the three of you as well. Skip and I will drive her out this afternoon. Elaine can come if she wants to. Marme knows she is going, but forgets every few minutes. I'll load my truck with her chest of drawers, her favorite chair, and enough clothes to see her through three or four days. We'll do the rest later this week."

Mom told Jumpy that when he came back she'd have Dad's suit and shoes ready.

"He didn't mention shoes. It's a good thing he's got you filling in the details, Lou."

Normally our family sat in the fifth row from the front on the pulpit side of the church. Jumpy, Melinda, and their family sat toward the back on the lectern side. Jumpy said it had more to do with politics than church. "Skip can't stand to be on the left, ever," he joked.

There was some truth to what he said. My dad was a supporter of Senator Robert Taft in the 1952 elections. Jumpy was an Eisenhower man. They only agreed on one thing, they didn't want Adlai

Stevenson to be president. Jumpy opposed Stevenson because he was an *egghead*. "He's not a man of the people."

Dad's reason for opposing Stevenson was much more simple. The man was a Democrat. Dad didn't trust the Democrats. Years later our greatest argument was when I supported Kennedy and Dad supported Nixon.

On this particular Sunday, neither family sat in their normal places. We all sat with Marme, who insisted on sitting in the front row under the pulpit. We had all heard her explain it many times, "You have to pay extra money for front row seats at a play because they are the best in the house. They're free at church. Why not take advantage and sit in the best?"

Once again most of the family disagreed with Marme. We were 100 percent in agreement that it just wasn't right or normal to sit that close to the preacher. Dad complained that when he sat with Marme he felt the pastor was talking directly to him.

You may wonder how all of this worked when we sang in the choir. At Maple Street Lutheran the choir sat in the congregation and came forward to sing their anthem. They tried several times to purchase robes and have the choir sit in the loft behind the organ, but singers threatened to quit. Young parents felt it was necessary to sit with their children, and grown men who loved to sing disliked wearing what appeared to be a glorified dress. There were no robes at our church.

Somehow, though most of us felt like cows in the wrong stanchion, we had a good morning together. Pastor Hauge's sermons were normally very good, but the highlight of worship was the hymns. Every Joseph loved to sing. Dad and Jumpy with their creamy tenor voices, Mom with a rich alto. Tim and I were on our way to becoming basses, and Melinda and Karen sang soprano. The entire family sang parts on all the hymns. Most of us not only sang in the church choir, but formed a mini choir when we were in the pew.

As we left, Pastor Hauge shook my hand and said, "I'll see you tonight, Jake."

Tim overheard what the pastor said and asked, "Does pastor come to the games?"

I didn't realize that I hadn't told Tim about my conversation with the pastor at Little Oslo or what Buck had told me at the Paradise Dance Hall. "Buck thinks Pastor should have tried pro ball. Says he was a terrific catcher."

Tim was impressed and told me that he could see Pastor Hauge behind the plate. We stood and watched him greet people as they came out of the church. We were pretty fortunate. Our pastor was the kind of man you could talk to if you ever had a problem. He was smart and he was kind.

· · · · · · ·

Normally, if I got to the ballpark at 5:00, thirty minutes before batting practice, I'd be the first one there. That night nearly the entire team arrived forty-five minutes early. As usual, Smokey threw to the hitters for the first fifteen minutes before the infielders took turns.

When I finished hitting I heard a growl coming from the Harden dugout. "You just had your last hit of the night, Kid." It was Lombardo.

I moved in his direction and said, "I love competing against you. You're going to see me at my best tonight."

When I came back to the dugout Buck, who was playing short toss, greeted me. "Talking with the enemy?"

I smiled at Buck and said, "I told him we'd talk after the game."

"Do you feel ready to face him?"

"Ready as I'll ever be."

Buck took a step toward me and said, "You'll do okay if you re-member what you're told."

As I trotted to the outfield I was shaking my head. "Buck is talking in riddles," I thought.

When it was Harden's turn for batting practice, Smokey pulled us together down the left field line for his pre-game speech. "We've played all year to get to this place. This is our big opportunity to win the prize. It will come down to this, can we handle the big guy's pitches? He'll try to overpower you with his speed and keep you off balance with his change. He seldom strikes out anyone with his curve. Pick your pitch. Either go with his fastball or stay back and wait for the change. If he throws his palm ball hit it to the opposite field."

He then read the starting line up. When he came to the seventh spot he paused. It was almost as if he hadn't made up his mind. Cam had been starting and doing well. He looked up and down the bench before he said, "Seventh hitter will be Sherm. Of course, he'll play second."

When we finished the brief confab we drifted back to our dugout. Several of the older players patted Sherm on the back and talked to him. I walked with Cam. "Did you know you weren't going to start?" I asked.

"No, but I'm not surprised," he responded. "I figured Smokey would play Sherm at some point in this game. He's been an important part of this club for several years. I'm okay with it. If he does well, the team will do well. If he doesn't do well, I'll get in late in the game. I'll be ready either way."

Buck set Harden down in order in the top of the first, striking out the second and third hitters.

I got behind on a Lombardo fastball and popped up to start the bottom half of the first. The next two Jewelers' hitters, went down swinging.

In the second Lombardo singled, but was erased on a double play. In our half, Buck singled and was stranded at first.

The pitchers didn't allow a base runner in the third, fourth, or fifth innings. In the top of the sixth, with a runner on second, Sherm fielded a ball behind second base and threw wide of first. The base runner went to second and the man on second scored.

We all expected that Smokey would now substitute Cam for Sherm. Instead, when we came to bat in the bottom of the inning, he put Cam in at first. That meant Cam was leading off in the sixth.

Lombardo walked him on five pitches. Terry bunted down the third base line, trying to get Cam into scoring position. The throw from third pulled the first baseman off the bag. That brought me to bat with two on and no one out. I was headed to the batter's box when I heard a voice calling me. It was Buck. "Heed the advice of your elders," he shouted. When I looked a bit confused he nearly hissed, "For God's sake, listen to your pastor."

Buck smiled and ran his right hand down his pant leg. I was amazed. In my excitement I had totally forgotten what Pastor Hauge had told me. Not once had I watched Lombardo to see if he tipped his change. It was so stupid. I had information that could make a huge difference and in the heat of battle, and I hadn't been paying attention. I stepped into the batter's box determined that I would wait for the change. I stared at the pitcher. His hand stayed on the ball and he fired a strike letter high. The same thing happened on the second pitch, except it was slightly outside, 1–1.

As Lombardo leaned to get the sign for the third pitch, I saw it. Clearly he wiped his hand on his pant leg. If Pastor Hague was right, this was Lombardo's change. When he went into his motion I moved the weight to my back foot and watched as the palm ball came my way, big and fat and juicy. I shifted ever so slightly and swung inside out. The ball was lined over the head of a jumping second baseman. I was thinking double from the time the ball left the bat. The coach at first waved me to second. Three steps past the bag I caught the eye of Smokey, coaching at third. He was waving me on. I hit the bag full stride with my left foot and pivoted for third. Seeing that Smokey had his palms down. I slid into third ahead of the throw, knowing two runs had scored.

Smokey immediately called time out and slapped me on the back. "What happened in right?" I asked.

"The center fielder cut in front of the right fielder. If the right fielder had handled it, he would have had a great shot at third. The minute I saw the center fielder pick up the ball I knew he had to turn to throw to third. Jake, I'd bet a month's salary that you can beat an outfielder making a pirouette. Watch me for the signs."

I looked at Smokey pacing out of the coach's box. I knew what sign he wouldn't give me, the suicide squeeze. Everyone on both teams remembered the last time that was tried. Lombardo pitched out, and I was lucky to score. There would be no bunt this time.

The infield moved in. Our batter hit the ball directly to short. I took three steps toward home and then dove back to the bag. The short stop watched for a moment and satisfied that I was going nowhere, threw the runner out at first by two steps. One out.

Smokey called time and drew me off the bag to talk. "I want you to be off at the crack of the bat. Even if it is hit to short go for it. We'll make them beat you with a great throw." I nodded.

On a two and two pitch LaVon hit the ball hard. I put my head down and took off for home. I peeked and saw that it was to the left of the second baseman. I didn't see him field the ball, but I guessed that he would have to throw off balance, and that it wouldn't be a strong throw. Later I was told that my hunch was correct. Though he fielded the ball cleanly his weight took him toward first. He had to stop, plant his feet, and throw a bit off balance to home. I did what coaches tell you not to do; I went head first into home. I dove to the right and dragged my left hand across home as I slid past, beating the throw by an eyelash. 3–1.

Buck came out of the dugout, hand extended. "You did exactly what Davy told you to do. I'll take it from here." Moments later LaVern hit into a double play, and we entered the seventh.

It was not quite as easy as Buck suggested. In the seventh Lombardo hit a two-run homer to left-center, and the game was tied. In our half of the seventh Buck led off with a double and scored on a single by our catcher.

I had one more shot at Lombardo. Batting with one on and two out, he wiped his hand on a 2–2 pitch. I did everything the same as my last time up, only I got under the ball a bit and lined the ball directly to the right fielder.

In the eighth Harden scored again, to tie the score.

In our half of the eighth Lombardo walked the lead-off hitter. On a hit and run LaVon hit a ball to third. The third baseman had no choice but to get the sure out at first. Before he went to bat LaVern walked over to me on the bench and said, "You've hit the change hard the last two times up. Anything that I should know?"

I whispered, "Lombardo is tipping his palm ball. He wipes his right hand on his pant leg before he throws it." LaVern grinned and headed to the plate. Three pitches later he hit a towering fly ball over the fence in right center. He circled the bases waving his cap in his left hand. We all greeted him at the plate. He picked me off the ground and said, "He did exactly what you said. When you know what is coming it is like hitting a driver off a tee."

We were two up going into the ninth.

Buck was ready to close. He struck out the first two batters and the third hit a lazy fly ball to center field. LaVern squeezed it with two hands for the final out and we had won the championship.

We all rushed the mound and piled on Buck. He was clearly our MVP, and we all let him know how much we appreciated him. When I came out of the pile I saw that two people were missing. Smokey had walked over to the box and shook hands with Ted Towne. He was just taking care of business.

The other person who was absent from the celebration was Sherm. I turned and saw him walking across the edge of the infield on his way to his car. Two years ago he had led the team in hits, batting average, and steals. It was a shame he couldn't have been a bigger part of the championship.

Buck grabbed me by the arm and led me away from the crowd over to second base. He pointed to a spot down the left field line. Then he waved at a man with a Cubs hat, wearing a long jacket and holding a pair of binoculars. The man waved back. "Wave at your pastor, Jake," Buck said. I did, and Pastor Hauge put two hands together over his head in a sign of victory. Then he turned and walked up the hill.

"It was a great season," I told Buck. "I'm honored to be on your team."

"Keep working," Buck said to me. "With a little muscle you'll be an even better player."

As we walked toward the cars a pretty woman ran toward Buck. She jumped into his arms and kissed him. "This is Pearl, the love of my life," Buck explained.

"I was sure hoping it was Pearl," I said. And we all laughed.

"Buck has talked about you a lot this season," she said. "He loves your attitude and the way you play the game."

I thanked her and was about to say something nice about Buck when we saw the big man from Harden heading our way. When he reached second base, where we were now standing, he said, "You took us this year." He shook hands with Buck. "Always a pleasure to play against you," he growled.

Then he looked at me. "I hope to hell you go to college a long way away. Have you thought about the West Coast?"

"Why Mr. Lombardo," I said with a big grin. "I've decided to finish high school and play for the Jewelers next summer. You'd miss me if I wasn't here, right?"

"Like I'd miss poison ivy," he muttered. "Damn, I was hoping you had graduated. See you next summer." And he was off walking toward a car that was waiting for him.

"That was nice of him," I said to Buck.

"He's okay," Buck said. "Last year after he beat us for the last time he visited the store the next day to solicit our business."

Pearl laughed, "We told him that as long as Wahissa was paying Buck we'd stay with the Wahissa bank."

I could see Candy waiting impatiently for me. I thanked Buck again and headed to her car. I hoped we could celebrate a bit before the night was over.

Undercover

*E*arlier in the day, after church, I pulled Candy aside to tell her about my visit to Paradise. She told me it would have to wait because she and her family were leaving to have lunch at the Paulson farm. We decided that she would meet me after the game that night. "I've got some important things to tell you," I said.

She gave me the kind of look that said, "I've got a couple things to say to you, also."

We met at the dugout and were heading toward the cars when she asked if I was willing to walk home. I told her that was fine but it would be easier if Mom and Dad took my glove, cleats, and bat. I tossed those three items in the backseat, kissed Mom, who told me she was proud of me, and caught Candy before she headed up the hill.

We didn't get far before she found a bench at the edge of the park and sat down. "Before we go any further I want to know why you went to Paradise without me," she said sternly. "I've come to expect that we spend Saturday nights together."

It was true. We either went to a movie or did something with Tim and one of his many girlfriends. "I didn't know what I was going to get into," I said slowly trying to weave my way through what was feeling like a minefield. "I thought I might end up spending the whole night with a group of guys. I know you would have been bored if I started talking guy stuff. I thought this was easiest. By going alone I didn't have to worry about how you were doing." She looked totally unconvinced. I tried to hug her and concluded, "Candy, I didn't have a plan and I felt that traveling alone was easiest."

"And did you spend your whole night with a group of guys?" she asked skeptically.

I didn't like the way this was going. "No. Not the whole night. I started out by talking to a couple fellows who scrimmaged us over Christmas vacation. We talked about the men who got beat up, and they introduced me to a girl who was a neighbor to Lloyd Swenson. She gave me some information that I want to tell you about." I paused to see how that was received.

"Tell me more about the girl," Candy said.

"In just a second. I'll tell you everything," I said fumbling for more time. "First, I want to tell you that I also had a talk with Buck. He told me the Sheriff visited him to talk about the beatings. He swears he had nothing to do with them. He also knew Lloyd and Kid. In the past you've believed it may be Buck who is doing this. I have completely eliminated him."

Candy nodded. "Good information. Now tell me about the girl."

"Her name is Courtney, and she lives on the farm next to Lloyd Swenson," I said weakly. I started to tell her about the visit by Mr. and Mrs. Carlson but Candy interrupted me, asking for more information.

"Did you dance with her?

"I did. I also took a walk with her. It was on the walk that I found out that Mrs. Carlson visited the family and that Woody was with her!"

Candy turned sideways and her eyes narrowed. She looked at me, cocked her head, and then said, "I'm not done with this Courtney chick, but what did you find out about the Carlsons?"

"Courtney told me that Lloyd's wife is named Sonia and that he beat her many times. I didn't know Mrs. Carlson was a social worker, did you?"

"Of course I knew. I see her almost every day in the courthouse. She works out of the Department of Social Services, the department I'm working in next week."

"Wow. How great is that?"

Candy wasn't done. "I have no idea why you think that is so terrific, but what else do you have to tell me? Do you have something else to tell me about the Swenson family? Perhaps you have more to tell me about this Courtney girl?"

"There isn't much more to tell about either one," I explained. "I think Courtney was wondering why I was so interested in her neighbors. She wanted to talk about us, and I wanted to know about Lloyd Swenson."

"So, which was it? You and Courtney or Lloyd Swenson."

"From the time I found out that the Swensons were neighbors it was all about them. Now I want to know if Mrs. Carlson had a connection with any of the other victims."

"And I want to know," Candy said firmly, "what happened to you and your dance partner."

"Nothing happened," I said. "We weren't outside very long until I asked where she lived. She pointed up the hill toward the ridge. I recognized the direction as where Lloyd lived. I asked if she knew the family, and she told me what I've just told you. After awhile we went back to the dance hall and I met Buck. Actually, Buck spotted me. We talked about baseball. He told me he was impressed with my catch against Kickapoo City. Then we talked about his visit from the Sheriff. He told me that he was miles from Vang the night that happened, but that he knew several of the victims. They had all played with him, but he was friends, not enemies."

We sat quietly on the bench for several minutes. "Oh yes, one more thing." She leaned close to hear, "Buck knows Pastor Hauge. They played ball together. Buck says Pastor was a fine catcher. He could have played at a higher level."

She smiled, "You were a busy boy Saturday night. Fortunately, your story holds true."

"What do you mean?"

"At breakfast Dad told me he had seen you at Paradise last night. He told me he saw you walking down the street with a redhead. He told me that you had a conversation with Buck. He also told me that Sheriff Silver talked to Buck earlier in the week and that Buck was no longer a suspect."

I turned and looked at her in disbelief, "You were attempting to trap me."

"I was giving you an opportunity to clear your name. Hearing you were walking down the street with another girl on a Saturday night didn't put me in the best of moods. I've thought about little else all day. I didn't know you were going to Paradise, so I was a little surprised. When dad told me that you were with a redhead, I have to admit that I got my dander up." She took my hand, "I should have known that your intentions were honorable. I really do trust you, Jake Joseph."

She heard me sigh. "Unless there is something else you want me to know."

I thought for a few seconds, wondering what Phil Paulson saw. I decided to let things stand. "That is pretty much it," I said.

Candy stood up and we began to walk slowly toward her house. "What is next? What do you plan to do now that you have this delicious information?"

"If you want to be a part of this, I think the next step could be yours."

Candy stopped and looked at me with deep suspicion. "You've lost me," she said.

"You are working in social services. I'm sure they have records of all the visits made by the social workers. You have access to the records. You could look them up when people are out of the office. It would be helpful to know if anyone has visited the other victims. There's only a total of four. That can't take too long, can it?"

"Reports such as the ones that Mrs. Carlson wrote go to the Sheriff's department," Candy said calmly. "Fig Olson, one of the other deputies, is usually the person who follows up on these reports. He then investigates and makes a recommendation to the district attorney."

"Okay, so Mrs. Carlson's report is sent to Deputy Olson, but she surely would keep a copy of her report, wouldn't she?" I asked.

Candy thought for a moment. "I'm sure she would keep a copy, but where would she keep it? It could be in one of the file cabinets in the outer office, or she could keep a copy in her desk."

"I'll wager she keeps two copies," I said. "She certainly would have a copy in her office, but I'd be surprised if she didn't have a copy that is available for her supervisor to see."

Candy nodded. "You are probably right. No doubt there is a copy of the report somewhere in the area where I work. Now, I have another question. What happens if I get caught going through files. I could get fired. Have you thought of that?"

"You're very smart. You know when to look and when not to look. You must be able to find a time when no one is in the office. Maybe you work through a noon hour. I know you can figure it out."

"Jake, if I get caught the person who arrests me will be my father."

My first impulse was to laugh it off and say, "There you go. Your father will free you." My second impulse was to say nothing stupid. "It's up to you. If you think you can help, great. If not, we'll have to find a different way to get information."

"I ate my lunch with Sharon the other day. She says that the Kid Hill family has suffered terribly this entire summer since he isn't able to work. I want to see these beatings end before others get hurt."

She thought for a few moments before she spoke. "Mrs. Gamble often eats her lunch in her office. She does have an occasional meeting elsewhere in the building. Several other women have desks in the office. There is Miss Custer, the visiting nurse, and two social workers. Mrs. Carlson comes in early and then leaves mid-morning. Only occasionally does she return and then it is late in the afternoon. Mrs. Krohn's schedule is similar, except she doesn't come in at the end of the day. It may take me a couple of days, but I'll see what I can do."

We didn't speak for the last few blocks before we reached her house. I stopped and took her hand and said, "One more thing about

Saturday night. After Courtney told me she was a neighbor I asked her to show me where she lived. We drove up on the ridge past her place and the Swenson residence. Then we turned around and came back."

Candy immediately kissed me. "Thank you. Dad told me he saw this girl get out of your car. He then parked the squad car and saw you walking alone into the dance hall. I'm so glad you decided to tell me the whole thing." Then she kissed me again.

We walked around to her back door and said good night.

As I walked home I realized I came within inches of being totally embarrassed.

. . . .

That next morning at work Moose approached me after the early buzz. His cap was off, a sure sign he was uncomfortable with what he was about to say. "Charlotte's back," he said. "She wants to come back to work at the end of the week. Is that okay with you?"

"Sure," I told him. "It's her job. What day does she want to start?"

"Friday. Not many people start on a Friday, but that is what she wants. I'll need her to get me through the winter."

I laughed. "Moose, this is such a relief. With football practice every night and working every day and school starting on Monday I could use a couple of days off. If she wants to start on Thursday it would be okay with me."

Moose sighed as he held out his hand. "You are officially a part of the Little Oslo family. You've filled in great this summer. You show up on time. You get the orders straight, and you are always polite to the customers, which is more than I can say for Charlotte. Thursday will be your last day. I'll probably need you over Christmas, but that is a long way off."

That afternoon when I got on my bike and headed for home. I felt like a 100-pound weight had just been lifted from my shoulders.

. . . .

I had just started munching on my second cookie when the phone rang. It was Candy. "Can you come over soon? I have some news."

I reminded her that football practice began that night, but I'd come over as soon as practice was over.

She sounded disappointed, "I've got something important for you."

"I'll be there as soon as I can get away," I told her.

I showered and left practice early. When I arrived at the Paulson house Candy was waiting for me in the back yard. We took two lawn chairs and placed them under the oak in the corner furthest from the house. "I was able to see two of the records," she said triumphantly. "Mrs. Gamble told me she would be out of the office from 11:00 until 1:00. I waited until 11:30 before I began my search. If there is a file on Thomas Knight, I couldn't find it. It took me a long time to find nothing. I looked everywhere. There is an alphabetical file, and there are separate files under each social worker. I found nothing."

"Anything else?" I asked eagerly.

"Yes. I found a file for Richard Hill. It was in Mrs. Carlson's section. I didn't double check in the general files."

"What did you find?

"Richard was also a client of Mrs. Carlson."

"Really. What was the issue?"

"Guess."

"He beat up his wife?"

"Right you are. More than once. Mrs. Carlson filed papers with the district attorney three times and nothing happened. After the third time she wrote a very strong letter protesting the DA's lack of action."

"Did you notice a date on that letter?"

Candy reached into her pocket and pulled out a small note pad, "Sure did. Date was April 22, 1952."

I let out a whistle. "This spring. Did you read the letter?"

"I scanned it. It was a protest. She said that he was putting Mrs. Hill in danger by his failure to act."

I gave Candy a big hug. "You are terrific. We have made great progress."

"There's more," she said.

"What else."

"I found the Lloyd Swenson file. It looks and sounds very much like the Hill file. Same visits. Same reports. Same letter of protest to the district attorney."

"Was there a reply from the DA?" I asked.

"Yes. He said that one of his staff had visited with Mrs. Hill who declined to press charges. He said that he did not have enough evidence to pursue battery without her cooperation."

"Wow! You have made great progress."

"It looks like we are a long way from figuring this out," she protested.

"Look at what we have. We know that Mrs. Carlson was the case worker for two of the four men who were beat up."

"We know that one of the men was not her client," Candy said. "We don't know if she even knew the fourth man. I say you have made a little bit of progress, nothing more."

"We know her husband was with her at one of the homes."

"We know that her husband is one of the kindest men we have ever met. Granted, he is strong. He could do it. But Sheriff Silver doesn't even know if this is the work of one man. It could be two or three."

I was stunned. "Two or three? Where did you get that information?"

"From my dad. The last case, Fuzzy Kvamme, looked very strange. Two of the fist marks didn't match the others. There was a big fist and a small fist. At least that is what the crime lab thinks."

"That information isn't public, is it?"

Candy thought for a moment, "I guess not. Maybe that is something I'm not supposed to tell. Oh well, I know it is what dad said."

I thought for a couple minutes. "It will still help if you can look at the Fuzzy Kvamme file. It would help to know if Mrs. Carlson visited the Kvamme household."

"If you are really nice to me I will go undercover tomorrow and see what I can find."

The rest of the night I tried to be really nice.

Caught

CHAPTER 26

O n August 25, the day after the Harden game and about a week before classes were to start, evening football practices began. All of the returning lettermen were invited to check in to select our pads and helmets. The seniors got first choice.

Tim, who took off a couple hours of work, picked me up from Little Oslo. There were only six pairs of girdle hip pads and we each wanted one. If you didn't get the girdle variety you had to tighten the conventional type with a belt. Since it was difficult to do it perfectly they were always slipping and sliding. The girdle fit in something like a pair of elastic underpants and usually stayed put.

We played before facemasks were mandatory. Although we didn't have a bar across our mouth Tim bought a tooth guard. I think he was the only guy on the team that had one. Since I was the quarterback I decided not to get one. How could you shout out the signals when you had something in your mouth? I know they do so today, but it seemed strange in the fall of 1952.

．．．．．．．

When we finished our second practice that Tuesday night I saw Candy standing in front of the Paulson family car. I trotted over and she said, "Get in. I'll give you a lift back to the showers." She looked tense.

"What's up? Are you okay?"

She just looked at me and shook her head. "I'll be shocked if I get through this without damaging my reputation," she said. She didn't speak another word until we reached the school. "I'll wait," she said tersely.

Normally, I was slow to dress. Not that night. I threw everything in my locker, ran my head under the shower (it didn't take long to wash a flattop), and was out of the dressing room before anyone else.

Candy drove the car to the park, turned off the ignition, and got out of the car. When we found a place to sit she said, "Mrs. Gamble caught me."

I threw my arms around her and said, "Candy, I am so sorry. What happened?"

She sighed and said, "I'll start at the beginning. At about 11:15 she told me she would be leaving in fifteen minutes for lunch. No one else was in the office. At 11:40 I started looking in the files. I found the Kvamme file immediately. I read Mrs. Carlson's report. It was nearly identical to both the Swenson and Hill reports. In fact I read it very carefully to make sure it was not a duplicate of one of the other reports. I don't think I told you that in the Swenson report there were some private notes that she had made after her second visit. She indicated that she felt so threatened by Mr. Swenson during her first visit that she decided to have her husband accompany her on her next trip. He stood in front of the car the entire time she met with Mr. Swenson. By the way, she never went into his house. She met him on the porch even though it was about forty-five degrees. It's all in the report."

When Candy's eyes got moist I moved close to her, but she held up her hand to tell me to stay back. "In the Kvamme report she again indicated that she thought there was enough evidence to convict. Once again the DA answered her first letter saying that he again sent a person from his office to the Kvamme home to talk to Mrs. Kvamme and like Mrs. Swenson, Mrs. Kvamme refused to press charges. There is no response in the file from the DA to the other correspondence. I don't know if he replied or whether Mrs. Carlson just didn't include it. My guess is that he didn't respond in writing. By the way, in the file there are handwritten notes from her conversation with Mrs. Kvamme and the Kvamme children's teacher."

"Candy," I said, "why are you giving me all these details? Just tell me about getting caught."

She wiped her eyes and said, "If I don't tell you these things first I'll never get through it. One more thing. Mrs. Carlson wrote a letter to the district attorney in early May suggesting that *a substantial pattern of abuse exists in the Kvamme household.* I just finished reading the Kvamme report when Mrs. Gamble walked in. She walked up to me, snatched the file out of my hand and shouted, 'Candy Paulson, what are you doing?'"

Candy began to sob. This time she let me hold her. "I am so sorry," I said several times.

Candy gathered herself and continued, "She kept on shouting at me though I'm not sure what she said. She talked nonstop for a couple of minutes and then I heard her say, 'I don't know what I am going to do with you. I just do not know what to do. I obviously can't run to the Sheriff's department, not with your father employed there. Stay right here. I'm going directly to see Judge Swiggum.'

"She stomped out of the room and soon entered again with the Judge right behind her. She told the Judge that she had caught me red-handed going through private case files. 'I need advice, your honor. What should I do with this girl? Should I file charges with the district attorney's office?'

"As Mrs. Gamble talked she waved the Kvamme file in the air in front of her. The Judge walked over to her, took the file out of her hands, and read the name, 'Orvis Kvamme.' He thought for a moment and then looked at me and said, 'Is this the fellow that was beat up not very long ago?'

"I nodded. Then the Judge spoke softly, 'You were not filing this file in the cabinet, correct? You were reading or were about to read this file, is that correct?'

"'I have not yet read the file,' I answered.

"He nodded, thought for a moment and spoke to Mrs. Gamble, 'Is it written policy that secretaries are forbidden from reading client files, Margaret?'

"'I believe it is. Yes, I think so.'

"'Has Miss Paulson seen this written policy?'

"Mrs. Gamble was no longer angry. She was looking a bit frightened. 'I certainly hope so.'

"The Judge frowned and said, 'Was that a yes or a no?'

"Mrs. Gamble thought for a moment and said, 'I don't know if she was provided with a written copy of office procedure or not. She is not a full-time employee. I know that all full-time employees are provided with a complete personnel policy. Whether Miss Paulson received one or not, I'm not sure. I certainly hope she was.'

"The Judge turned toward me, 'Have you ever been provided with a written policy stating that it is forbidden for a secretary to read client files?' The Judge addressed me with a softer, kinder voice that he addressed Mrs. Gamble.

"I shook my head. ' I have never been given any written policy statement on any subject.'

"The Judge wasn't done. 'And Margaret, did you give Miss Paulson an oral summary of what is required and forbidden? Did you ever tell her orally that she was never to look in a client file?'

"Mrs. Gamble thought for a moment and then said, 'I don't remember. Perhaps not.'

"The Judge, now totally in charge, spoke directly to Mrs. Gamble, 'Margaret, will you please go to my office and sit in the outer lounge. I'm going to meet with Miss Paulson alone for a few minutes. I'll come and get you soon.'

"Mrs. Gamble looked confused and a bit frightened, but she did as the Judge told her. As she shuffled out the door she made some noises that sounded like an animal huffing and snorting.

"The Judge waited for her to get out of sight and then turned to me and said, 'I'm hoping there is a very logical explanation for this curious action.'

"I said, ' I certainly hope so, too. I thought so when I first located the file, but I'm not as sure right now. My boyfriend and I have a theory about the beatings, and I was looking to see if the theory was valid.'

"The Judge cocked his head. 'Not only do you and Mr. Joseph pick up strangers along the highway at night, acting as Good Samaritans of the road, you solve mysteries?'

"'Now that you put it that way it doesn't sound as noble as I hoped,' I responded. 'We've both heard a lot about the beatings. My dad comes home at night and talks about the investigation. Jake, my boyfriend, works at Little Oslo and hears the Sheriff and others speculating about the victims and the perpetrator. We've noticed that a couple of the beatings were clients of this department. We've noted that at least two of the men were examined for beating their wives. We wondered if all four fell into the same category.

"The Judge paused for a moment and then asked, 'And what did you find? Were all four of the men wife beaters?'

"'There are only files on three of the victims,' I said quietly. 'I don't know what is in Mr. Kvamme's file. I hadn't read it when Mrs. Gamble entered the room.'"

"'You have already read two of the files of men who were beaten?'

"'Yes sir. I did that yesterday.'

"'And what did you find?'

"'Both men received a visit from a country social worker when they were reported for beating their wives.' I wasn't sure if I should say anything else, but the Judge seemed interested, so I continued. 'The social worker, Mrs. Carlson, recommended that charges should be pressed.'

"'And?'

"'And nothing was done.'

"The Judge nearly spit out his next comment, 'The bastards.'

"I was baffled because I had no idea why the Judge was upset. Since I was in no position to ask questions, I remained silent.

"The Judge thought for a moment while still holding the Kvamme file in his hand. Finally he said, 'Suppose we look at this one together.'

"He opened the file and began to page through it. Then he looked at me and said, 'You are probably better at this than I am. Show me what you can find.'

"I laid the file on the top of one of the cabinets and began to turn the pages. Noticing that he was barely tall enough to read the paper on the cabinet, I picked it up and held it in my hands. 'Here is the report of Mrs. Carlson's visits,' I told him. 'Someone reported abuse the last week in November. She visited Mr. and Mrs. Kvamme in their home three days later. It looks like Mrs. Carlson made another visit in February, and still another in March. Each report was copied to Deputy Olson in the Sheriff's office.'

"'As I understand it,' I said quietly, ' the deputy continues the investigation and makes a report to the district attorney. Is that right?'

"The Judge nodded. 'That is correct.'

"I turned over two more pages. 'Evidently the deputy did nothing because here is a letter from Mrs. Carlson to the district attorney.' I quickly scanned it. 'It appears to be similar to the letter she sent regarding Mr. Hill.'

"'The wimpy bastards,' the Judge muttered. This time he decided to explain his remarks, 'When you are dealing with Deputy Olson and the district attorney you are almost dealing with one person. The two of them are related. They married sisters. Olson does whatever the DA asks of him. The district attorney has his eye on my seat, and for some strange reason he does not want to act on a number of cases that he thinks will be controversial. God help us if he is ever elected. He doesn't have balls enough to be a judge.'

"He looked at the file and then he looked at me. 'What is your next step? What are you going to do about all of this?'

"I stepped back and said, 'I don't know. I suppose the answer depends on whether Mrs. Gamble files charges against me.'

"The Judge walked to the door and looked down the hall. Then he turned and said, 'Mrs. Gamble won't file charges. She doesn't have a legal leg to stand on. If she did I'd throw the charges out.' He paused for a moment, looked at me and smiled, 'I owe you that much.'

"He walked around the office for a bit and then spoke, 'You have an interesting theory. Very interesting. Let me guess. The man without the file is Tom Knight, correct?'

"I looked surprised. 'You are right, sir,' I said. 'How did you know?'

"'Call it the Judge Swiggum theory. Like your theory it is based on a little bit of information and a hunch.'

"Again he walked to the door. This time when he returned he asked, 'Are you comfortable working in this room next to Margaret the rest of the afternoon?'

"'Assuming that you are going to talk to her before she comes back, the answer is yes.'

"'Margaret and I will have a little conversation. She will listen to what I have to say. Tomorrow Mavis, my secretary, will move into this office for the rest of the week, and you can work with me. I have Mavis working on a project this afternoon. It would not be in our best interests for her to leave at present.'

"He started to walk out the door before he turned and spoke, 'Helen and I are eternally grateful for you kindness the night of July 20. You and your friend did everything in the proper manner, or at least the manner that benefited the two of us. Ken Brown also holds you in highest regard. Thank you. I am glad I can do something in return. One more thing. I think Helen may have the final piece of your puzzle. Later this week take the time to talk to her.'

"About ten minutes after he walked down the hall a grim-faced Mrs. Gamble returned, walked into her office, and shut the door without looking or speaking to me. The door was still closed when I went home at five."

I took a deep breath and said, "We'll drop the whole thing. I never thought that you'd get in trouble."

Candy looked at me dumbfounded. "If you think I went to all this trouble only to drop it after a bump in the road, you are absolutely wrong, Jake Joseph. We are very close to solving this crime. I don't know what the next step is, but we can't stop now."

I looked at her and thought, "This is the most beautiful and courageous girl in Wahissa. I kissed her and then said, "The next step is a conversation with Helen Lewison. You can do it alone or I can meet with you."

"I'm not about to meet with her alone," Candy said clearly. "I don't know when you are free now that you have football practice, but we ought to see her before the end of the week. I wonder what she knows?"

· · · · · · ·

On Wednesday I received a call from Candy while I was still at Little Oslo. "I'm in the Judge's office," she said. "Everything is fine. He talked to me this morning, but I haven't seen him since noon. I think he left for La Crosse. Anyway, Helen called me a few minutes ago. She asked if I could meet her this afternoon. I told her that I wanted you to come with me, and that I wasn't sure I could reach you in time for a meeting today. She said that was fine and suggested that we meet at the park at 2:30 tomorrow. Will that work for you?"

"It's perfect," I told her. "I should be done at the restaurant by 2:00. I'll peddle over immediately after I'm finished. Did she give you any idea what this is about?"

"All I know," said Candy, "is what the Judge said. This could be the final piece of our puzzle."

"What does that mean?"

There was a pause on the other end. "What piece is missing?" she asked.

"It seems to me," I told her, "that there are several pieces of this puzzle that are missing."

Moose was giving me the evil eye, so I told Candy I had to go.

That night after practice Tim and I headed to Ham's Station. We each bought an ice cream bar and a Coke and headed to the back bay. Six or seven of the football team were sitting on tires and sharing the news of the day. We found a bench and pulled up next to two juniors, Ricky Overbo and Dan Thomas. Ricky had been gone most of the summer working for Ken Brown up on Loon Lake. "What did you do?" Tim asked him.

"I ran the rental shop on the lake," Ricky informed us. "Ken has quite a business, renting out canoes and motor boats. We also do a fair business with paddle boats."

"Once they close the shop Ricky is free to hustle," Dan said. "I was up there one night and there were some serious babes that were hanging around."

"The night Dan came up there were several families from Eau Claire. The babe that Dan ended up with had some mighty big melons," Ricky bragged.

"Got my hands on 'em too," Dan told us. "I wish I could have stayed up there for a weekend. There was some great action going on."

Tim and I flashed a look at each other. Ricky and Dan hadn't had a date in Wahissa in over a year. Fat chance they were scoring at Loon Lake.

Dan and Ricky were so caught up in their fantasy tale that they didn't pay any attention to us. "You meet the most interesting people at a resort," Ricky was saying. "One of the people I met was Coach Carlson's sister. She was there with her son and her daughter. The daughter, Liz, was always hanging out around the boathouse. She's going to be a freshman next year and a real looker. She really is. Anyway, I had to take a motorboat out to see why one of the canoes was late coming back and asked her to go with me. Turned out to be nothing, just a couple of people making out on one of the beaches who had lost track of time. Coming back she told me that her mom and dad were splitting. Her dad had beat her mom something fierce. A half dozen times! She said that Woody came up to stay with her mom the last time it happened. He was so mad that he threatened to get even. It was all Liz's mom could do to hold him back. Her mom had said, 'If you beat him I'll never have a chance to get back together with him again. Woody, you have to let me handle this on my own.'"

"When did all this take place?" I asked.

"I think it was last spring," Ricky said. "I wasn't really paying attention. I was just pretending to be interested so that we could spend some time alone later. It never happened though. I really thought I had a shot at her, too."

Tim rolled his eyes, "Strange how those things work out, isn't it. You think you've got a shot and then all of a sudden things evaporate."

"Happens to you, too?" Ricky said.

Tim never answered. He just motioned to me to follow. We headed for his car and then on to home. About a block from home he said, "Well Sam Spade, that ought to get you going."

I tried not to look too interested. "I don't know what you are talking about."

"You think I didn't see you leap out of your skin when "Rick the Prick" talked about Woody's sister? Surely you are processing this information in that big brain of yours. Woody is pissed off because his sister is knocked around by her husband. Doesn't that add fuel to your fire?"

"I'll have to think about it," I said cautiously.

"Think about it, my foot," Tim said. "You've been hot on this for weeks. You spend a Saturday night in Paradise rather than with Candy so you can gather information. You pump everyone you meet who knows anything. You've been thinking about Coach Carlson for weeks, and now you have powerful new information. Tell me that you aren't ready to jump up and down."

"Up to now you've been telling me to back off. You tell me that I'm no Sam Spade, and ask why I'm concerned about a couple of bums who got beat up. What's with you?"

Tim stopped the car. "Damn, Jake. I wish more than anything that I would have gone with you to Paradise. I had a date and thought that was more important. I've regretted my refusal ever since you came back. I think you are on to something. I'm trying to tell you I've been wrong. If you can solve this thing I think it would be great."

"Really?"

"Really."

"Well, this does help us with the motive. Woody's wife is frustrated with the reaction of the district attorney's office, which makes Woody upset. Now we find out that Woody's sister gets beat up by her no-good husband. The motive is becoming clear or at least appears to becoming clear."

Tim was anxious to know more. "What do you know from Candy's dad? Have you learned anything new at Little Oslo?"

I decided he needed to know what I knew, so I began to tell him everything. I told him about Candy finding the information, though I didn't tell him she got caught. I told him how I had found out about Mrs. Carlson from a girl in Paradise.

"What did the girl look like?" he asked. "Was she pretty?"

"Will you keep your mind on the issue at hand?" I asked. "Yeah, she was pretty, a redhead, but that isn't the issue. The issue is,"

"Big knockers?" Tim asked.

"Tim! Soon you'll start sounding like Ricky. Let's stay on course, okay?"

He was roaring with laughter. "I'm just teasing you man. I know something happened at that dance. Ninety percent of the guys at Wahissa High would be bragging about a conquest, but you are so straight that you come home and go silent. I'm pulling your string. Go ahead. I won't interrupt."

"Where was I? Oh yeah, this girl told me when Mrs. Carlson investigated Lloyd Swenson, Woody rode along with her as her protector. Mrs. Carlson never entered the Swenson home. Woody stood outside the car listening to every word. This helps explain why Woody got involved. He shared in his wife's frustration as she tried to help women who were being mistreated."

Tim said, "It would explain how Woody knew what Lloyd Swenson looks like."

I was startled. "I didn't even think of that," I said. "It does explain how he knows what Lloyd Swenson looked like, but it opens another mystery."

"Which is?"

"How did he know what Fuzzy and Kid looked like? He not only had to know what they looked like, he had to identify them in the dark."

We both sat in silence for a while before I thought out loud, "Of course, he knew what Tom Knight looked like. Everybody in town knows Tom."

"Where does Tom fit into this puzzle?" Tim asked.

"I don't know yet," I admitted. "I don't know what to do with him. He's in the wrong town, as far as we know. He is neither a drinker nor a mean bastard."

I was dying to tell Tim about the Judge and Helen, but I decided that was off limits. The whole conversation made me wonder what Helen had to tell us. The Judge told Candy that Helen had "the last piece to our puzzle?" What did that mean?

It was late and we both had to be at work early the next morning. It was our last day at work. When Tim found out that I wasn't working on Friday, he took Friday off as well. We didn't have any plans, but it would be the last day before our senior year began.

Another Piece to the Puzzle

CHAPTER 27

hen I got to work on Thursday morning there was a big handmade sign that said, "Jake, Thanks for a great summer."

"Cookie made it," Moose said.

I was astonished. Cookie wasn't the sentimental type. He had given me no indication he cared that I even worked at Little Oslo. I walked to the kitchen and said, "Cookie, did you make that sign?"

He looked embarrassed and said, "Ah, shit."

I put on my apron, grabbed a coffee pot, and began to make my rounds. The Silver Table had perfect attendance. I took their orders and asked Ken, "Double this morning?"

"Might as well," he said with a shrug. "Dani's got me on a diet starting the first of September. Sounds horrible."

Everyone filled their spots at the Painter's Table also. "I assume it's combos all the way around?" I asked the group. Swish polled the group and nodded. "Are you just about done?" I asked.

"We're down to finishing work on the last two houses," Swish said. If it doesn't rain we should wrap it up shortly after noon. Thanks for your help this summer." Everyone at the table seemed to agree, even Sherm.

As he left that morning Ken slipped some bills in my pocket. I could tell that there were more than normal. Later when I counted it there was a twenty, a ten, and three fives. I felt flush.

The 10:00 group all applauded when it was announced it was my last day. Similar things happened at noon.

The Bolstad family came in for an early lunch. April and May sat on one side of the booth while June and August sat on the other. They hardly spoke to anyone but their immediate family. They all thanked me and each gave me a quarter tip. Since it was their first tip of the summer, I was moved.

When the buzz was over, just before 2:00, I shook hands with Moose. "I'll come by in a couple days," I told him. "Just don't expect me at 6:00 tomorrow."

He handed me the envelope with my weekly check. Later I found out that he gave me a fifty-dollar bonus for the summer."

I went to the alley, picked up my bike, and rode the five blocks to the park, which was just two blocks from the courthouse. Up ahead I saw Candy walking briskly. I looked at my watch. It was 2:20. I dismounted, walked my bike alongside her, and then hid it behind some bushes. Helen, who had already arrived, was sitting on a bench under a big oak tree.

"Thanks for coming on such short notice," she said sweetly. "I've picked out a place to talk where we won't be seen." We walked several hundred feet to a remote place on the edge of the park where two benches faced each other. She sat on one; we sat on the other.

"Buzzy tells me that you have some clues about the beatings." Looking at Candy she said, "He tells me that you had the opportunity to look at some client files and that there are records on three of the four men who were beaten. He also tells me that the man without a file is Tom Knight. Is that correct?"

Candy nodded. "Yes," she said quietly. "As usual the Judge has observed and listened to everything quite well."

Helen nodded. "It is one of his gifts. It is one of the reasons he is a respected jurist."

"How is your leg?" Candy asked. "When we left you in July you were hobbling."

"Did you have to see a doctor?" I asked.

"I'm fine," Helen said with a small smile. "I decided not to see a doctor. You never know who is in the office when you see one of the Quincys. I washed the wound and treated it myself. During the day I wore slacks. Fortunately, or unfortunately, depending on how you see things, Sherman doesn't pay much attention to me at night. I'm certain that he never observed my wound."

She paused, looked around, and seeing no one approaching, continued. "I made a discovery the other day about Tom Knight, or at least about his family. It was quite by accident. I believe I told you that I suspected that my husband was seeing another woman, and that the reason I suspected it was that I had smelled perfume on his clothes. Whoever he is seeing wears a cheap lilac-smelling scent that one can detect easily. I've never encountered it anywhere else."

We both nodded. Candy said, "You mentioned all this on July 20, when we first met you."

"Both Buzzy and I are indebted to you, more than you can know," Helen said. "I hope this information is a small way of saying thanks."

She paused as if she was collecting her thoughts before she spoke. "The other day I was at the library. I was looking for material on Alaska. Since there is talk that it will soon become a state, I have decided to do a geography section on it early in the semester. As I was looking at the books in the Alaska section, I became aware of a strange aroma. At first I couldn't figure out why it was so familiar, and then it became quite clear. It was lilac, that same sickening lilac smell that I found on Sherman's shirts. I began to sniff like a Labrador retriever to locate where the smell originated. I know it sounds screwy, but I literally whiffed the air and followed the scent. It wasn't far away. I walked around the stack where I was searching and found a woman standing with her back to me. I couldn't tell who it was, so I moved closer. Just then she turned around and looked startled. She actually blushed. I'm not quite sure how to describe the look on her face except to say it was somewhere between fear and embarrassment.

"She had three or four books in her hand that she was returning to the shelves. 'Hello, Helen,' she said turning crimson. 'You startled me.'

"'Karen, I apologize. It was totally unintentional,' I told her. I then looked at the book cart that was just a few feet away. 'Are you working at the library these days?'

"Still looking embarrassed she answered, 'Yes. I just began a few weeks ago. My kids are old enough for me to be gone part of the day, particularly when school begins.' With that she turned and walked away.

"The woman was Karen Knight, Tom's wife. I knew immediately that Karen and Sherman have been spending time together. I couldn't prove it of course, but in this case the nose knows."

Helen paused and looked around again. "Do you think that Karen believes you suspect her?" Candy asked.

"Most definitely," Helen responded. "This was totally a woman thing. We both are sleeping with the same man, and we both know it without talking about it. I don't know either of the Knights very well," Helen said. "A few years ago Karen and I bowled together on Tuesday evenings. I know who Tom is, but know nothing about him."

Once again Helen gazed around the park. "Pam, one of women who bowled with Karen, teaches three classrooms away from me. When I took my materials to school Pam was in her classroom. I walked in and said, "Pam, I need to talk to you.'

"Pam burst into tears and said, 'Oh, Helen, I should have come to you months ago. I am so sorry.'

"'How long have you known?' I asked.

"'Since spring. For several weeks I had noticed that Karen put her shoes on and left immediately after the last frame. I just figured that she needed to get home to put her kids to bed. Then one night when I also had to leave early I saw her get into Sherm's car. I'd know his car anywhere, of course since we often park next to each other in the junior high lot.'

"I asked her what else she knew. 'Nothing,' she said. I've only talked about it to one other teacher, Barbara Fossum, who teaches sixth grade in Harden. That's it.'"

Helen shook her head, "I believe her. Pam is a good person. I can see that she feels torn. She is a friend of both of us, and she doesn't really know anything firsthand."

I was confused. "I'm not sure what this solves," I said. "You said you might have a piece to the puzzle. How does this fit?"

Helen looked as confused as I felt, and then said, "Oh. I didn't finish the story. I'm sorry. I'm nervous. I'm worried about being found here and not knowing how to explain why I am talking to you. Sherman isn't your number one fan, Jake, I think you know that."

I nodded. "For some reason he dislikes me strongly."

"Maybe I can shed some light on that as well," Helen said. "I'll try to finish what I set out to do, to give you important details that fit this whole mystery. I remembered that Dorothy Davis, who is a kindergarten teacher, whose husband Mike coaches junior high basketball with Sherman, lives two doors away from the Knights. I stopped in her classroom to chat—nearly all the teachers are putting up bulletin boards and writing lesson plans these days. It took me a couple of visits but early last week I found her alone. We talked for a bit, and I told her that I had run into Karen Knight at the library the other day. "Karen told me she is working there part time," I said.

"I heard the same thing," Dorothy said. "She hasn't been working outside the home, though I think she has hosted Tupperware parties in the past."

Then Dorothy shook her head. "I'm worried about Karen," she said sadly. "I don't think things have gone very well for the two of them lately."

Helen looked at both of us and said, "I thought for sure she was going to say she knew that Sherman had spent time with Karen. But that wasn't it. She said to me, 'I think Tom has a fiery temper, and I think he has been doing a lot more drinking lately. I heard screams coming from the house one night in mid-May. The next day I saw Karen with a Band-Aid on her cheekbone. Another time she had a bandage on her forehead. When I asked her what happened she told me she had forgot to duck when she was mowing the yard. 'I hit my head on a tree branch,' she said. 'I can be so clumsy.'

"Dorothy shook her head again. 'I don't believe it for a moment,' she said. 'I think Tom hit her. I really do.'"

Candy and I looked at each other. We both knew we had another piece of the puzzle.

Helen saw us nodding to each other. "What just happened?" she asked.

"You've just helped us fit Tom into a pattern," I told her. "It might just be what we need to help people solve the mystery of these beatings."

"Oh, I hope so," Helen said. "I do hope so. People are getting hurt so badly. Are you able to tell me what you are thinking?"

"Not right now," I said. "We are not quite finished, but we are getting close. This has been very helpful."

Helen said, "Buzzy, was impressed with the work that Candy has done. He insisted that I share what I know. He didn't give me a lot of details, but I trust him. I told him I would talk to you before school starts."

Candy changed benches and sat next to Helen. "Helen, you are a very fine woman. Thank you for trusting us. You must be facing some difficult times yourself. My guess is that you aren't sure where things are going for you."

Helen stared at Candy. For a moment I thought she was going to tell Candy to mind her own business, but then she burst out crying. "My life is a mess," she said putting her head into her hands. "It feels like it is spinning totally out of control. I've always wanted children, but we haven't been able to have them. This is the first time in my life that I'm relieved that we are childless."

"You said you might be able to cast some light on Sherm's attitude toward me," I said hesitantly.

Helen had already stood up. She turned toward me and said, "Sherman thinks that you are in your position not so much for merit, but because Smokey is fond of you. He thinks that your presence on the team has somehow turned the other players against him."

I became a bit defensive and said, "Sherm hasn't played up to his usual standards this season. I think . . ."

Helen interrupted. "Please understand that I know what Sherman is thinking is totally illogical. If there is anything I know about Smokey is that he plays the men he believes will win games. Sherman's mom is quite religious. He grew up a very devout Baptist. He lives every day knowing that when he commits adultery he is violating both his own moral code and the code of his religion. He is not in a very good place, right now."

She wiped her face and said, "I need to go. I think of you both as friends. She hugged Candy and then shook my hand. "Jake, you need to know that there was one Lewison in our family who was cheering for you every game this year. I loved to watch you play. I loved to watch you run." Then she turned and walked away.

. . . .

Candy and I watched Helen and then started walking toward the courthouse. "I'd love to talk right now, but I need to get back to work," she told me. "When can we get together?"

"How about after practice?" I asked.

"Okay, but let's make sure it happens," she said. "I want to talk while everything is fresh."

I picked up my bike, and we walked back to the steps of the courthouse. When she went into the building, I rode out to Calvary Home to see Marme. I found her sleeping in her easy chair. When I kissed her she woke up but seemed to be groggy. "Jumpy is picking me up at 5:15. We're going out for supper," she said beaming.

I felt relieved. The last time that Dad invited her for supper she refused. "I'm not up to going out in public," she had told him. It seemed to me she had more ups and downs than a teeter-totter. One day she was feeling good, and the next she felt terrible.

We sat and talked until she told me she needed to clean up. "I've got to look good. I've got a date," you know. We hugged and I left.

It was nearly 5:00 when I got home. Football practice started at 6:30. Mom told me Tim was waiting for me in the Loft. I'll fix a couple of hamburgers and bring them over," she said.

I made my way over to the shed and climbed the ladder. "It's about time you got here," Tim yelled. "I've got fast-breaking news."

"Me too," I said. "You go first."

"Early this morning," Tim began, "Earl Prince from Prince Plumbing brought one of his trucks into the shop. It had a severely dented left-front fender. 'Can you straighten it out so we can drive it without the tire rubbing?' he asked Crash. Crash looked it over and told him he could, but added, 'Your front end is out of alignment. You better not drive it too far or too fast. What happened?'

"Earl cussed a few times and then told Crash that Tom Knight had ran into a tree last night. 'He says he drove off the road to avoid a deer,' Earl said, 'but I suspect he's been drinking again.'

"Crash said, 'I thought Tom was laid up. I thought he got beat up so bad he couldn't drive or work.'

"Earl shrugged. 'He didn't get hurt nearly as bad as those other fellows. Sid's got a theory. He thinks what happened to Tom was a copycat beating. Some guy beat on him and hoped to make it look like this Superman fellow did it. But Sid says he doesn't think the guy that beat on Tom was as strong. The arms of those other guys were nearly shattered. Tom has a very simple break that is healing nicely. The other fellows had broken fingers, but Tom's fingers were only bruised. Don't tell anyone I told you. I think Sid is hoping someone will spill the beans, and we'll know who did it.'

"Crash asked him if Tom was working again. 'I give him simple jobs,' Earl said, 'and I send a kid with him. The kid provides the muscle and Tom kinda supervises, if you know what I mean.'

"'He must be healthy enough to drive,' Crash noted.

"'It's too bad he wasn't hurt worse so he couldn't drive. He goes out drinking nearly every night, and when he drinks he gets ugly.'

"Crash asked him what he meant by ugly.

"'He gets mean. He swears at people. He offends people. And he comes home nasty making poor Karen pay a price. I know for sure that he has hit her on two different occasions. Only recently I saw her with a bandage on her forehead. He didn't admit hitting her but he did tell me he suspects she's been running around on him.'

"Earl continued, 'I told him to stay home nights and she'll stay home with you. It's no fun being married to someone who comes home drunk three to four nights a week.' But Tom just ignores me. I have no idea how Karen is handling it. She may be seeing someone else, for all I know. Who could blame her?"

When Tim finished I quickly told him what I had learned that day. When I completed my story he said, "How do you know? Who told you?"

I told him it was Helen Lewison, but that I couldn't explain the circumstances under which we talked. That seemed to irritate him, but he noticed we were nearly late for practice, so we slid down the pole and headed to school.

Practice went terrible. I overthrew receivers and missed hand-offs. My mind was somewhere else. Coach knew it too and yelled at me all night. Before we headed back to school he pulled me aside, "Jake, you haven't made any progress from last year," he told me. "Your passes aren't crisp. Your spirals are not tight and your hand-offs are slow. What is going on?"

Before I could answer Woody stepped over. "I'm not worried about Jake," he said. "He's shifting over from baseball legs to football legs. He'll be ready to go by the home opener."

I thanked him and told him that now that I was done working at Little Oslo I could put my full attention on football. "It will be different starting Monday, I promise."

He said, "I'm depending on you, Jake. We need a good season out of you."

"You'll get one, Coach," I assured him. "Sorry about the last few days."

Since we practiced more than a mile from school we rode in cars from the locker room to the field. Riding back with Tim I confessed, "My mind isn't on this game at all. I've got to have a better week at practice next week or I'll stink up the place a week from tomorrow night."

I took a quick shower and told Tim that Candy was picking me up. When I got to the parking lot she was waiting. We drove to her place where she parked the car in the garage. We stayed in the car to talk. I told her what Tim had told me. "The evidence is piling up," I told her.

"Right," she said. "We've got more evidence, but we've got holes so big you could drive this car through them."

"Okay" I said, "Let's see what we have."

Candy agreed. "Start with what you think we can prove."

"Prove may be a bit strong, but we know, and can verify, that three men who were hurt were clients of Woody Carlson's wife. We know that she wrote reports to the district attorney saying that there was enough evidence to arrest each man for battery. We know that she appealed to the DA by letter, and that he totally ignored her correspondence."

Candy nodded.

"We know that Woody's sister was a victim of violence, getting beat up by her husband, and that Woody threatened to return the favor to her husband."

Again Candy nodded.

"Everyone knows that Woody is strong enough to break bones and beat men senseless. We have evidence that Sherm Lewison has been having an affair with Karen Knight, and that Tom Knight hit his wife multiple times. We have been told by a reliable source that the injuries Tom Knight received were not as serious as those received by Lloyd Swenson, Kid Hill, and Fuzzy Kvamme."

"So what?" Candy said. "That doesn't prove anything."

"Okay, so it doesn't prove it, but it leads me to believe that Sherm Lewison was the one who beat up Tom Knight. He doesn't have the strength of Woody Carlson so the injuries weren't as severe."

"You have no evidence that Sherm hit anyone," Candy said.

"The truth is we don't have an eyewitness report that Woody hit anyone. We know that Sherm and Woody's hands were bandaged, and that Sherm lied about why they were bandaged. It isn't proof, but it does fit. Kind of."

"Why do you think Sherm got involved in these things?" Candy asked.

"I have a hunch that he wasn't involved in the first one, the Lloyd Swenson beating. I think when he and Woody were painting together they got to talking about men who beat up their wives. Sherm somehow mentioned that he was angry at a man who was hurting his wife. Woody, who shared Sherm's revulsion toward men who beat their wives found a companion, a person with whom he could talk."

"Wasn't Woody taking a risk by sharing things with Sherm?"

I shrugged. "Probably, but perhaps he wanted someone to talk to. Maybe he needed someone to keep watch and make certain no one saw him."

"Or," Candy exclaimed, "I guess it could be that Sherm asked Woody. Maybe he said something like, "Please, let me get involved.""

"Or," I said thinking slowly, "it may have just evolved to get Tom after they worked together."

"The truth is, we just don't know," Candy concluded. "We know a lot of things, we have a good deal of evidence, but we don't know everything."

Neither of us spoke for a long time. Then Candy said, "When you say you have evidence, do you think it would stand up in a court of law?"

I thought for awhile and then said, "No, but it would make for a great argument."

Candy kissed me and then said, "But you can't go to my dad or Sheriff Silver and say, 'I've got all the evidence you need to solve your case.'"

"No, but I could go to them and tell them what I know, hoping that they will follow up the leads and solve the case."

"Hope? All this work and the best you can do is hope it would work?"

I nodded. "Yeah. That is the best we can do." I thought for a few moments and said, "Darn. All this work, all of the sleuthing, and I don't have the hard evidence I need."

Candy took my hand, "But you really feel that you are on the right track. You really believe you have identified the two men involved. Right?"

"Right."

"Then," Candy said, "we need to find another way to share the information. If we can't go to law enforcement, where can we go?"

Since neither of us had any good ideas we spent the rest of the night necking. At least the night wasn't a total waste.

A Shot in the Dark

On Friday I heard Mom's voice trying to break into my subconscious. "Jake. Jake. Are you awake? Tim's here."

I finally rolled over and looked at the clock, which read 8:30. As I lay there I thought, I can't move, my bed loves me." Finally, when I heard her voice again I answered, "I'll be right down."

Tim was sitting at the kitchen table eating pancakes. "These were meant for you. They are delicious, just like everything your Mom makes. Too bad there isn't enough for you."

Mom, who didn't like anyone to be teased replied, "Jake, I've got a stack ready for you. You slept in a long time."

When we finished breakfast I changed before we headed to the Loft. On the way Tim said, "Do you feel like swimming? Let's pack some sandwiches and head for Herrick's Hollow."

"Do you want to ride bikes?" I asked.

"Are you crazy?" Tim responded. "We'll get enough exercise to-night at practice. My car has a full tank of gas. We don't have to be back 'til mid-afternoon."

We ran to my house and told Mom about our plan. She thought it was great and immediately opened the refrigerator and showed us what was available for lunch. In five minutes we had made sand-wiches, packed some chips, and found four bottles of Coke. We were off for a day of leisure.

About a mile from the bridge that gave us access to the swimming hole, we spotted a police car. We slowed down and saw Sheriff Silver walking alongside the road. I rolled down my window, "Everything okay, Sheriff?"

He looked in the window before he recognized us. "Oh, hi Jake. Is that you Tim? He stood up and said, "I've got a report of stolen cat-tle from the farmer just over this hill. He's says three beef cows are missing from his property. He isn't quite sure when they were taken, because he doesn't come out here every day. Looks like there was a truck here recently. "

He looked at the field and said, "You boys got a minute to give me a hand with a tape measure."

Tim turned off the engine and we got out of the car. He handed one end of the tape to me and started walking toward a gate that was off the road. After he reached his destination he wrote something on a piece of paper before he moved us. Then he took another measure-ment. In all he wrote down four different numbers. Neither of us had a clue as to what he was doing.

When he finished he thanked us and headed toward his patrol car. Tim whispered to me, "Want to take a shot in the dark?"

I had no idea what he meant, but before I could answer Tim called, "Sheriff. Do you have a couple minutes? We've got something to share with you."

The Sheriff turned and walked back to us.

Turning to me he said, "This is your moment. Tell him your theory."

When he got to us I began apologetically, "This is rather spontaneous, but we've been thinking about this a lot lately and have an idea we'd like to share. I'll try to be brief."

The Sheriff looked just a bit irritated, but putting his hands on his hips he said, "Fire away."

"Well, we've got this idea about the beatings."

The Sheriff sighed. "All the men who were beaten played baseball, right."

"Well, I began, "not all of them. Tom Knight didn't, but you're right, the other three did, but that isn't it. What I've noticed is that all of the men, at least almost all of the men, have been accused of beating their wives. The word is that the three men from out of town have hurt their wives and maybe their children."

The Sheriff raised his hand. "Where did you get this information?"

Since this wasn't planned I tried to quickly decide how to identify my sources. "A lot of people are talking, sir. There is a lot of conversation. I was down in Paradise a week ago at the dance hall. People there say that both Kid Hill and Lloyd Swenson have been brutal to their families."

"What kind of people?"

"Mostly people my age, sir. We were talking at the dance and . . ."

"You have information that you picked up at a dance from some teens, right? They said that someone told them that two of the victims were mean sons of bitches, right? You know what I ought to do, I ought to go arrest those two men right now for beating up on each other. I think you have the case solved. Lloyd beat up on his wife and Kid beat up on his wife, and when they got tired, they beat up on each other."

"Actually, there is more to it than that," I said. "Fuzzy has beat up his wife as well."

"This is a regular merry-go-round," the Sheriff said. "Everybody beating up on everybody else. Fellows, I've got work to do. Please understand, I get a dozen tips a day. Someone thinks that the owner of a general store has beaten up on all four of them. Another guy tells me that Axel Dunhouse is Karen Knight's brother, and that he has never liked Tom. This guy says 'ol Axel came up to the Minuteman to beat the crap out of his brother-in-law, just for spite. Still another guy tells me that he saw a schoolteacher down in Paradise the night of one of the beatings. He says, "Woody Carlson is the one guy who is strong enough to beat all four of these men at the same time."

The Sheriff shook his head, "Can you imagine a man like Woody Carlson beating a man until he is nearly dead? I see Woody at Little Oslo five days a week. He painted my house. Along comes some guy wants me to believe that just because Woody was in Paradise the night of the beating I should treat him like a suspect. Finally, I have to listen to two guys who are still in high school, for god's sake, pardon me for being so blunt, two guys who picked up their information from two other guys all of whom are kids, not even eighteen-years-old."

He started to walk away, "Fellows, I got work to do. Thanks for sharing, but I don't have time for any cockeyed theories today." He walked back to his car, got in, and left a trail of gravel flying as he sped away.

As he drove out of sight Tim apologized, "Man, I am so sorry. He ripped you terrible. I should have thought this through. It looked to me like we had his ear and it was worth the attempt."

I looked at him and said, "Did you hear him Tim? He has identified Woody Carlson in Paradise the night Fuzzy was beaten. That seals the deal. We finally have him on the site. You are a genius. You provided us with the evidence we need."

"Yeah, but what are we going to do with it? Who will believe us? The one man assigned the task to solve these cases won't listen to us because we are just kids. And do you know what, he's right! I'm not sure even I believe us."

"Okay, so we're young," I responded. "Our first task is to solve the crime. The second part of this is to find people who will believe us and present our case for us. Maybe we can go back to Judge Swiggum. Maybe we can talk to Candy's dad. Maybe we contact the chief of police. Buster would love to solve this while Sid is still spinning. Overall, we are better off than when we left home. Let's go swimming."

The water was terrific. We were all alone until 1:00 when a group of junior girls showed. Tim had dated Shirley, a pretty blond who drove the car that brought the girls. He and Shirley spent some time in the shallow end of the swimming hole. I talked to the other girls, but with the lessons I learned from my encounter with Courtney still fresh in my mind, I kept my distance.

When we got home I called Candy on the phone to tell her what we had learned. I told her that we had run into the Sheriff and had started to share some information, but that he had rejected it out of hand. She laughed.

"News travels fast in Wahissa," she said. "Sheriff Silver came back to the station, told my dad that he had run into you. He said that you had some cockeyed tale about men being beaten. He threw his hands in the air and said, 'It's bad enough that every farmer and housewife is an expert on these beatings, now we have children who think they can figure this out.' Dad picked me up for lunch and told me the whole thing. He wanted to know if you were getting a bit carried away. 'Just because he plays baseball, it doesn't mean he is a cop,' he said. I'm not sure what he meant, but I know that he thinks you are out of your league. And another thing, this teaches us that we are only minutes away from having everyone in town know everything you do and think."

. . . .

I took about an hour and a half in mid-afternoon to study the "Wahissa High Play Book." It contained all of our plays on offense and showed the alignments we were to use on defense. I imagined the routes that Tim would run, and I thought about the blocking assignments. I studied the formations, where all the backs were to line up. A year ago, after running the single wing for a decade, we had switched to a straight T. On occasion we split one of the running backs to one of the wings. I had to know where each back was to line up on every play.

When practice was over that night, Coach patted me on the back and said, "That is more like it. Great practice tonight, Jake. If you can make as much progress next week we'll be ready for our home opener."

Coach Carlson was standing near him. "You are our leader, Jake. The offense rides on your shoulders. Get a good weekend rest."

I thanked them both and started heading to the car. As I left Woody said, "See you in church on Sunday."

Tim was waiting with the engine running. "You were sharp tonight, man. You hit me in stride on every pattern. Your arm seemed stronger. I hope you felt good about it."

When I didn't answer him immediately he said, "What's up?"

"I'm feeling strange," I told him. "For a month I've been putting together information about the man who beat the living daylights out of four people in our county. It is information about four brutal acts. The man who I think is guilty is one of the finest men I've ever met. What is worse, he likes me. He is kind to me. And though he is kind to me, I'm planning to find a way to turn him in. What is wrong with this picture?"

"What just happened?" Tim asked.

"As I left Woody Carlson told me he'd see me in church on Sunday."

"Crazy," Tim said.

· · · · · · ·

As I lay in bed that night it was the first time in weeks I wasn't so tired that I fell to sleep immediately. I hadn't taken time for devotions all summer. I picked up my Bible and opened to the Gospel of Matthew. I read all of chapter five and most of six before closing the book. I said my prayers and got ready to sleep. I slept well that night because I had a plan.

A Visit with the Pastor

I was out of bed at 7:00 on Saturday, August 30. At first I was disgusted with myself. The first Saturday all summer I could sleep in, and I was wide-awake. As I pulled back the curtain, I looked out the window to see bright sun and a beautiful blue sky with cotton candy clouds. Dad often said, "Treasure the early hours, they're the best God made."

After a quick shower I went downstairs to the kitchen. Dad was sitting at the table reading the morning paper and eating a bowl of cereal. I filled a bowl to the top, added some berries, poured a glass of orange juice, and joined him. Without a word he handed me the sports page. I scanned it quickly noting that the Cubs beat the Dodgers 4–1 at Wrigley Field, and that the Yankees got beat by the Washington Senators 3–2 in New York. The Phillies beat my team, the Cards, 10–6 in St. Louis.

"Do you have any plans?" Dad asked casually.

"Tim and I are planning to go to the park and work out from eleven to noon. We haven't had enough time to work on pass patterns. This afternoon Candy and I are planning to go for a bike ride. I thought we might go swimming."

Dad never looked up. I wasn't sure he was listening. "When I finish breakfast I thought I'd drop by the church and see if Pastor Hauge is in."

Immediately he put down his paper, took off his glasses and said, "Do you *need* to see him . . . ?"

I waited while he was processing. When nothing happened I tried to help, "Do I need to see him?"

"About a problem? Is something wrong?"

"No," I said as nonchalantly as possible. "I haven't had a chance to thank him for the tip he gave me about Lombardo's change-up. Besides, Buck says he knows a lot about baseball. Maybe I can learn something from him. I know he was at the Harden game."

Dad didn't look convinced. "Actually . . ." Again I waited, but this time he got going himself. "Actually he was at most of the Jewelers' games." He thought for a moment. "I'm not sure Saturday is a good day to see Pastor. He is probably working on his sermon or doing something very important."

"If he is busy I'll just come home," I told him. "It's not essential that I talk with him.

Dad looked a bit relieved, but he seemed determined to test me one more time. "Of course, if he isn't in and you really need to talk, Mom is going to be around all morning."

"I'm sure she will be," I said. "I won't go right away. No one wants a visitor too early on a Saturday morning."

I walked outside and looked down the hill where I could see people starting to stir at Tim's house. Mark was outside putting streamers on his handlebars. Karen, who was in the kitchen, saw me and waved. No sign of Tim. I was virtually certain Jumpy was already in the garage. He often made a run on Saturday mornings while Dad cleaned his truck and did inventory.

It was strange not to be at Little Oslo. I wondered if all the tables were filled and whether Cookie was as crabby as usual. I also wondered if people were glad Charlotte was back. I closed my eyes and could see the various tables with people I had served that summer. I wondered if the painters had decided to work one last day.

About this time Mom came to the doorway and said, "I made sweet rolls last night. I'm warming them up now."

I strolled around the house, went inside, grabbed the rest of the paper, poured another glass of OJ, and began reading the comics in the living room. Mom came in the room with two warm rolls on a plate and sat down near me. "Is everything okay?" she asked quietly. It was clear that Dad had given her a warning.

"I'm fine," I assured her. "Dad is concerned that I plan to see Pastor Hauge. I'm not in trouble, and I have no great problem to solve."

Mom sighed and said, "I love you Jake."

"I love you too, Mom," I said.

She appeared to be relieved as she went back to the kitchen. I began to read the comic section of the newspaper. I enjoyed Alley Oop, Priscilla's Pop, and Dick Tracy, and read them daily during the school year. I put down the paper and reflected on how strange it was to be sitting with nothing to do. I used to look forward to doing nothing, but after a summer of having nearly every minute planned, I found it awkward.

When I finished the paper I picked up *The Saturday Evening Post* and realized I hadn't read a single magazine all summer. By the time I paged through the stack that was sitting by the radio console it was 9:20. I told Mom I was going to take a ride and left for church.

Maple Street Lutheran Church was nearly a mile from our house. Until a year ago Pastor Hauge's office was in the parsonage, which was only two doors away from the church building. When the congregation decided it was better for everyone if the pastor worked out of the church, they built an addition that included an office. One night at dinner Dad explained the need to move the office out of the pastor's home. "Not many people want to talk with the pastor if they have to walk through his living room when his family is home."

I circled the church, parked my bike behind some bushes, and tried the door. It opened easily, and I entered into a dark hallway that smelled musty. Thirty-six years later I realize that all churches smell musty whether you enter them in the winter or summer. The only times they smell good are Christmas and Easter when there are lots of flowers, and days when there are church suppers.

The pastor's office was the first room off the parking lot. As soon as I knocked on the door he spoke, "It's open. Come in."

I walked through the door and immediately Pastor rose, walked over and extended his hand, "Jake. What a pleasant surprise. It is so good to see you. Please sit down."

As I settled into an overstuffed chair he sat directly across from me. He was a tall man, but sitting just two feet away I found myself not marveling at his height, but the size of his hands. On Sunday mornings I always thought the two most expressive aspects of the pastor were his voice and his hands. Now, sitting just inches away, I realized that they were at least a third larger than my own.

"You had a great baseball season," he said smiling. "I think outfield is your natural position, though you did a credible job behind the plate. Your speed and your ability to position yourself make you a valuable asset in the outfield."

After I thanked him for his kind words I spoke hesitantly, "One of the reasons that I came to see you is to say thanks for pointing out that Lombardo tipped his change-up. It was, as you know, a real gift to us."

He smiled, nodded, and said, "I am glad that it helped."

We sat for the next few moments in awkward silence as I tried to organize my thoughts. Finally, he broke in. "Earlier you said that one of the reasons was to talk about baseball. What is the other reason?"

I took a deep breath and then began, "This next item is difficult. I'm not sure how to tell you. I have some information that I'd like to share."

With his hands folded his eyes told me he was listening and invited me to continue. "I think I am apologizing because this may be a bit jumbled," I said. "It's about the beatings."

When his eyes narrowed, I quickly added, "I had nothing to do with them. Neither did anyone in my family." He seemed to relax.

"But I think I know who did, and I don't know what to do with the information. It's a discovery I've made by listening to conversations at Little Oslo and by some information that Candy has gathered."

Suddenly I needed to check something out. "I'm assuming that what I tell you will not be repeated. You won't talk to anyone, unless I say it is okay, right?"

"What you tell me is entirely confidential. I don't talk to anyone. Not your parents. Not the police. No one."

I nodded. Then I started again. "There have been four men who have been beaten. Three of them played baseball sometime in the past. That isn't the most important thing, but it has some bearing on who did it. The only one who didn't play a lot of ball is Tom Knight."

Pastor Hauge nodded. I wasn't sure that a nod meant he knew what I said was true, or that he was telling me that he understood. I continued, "What I, well, we, have discovered is that each of these men have something in common. They are all wife-beaters. In some cases, they also beat their kids. I know that to be true. Without telling you everything, I can tell you I'm sure that every victim has been a perpetrator of violence in his own family. Candy has seen the records at the courthouse, and I have heard testimony from people who know the men themselves."

Pastor attempted to appear as if he was totally relaxed, but his eyes betrayed how intently he was listening. I knew he was hearing every word I said. I thought for a moment before I spoke, "Would it help if I went through the beatings one by one?"

Pastor Hauge thought for a moment and then replied. "I suppose it would help, though I'm not sure what you want me to do about it."

"I want you to know what I know, and then I want you to help me decide what I can do about it." I was surprised at how clear it sounded. Up until that moment I wasn't quite sure what I wanted to accomplish.

"If that is what you want," the pastor said, "then it is important for you to share as many details as possible."

I felt better. I now had a plan. After a very brief pause I began, "The first beating took place on June 13 in Vang. The victim was Lloyd Swenson. I heard about it the the following morning when Sheriff Silver told all the men who were having breakfast at Little Oslo that Lloyd's face was a bloody mess, his arm was broken as were all five fingers. We later found out that it was the fingers on his right hand. He was right-handed and that was the arm that was broken. The sheriff said that it was as if a machine had smashed him, except it wasn't a machine. It was a very powerful man. Later people began to refer to the assailant as Superman.

"In the days ahead we didn't learn a lot more about who did the crime, but we learned a lot about Lloyd. He drove a milk truck and the people on his route didn't like him. Many of them actually despised him. Quite frankly I don't know how he kept his job."

I realized I had been looking down as I spoke and I wondered if that made Pastor's job more difficult, so I decided to look directly at him. "People began to refer to it as the Bang at Vang. Lloyd Swenson was laid up for most of the summer. It was quite by accident that I discovered that he was a wife-beater. When I first heard about him beating his wife it really didn't mean anything, because I hadn't heard about the other men, and therefore I didn't see a pattern."

I paused and the pastor continued. "But when the next assault took place you began to see a pattern?"

"Not really. It is a bit more complicated than that. I'll try to help you see how we discovered things, but first I just need to tell you that the second victim was Kid Hill. His beating took place at Paradise, not far from the dance hall. He lives on Oak Ridge, about four miles out of Paradise, not all that far from Lloyd, though that doesn't seem to be too important. He is a carpenter. He too has a bad attitude and a bad reputation. I soon learned from an acquaintance who lives near Paradise that Kid had beaten his wife several times."

Pastor Hauge interrupted. "I know Kid," he said. "I played ball both with him and against him. Buck knows him fairly well, too. I know his reputation. I'm disappointed, but not surprised to hear that there has been violence in his home."

I had forgotten that Pastor Hauge had a connection with ballplayers. "Do you also know Lloyd Swenson?"

"No," he said thoughtfully. "I don't think I do. If I played against him I've forgotten. However, I do know another victim, Fuzzy Kvamme. I don't know him well, but I know him. Of the men who were victims I know Kid the best."

I tried to collect my thoughts before I continued. "At one point I thought that baseball and baseball players were the thread that tied all these cases together, but when Tom Knight was beaten here in Wahissa, it confused me, that is, us. Tom didn't play ball, and at first we didn't think there was any violence connected to him. Now we know that, though it has never been reported and though there are no records of his violence, he too beat his wife. A very reputable source informed us that Karen, his wife, has been seen with severe bruises. I'm sorry that this is so mixed up. I should have told you next about Fuzzy Kvamme. You've already mentioned that you know him. His beating took place on the night of August 17, a Sunday."

"Please remind me where that beating took place," Pastor Hauge said.

"It also took place in Paradise, only it wasn't close to the dance hall. Same M.O. Broken fingers, broken power arm—each of the men's major arm was broken—and his face smashed in. In all three of the cases the police were not able to figure out either who the assailant was or how the assailant traveled."

Pastor Hauge looked at me and said, "But though the police haven't figured this out you believe you have."

"Yes sir. I believe I know not only who did it, but why." I sat nodding my head thinking he was going to ask another question.

"Are you about to tell me who you think Superman is?" the pastor finally said.

"Yes. Yes, I am. But first I need to give you some background. Superman has to be very strong. He has to have a powerful reason for doing it. The man I have in mind meets both criteria. At first, I wondered if it was Buck." I saw a smile cross the pastor's face.

I must have responded to his smile, because he immediately decided to explain his reaction. "Buck told me that you had quizzed him a bit, and that he had told you about the Sheriff's visit. Buck is strong, but I don't think he beat up any of the men you have mentioned."

I was quick to reply, "Neither do I. I've gone an entirely different direction. It started when I talked to some friends in Paradise who told me that Mrs. Carlson was the social worker who visited the Swenson family. The second time she called on the Swensons, Woody came with her, probably for protection. I believe he accompanied her because she was frightened of Kid Hill. My friend thought that was a prudent move."

Pastor Hauge moved forward in his chair, his eyes narrowed, and he said, "Do you suspect Woody Carlson?"

"Sir," I stammered. "Please let me tell you what else I know. Please."

I then told him how Candy had read the reports that Mrs. Carlson had written. I told him that the reports indicated that she was extremely frustrated. I explained that Mrs. Carlson had written multiple letters asking the district attorney to act, but that he refused to do so. I told him how I knew that Woody's sister had been beaten by her husband, and that Woody had threatened to get even. I told him how his sister had begged him to let her handle her own affairs."

"And Tom Knight?"

"That is quite different. I'll tell you about Tom Knight after we finish talking about the other three."

Pastor Hauge sat back in his chair and appeared to be deep in thought before he spoke. "All of these beatings took place at night. The person who beat them would have to be able to identify his victims. How does Woody know these men well enough to find them and beat them?"

"Pastor, I know that you like Woody. I do too. He has been wonderful to me. I respect him as a coach and as a human being. I bear him no ill will. I'm just following things where they lead me. The answer to your question is that I think, beginning with either the second or the third beating, a second person was involved. It is possible that the second person was along on the first, but I am really wandering in an area where I have no facts. Here is what I do know. Tom Knight and Fuzzy had marks that were not identical to the marks of Lloyd and Kid. I have heard that the examiner believes that Fuzzy was hit by two fists, a big fist and a smaller fist. This is not a rumor. I head this directly from Phil Paulson. Sir, I believe the second person is Sherm Lewison. Sherm is able to identify the men because he played baseball against them."

"Sherm Lewison. What led you in his direction?"

I told him that I had come in contact with Sherm's wife, and that she had reasons to believe her husband was having an affair with Karen Knight. I told him that Karen Knight had visible signs of being beaten. "I figure that Sherm, who paints with Woody, helped Woody even his score with the other men, and Woody helped Sherm beat up Tom, the man who beat his girlfriend."

We sat quietly as Pastor Hauge thought. "Do you know Sherm Lewison, Pastor?"

"Only to say hello to him," he replied. "I've watched him play baseball for a number of years. In past years he was a terrific ballplayer. He played a solid second base, and he must have led the team in batting average. Until you came, he was the only player on the Jewelers with exceptional speed. This summer he was a mere shadow of the player he has been. Something has happened to him."

We sat awhile longer before Pastor Hauge spoke. "What do you want me to do with this information?"

"I don't want to answer your question with a question, but I would like to know if you believe me. Do you think I have enough information to draw this conclusion?"

The pastor was silent for what appeared to be a long time before he spoke, "All of your information is circumstantial. You have not been present to watch someone being beaten. The circumstantial evidence you have appears to be stronger in regard to Woody than it does Sherm. Rumor has it that you and Sherm have not had an ideal relationship. Sometimes our conclusions are colored by our likes and dislikes."

Perhaps he was right. It was not a secret that Sherm had been critical of me all summer. Did I think bad things about him because he was my antagonist? Did I think ill of him because I felt sorry for his wife?

Then I remembered that there were two more things I hadn't told him. "About Woody. In a conversation with the Sheriff he told me that an eyewitness told him that Woody was seen in Paradise the night of one of the beatings. I didn't dare ask him which one. Again, this is circumstantial, but it does put him at the place of the crime, right?"

Pastor nodded and looked at me as if to say, "What else?"

"Okay, there is another item about Sherm," I began. "It too is circumstantial, but it led me to my conclusions. On August 18, a Monday, the day after the beating of Fuzzy Kvamme, both Sherm and Woody came to breakfast with their hands wrapped. Sherm explained that the two of them had got involved in a wasp's nest on Friday. The problem with that explanation is that Sherm didn't have the bandage at the game Sunday night. Cam, who drove him to the ballpark, confirmed my memory. I conclude that he bruised his hand after the game on Sunday. We know that Fuzzy's beating took place late Sunday night."

"Jake," the pastor said slowly, "my point is this. No matter how many items you have that appear to link Woody and Sherm to these beatings, you didn't see it happen. No one did. The information you provide could have an alternate explanation."

"If I had proof," I said carefully, "I could go to the Sheriff, not the pastor."

He thought for a bit before answering. "Do you understand what I'm saying? If you were the prosecuting attorney and I was a member of the jury, I would not vote to convict on the evidence you just provided me. I am not certain beyond a reasonable doubt that Woody and Sherm beat the men in question."

I stood up.

"Where are you going?" Pastor Hauge asked.

"I have made a terrible mistake," I said. "It is so clear to me. It isn't to you. I don't have anything more to tell you. I should not have come. I'm sorry that I took so much of your time."

Pastor Hauge stood and moved in my direction. "You did not let me finish," the pastor said. "Though what you have told me bears no legal weight, though it may not be enough for a jury to be convinced beyond a reasonable doubt, I think you are probably right. It is just that without hard evidence, I don't know what to do with it." He looked at me carefully. "What do you want me to do next?"

"I came to ask you to help me decide what to do."

"What is your goal? Do you want to see the two men arrested and brought to justice, or do you want to see an end to the crimes?"

As he spoke I realized I hadn't thought about that. I paused before I spoke, "If there is a way to stop the crimes without punishing the two men it would be okay with me. I think that they ought to pay some price for their crimes, but I don't need to be a part of determining what that price ought to be."

Pastor Hauge extended his hand, "I need to do something else very soon. I'll think this over and talk to you in a couple of weeks. I need to consider what you've said and then I need to pray about how to proceed."

We shook hands and I left his office. When I arrived I was excited. I thought that Candy and I had cracked the case. Now I felt embarrassed. Actually, I felt like a junior high kid. I had gone to the teacher with a big idea, and I felt the teacher had kindly, but firmly, put me in my place—and I didn't like my place.

A Time of Redemption

I left Pastor Hauge's office and rode slowly back home. Tim was waiting to work out at the park when I arrived. "Mark wants to go with us," Tim said nodding to his younger brother who was throwing a football against the garage wall. He'll shag a few balls for us."

I ran in the house, picked up my cleats and two footballs, and joined them. When we arrived at the park there wasn't another person there.

About twenty minutes into our workout, Tim came back from running a route and said, "What's up with you? You don't seem to have your heart in it."

Since Mark was off chasing a ball he had kicked, I felt free to tell Tim what had happened. When I concluded, he said, "You did fine. Pastor is naturally cautious. He wants to think things over. You did the right thing."

Tim ran patterns for another fifteen minutes, and we headed home. After a light lunch Candy and I rode our bikes out to Herrick's Hollow to swim. It was the end of summer and the 'ol hole was packed. We spent a half an hour in the water, then found a place on the hill to sit in the sun. I told Candy what had happened that morning and how disappointed I was.

She echoed Tim's words, "You did fine. This is going to work out."

I was anxious to talk more about the situation, but she closed her eyes and tried to catch a bit of the late August sun. As we lay there I was convinced that I had messed up everything. When we rode back into town, I begged off our date. I felt like being by myself. Candy seemed to understand. Dad asked Mom what was happening to me. I overheard him say, "I've never seen Jake in a funk before."

The funk only lasted a few days. Once football season began my attention was diverted to game nights. We did well, going 6–2 for the season and finishing second in our conference. Most of our offense came on the combination of Joseph to Joseph. I threw, Tim caught. At the end of the season he was selected first team all conference on both offense and defense, one of only three players who was so honored. I was the quarterback on the second team.

Tim, Dad, Jumpy, Mom, and I sang in our church choir, which rehearsed Thursday nights. Pastor Hauge joined us most nights, but though I saw him at choir and at church each week, September passed without him saying anything about our visit. Then, in early October, as I was leaving the shower room after football practice, I saw him standing outside the gym next to his car. He smiled and waved me over. "Can I give you a ride home?" he asked.

"Sure," I responded, "but I'll have to tell Tim. He thinks I'm riding with him. I ran to the parking lot where Tim was parked and told him I had another ride home. "I'll check in with you this evening," I told him.

Pastor drove a green Chevy. It was the first car I had ever ridden in that had an automatic transmission. I think they called it *Fluid Drive*. He commented on our football season as we drove toward our house. He parked about a block away, in front of a vacant lot. When he turned off the ignition he turned to face me.

"There are two reasons I have not gotten back with you sooner.

Initially, I planned to talk after I had acted on the information you provided. The week after you came in to see me I asked Woody to meet me in my office. Without mentioning your name, I told him what I suspected. I told him that everything we said was totally confidential, and that the purpose of my conversation with him was to confront him. I told him that I had no intention of ever going to the police. I caught him totally by surprise.

"Once we completed our conversation, a new problem arose. I promised confidentiality to you, protecting your name as I talked to Woody, but once I talked to him, he also asked for confidentiality. Naturally, I agreed. I have painted myself into a corner. Do you understand?"

I nodded. "You aren't able to tell me how Woody responded, right?"

"Correct. On the one hand, you deserve to know what happened when I presented my, or rather, your case to Woody. On the other hand, I don't feel as if I can tell you what he said."

I must have made a rather loud noise, because he laughed and said, "That was a huge sigh, Jake."

Laughing, I said, "I guess it was. The truth is I didn't think you believed me. I have felt rather foolish for sharing what I did. My fear was that you thought I was just a kid going off half-cocked. The fact that you took me seriously and actually talked to Woody is an immense amount of relief to me."

Pastor shook his head vigorously. "I am greatly impressed at how you compiled the information you gave me. True, there was a bit of doubt. I asked myself what would happen if your evidence proved to have another explanation. What would I do next? I could have gone back to you. I could have asked you to continue the investigation, or I could have done some investigating myself."

The pastor thought for a moment. "There was another problem. Woody and I have been friends. Would my accusation destroy that friendship? Would I lose a valued member of our congregation?" As we sat in the car I realized I had put him in a very difficult situation.

He continued, "After I thought about it, however, I realized that you had provided me with an opportunity to assist a fine man. If he was indeed guilty, I could help him end his foolish and destructive ways. If what you told me were true, this was an opportunity to provide a time of redemption for him. If it were not true, he had an opportunity to deny it, and I could help clear the air with you."

We sat quietly, for a rather long time. It was clear he planned to say nothing more. "Thank you," I said. "Thank you for approaching Woody. I don't really need anything more. I'd love to know what he said, but I can live knowing that something was accomplished. I can close out the junior G-man chapter of my life. Tim called me Sam Spade. Early on I was hoping to get in on the arrest and be present for the conviction. Then, when the evidence led me to believe it was Woody, I decided that the only thing that mattered was that the beatings stop."

Pastor Hauge extended his hand. "Some day I will be able to give you a more detailed report. For now, all I can tell you is that I am continuing to meet with him." As I exited the car he spoke again, "One more thing. At the right time, do I have permission to tell him who provided me with the information? Can I tell him you came to me, rather than to the police?"

I thought for a moment. "Right now I see no reason for you to tell him that it was me, but I have trusted you with everything. If you think that it would be good for him to know, I'll let it be your decision."

"I don't think that it will be anytime soon," he said. Then he reached for the key, turned on the ignition, and drove away.

Walking into the house I knew that if Woody had nothing to do with the crimes Pastor Hauge would have said so. There was a lot I didn't know, but I must have been on the right track. Later that night I gave a brief report to Candy and decided that Tim didn't need to know anything more.

Four days later our beloved Marme died. It happened about 8:00 p.m. while she was sitting in her rocking chair. They found her with a copy of the Bible on her lap, open to the Gospel of John. Dr. Quincy said it was either a stroke or a heart attack. Dad and Jumpy decided at her age it didn't matter. They also decided not to request an autopsy.

The funeral was on a Saturday. It was a beautiful fall day with temperatures in the low 70s. The church was full, and people stood in the doorway. Marme had planned her funeral, selecting both the hymns and the readings. In addition to "Beautiful Savior" and "A Mighty Fortress," she requested that her sons sing, "I'm Going to Ride the Chariot." At first Dad said that there was no way he could sing, but in the end Jumpy convinced him that not only were the words appropriate, she was about to ride the chariot to see her Lord and it was one of their last gifts to their mother. They never sang it better.

Pastor Hauge's voice cracked several times during the sermon. We all understood. He had lost a dear friend. We all had.

Tim later told me that Mark had asked to sleep in his bedroom on the nights between her death and the funeral. When Karen heard that they were sleeping together she joined them as well. The night after the funeral Tim asked if they wanted to sleep with him again. Mark said, "No. I can be in my own bedroom tonight. Pastor Hauge said that Marme is with God." Then he said, "Tim, you are much more luckier than me. You got to stay overnight with Marme all by yourself. I was only allowed to stay with her when Karen was there."

Tim tried to explain that when he was a little boy Marme wasn't sick, but Mark wasn't having any of it. He felt cheated. Maybe we all did. Death often cheats us.

Hit and Run

On the 18 of October, a Saturday, Mom greeted me with grim news as I came down for breakfast. "There was a terrible accident near the Minuteman last night. The radio said a male in his mid-thirties was taken by ambulance to Madison. It must have been serious if they took him to University of Wisconsin Hospital."

"The report didn't give a name?" I asked.

"No," Mom replied. "It just identified him as a male."

A few minutes later Dad came in shaking his head. "Did you hear about Sherm Lewison? Terrible thing. Terrible."

Mom let out a squeal. "The man who was taken by ambulance to Madison was Sherm?"

Dad nodded. "He was hit by a car going 40 mph on a downtown side street. He flew in the air and landed, face down, on the sidewalk. I don't know any more. I was talking to Crash, and he hadn't heard who was driving the car that hit Sherm."

I put on my coat and headed toward the door. "Where are you going?" Mom asked. "You haven't finished your breakfast."

"Down to Little Oslo," I told her. "If anyone knows anything about the accident, they'll have told Moose by this time."

The bike ride to the restaurant was cold, but brief. I parked in my favorite spot, in the alley behind the garbage cans, entered through the back door, and was greeted by Cookie, Moose, and Charlotte who were standing in the kitchen.

"Did you hear about Sherm?" Moose asked. "Who would have believed we'd have a hit and run in downtown Wahissa?"

"Hit and run?" I repeated. "Have they identified the driver?"

"Noooo," Moose answered. "They may never find him. He is probably long gone by now."

"Nonsense," Cookie snorted. "The guy that did this is local. This was deliberate. He had Sherm as a target and waited for him. Now he is holed up somewhere in Wahissa County. I'd put money on it."

"You sure have a lot of opinions for a guy who hardly gets out of the kitchen," Moose snapped.

"Don't need to travel too far when you use common sense. He was hit on the south side of the road by a vehicle driving west. The vehicle was fifteen miles over the speed limit and had to cross the centerline to hit him. This was no accident. Someone was out to get 'ol Sherm."

By Sunday the town was informed that Sherm had a broken hip, a broken leg, internal injuries and had suffered a very serious blow to the head. The neurological report was not optimistic. Helen took a leave of absence and stayed in the hospital at his side for several weeks. When she returned after a week to help set up her classroom she reported that the prognosis was bleak. Early reports were that he would probably never walk nor talk again.

Once again our little town had a mystery to solve. Law enforcement accepted Cookie's contention that the driver intended to hit Sherm. Posters offering a reward for information leading to the arrest and conviction of the perpetrator went up immediately. Buster wanted to solve "his" crime before Sheriff Silver solved the beatings.

Almost immediately Sherm's affair with Karen Knight became

public. Tom, who became suspect number one, moved out of his house and filed for divorce within the month. It wasn't long before the police chief disclosed that Tom, who had been drinking at another bar when the accident took place, was no longer a suspect.

Karen's brother, Axel Dunhouse, who was an early suspect in the Lyle Swenson beating, was suspect number two. Witnesses told the chief of police that Axel had insisted that Karen stop seeing Sherm and spend more time with Tom. Though Axel didn't have an ironclad alibi, he could not be located in Wahissa at the time of the accident, and he didn't own a blue vehicle.

Blue was the color discovered on Sherm's clothing. Candy reported that Sheriff Silver ordered his entire patrol to cooperate with the police chief. Together, they visited every car repair shop in three counties looking for a car or truck that had a dented blue left front fender. Nothing was ever found. Phil Paulson told his daughter, "Nearly everyone in the county has been identified as a suspect."

A few weeks after the accident, word began to circulate that Sherm may have been Superman. Since he had been injured no further beatings had taken place, which was proof enough in some quarters. Though surely Sheriff Silver knew better, the injury offered an excuse for not spending more time on the investigation. Shortly before Christmas the Sheriff let it be known, that since he was unable to quiz Sherm and since Sherm was almost certainly the perpetrator, the case was now closed.

Initially there was great unrest in Wahissa because there were two unsolved mysteries. Candy's dad was one of the citizens who was disgusted, though he would not say so publicly. One night he told Candy and me, "Everyone, particularly Sid, knows that Sherman Lewison didn't have the strength to do damage to those four men by himself. The truth is, Sid is sick and tired of the whole thing. We have no policeman with any detective experience. The men on the force all recognize that there are dozens of clues that have not been tracked down. And they won't be. He'd rather have us patrol county highways looking for speeders than solve the beatings."

Privately, Candy provided her theory. As long as the beatings stop people don't care. When they don't care they stop putting pressure on the Sheriff. Without pressure he will declare the cases solved.

The entire Sherm Lewison situation was a tragedy. He never walked or talked again. The crime against him was never solved.

It was only three weeks later when we heard a knock on the door. It was Smokey. He stood in the doorway with his hat in his hand and tears in his eyes.

He cleared his throat and said, "This afternoon at approximately 3:00 Sherman Lewison died of a massive heart attack. Helen was with him when he died. She asked me to tell all the Jewelers that the funeral will be Wednesday at 11:00 a.m. at the Baptist Church in Duck Lake. She would appreciate it if the Jewelers would attend and sit together in uniform. She understands that this will be nearly impossible for those who live a distance from Wahissa. I don't know if you and Cam can get out of school, and there are others whose jobs will not permit an absence."

I invited him in but he said he was visiting almost all the players at their homes. "I'm not sure I can talk well enough on the phone," he said wiping a tear from his cheek.

It was a large funeral, with nearly all the Jewelers present, and the painters serving as pallbearers. Helen was elegantly dressed in a sleek black dress and wearing a broad rimmed black hat. She carried herself erect without a single tear in her eyes. At the reception she pulled me aside and kissed me lightly on the cheek. "You are still my favorite Jeweler," she said sweetly.

The Judge sat toward the rear of the church and wore a beautiful black suit. Candy visited briefly with him and then came to find me. "It is a shame," she said, that the Judge couldn't have accompanied her today. What a fine couple they would have made had they been together."

Two years later the wife of Judge Swiggum died. He retired and moved to Florida. At the end of that school year Helen Lewison also retired and spent winters in Florida. People said she had a special friend, though she never married again.

· · · · · · ·

As November turned into December, Tim, Candy, and I were busy making decisions about the next stage of our schooling. My heart was set on the University of Wisconsin in Madison, Marme's alma mater. Candy didn't have a school of choice and faced a barrier that didn't affect me. In our family Marme and Mom were college graduates while Dad and Jumpy were college dropouts. The brothers regretted not finishing school and wanted their children to continue their education after high school.

No member of Candy's family, the Paulsons on her dad's side, or the Whitcrafts on her mother's, had ever gone beyond the twelfth grade. Her parents didn't oppose her attending college, but let it be known that they viewed it as a luxury. Girls usually got married and didn't need a college degree. Candy knew that her parents would provide a small amount of financial support, but she would have to pay for most of it herself. The closest school was La Crosse State, which offered her the option of commuting if she was low on cash.

Crash offered Tim a full-time position at the shop, but as much as Tim loved cars, he didn't want to spend the rest of his life pounding dents out of fenders. Both Jumpy and Dad let it be known that a position with Joseph brothers awaited each of us after college. Though we admired the work of our fathers, neither of us wanted to drive truck the rest of our lives. Seven years later Mark attended college for three semesters and returned to learn the oil business. He became the president, and later, the owner of the company.

Tim's heart was set on engineering. The question was where? Two weeks before Christmas, the football coach from Platteville State College (now the University of Wisconsin at Platteville), a school with a fine engineering program, visited Tim and invited him to play wide receiver for the Pioneers. Though there would be no athletic scholarship, Tim's grades were good enough to merit academic aid. Tim was thrilled with the offer and accepted on the spot, even though he had never visited the campus. It was a great decision and he had a wonderful career, on and off the field.

That fall not only did I become convinced that I wanted to attend Madison, I discovered what would end up being my major. Mrs. Zahn's senior English was the best class I had taken to that point in my life. We started with some of the classics such as David *Copperfield* and *A Tale of Two Cities*. Next, we read some great American literature, *Moby Dick* and *The Great Gatsby*. We finished up with *East of Eden*, her favorite novel by John Steinbeck.

Mrs. Zahn convinced me that literature and writing were not only my favorite exercises, but my strengths. When I applied to the University of Wisconsin my intention was to enroll in the School of Education with a major in English and a minor in history. My goal was to teach at the high school level.

During that fall I also found time to read several books, just for fun. In past summers I thought I had read everything that John R. Tunis had written. That fall, for pure enjoyment, I read *The Kid Comes Back* and *Rookie of the Year*. I realized that during the summer when I was so busy, I had missed reading, one of the things I enjoyed most in life.

At Christmas Pastor Hauge gave me a copy of the sermons of Peter Marshall, entitled, *Mr. Jones, Meet the Master*. Dr. Marshall was a Presbyterian pastor who became the Chaplain to the U.S. Senate. He was a great storyteller. I think that Pastor Hauge hoped I would read it and decide to become a pastor. The book did just the opposite. It allowed me to admire Dr. Marshall, like I admired Pastor Hauge, while convincing me that I was headed in the right direction, a career teaching high school English and coaching.

Spread Your Wings

CHAPTER 32

S pring ushered in the final days of our senior year. So many things happened that all of the events seemed to blend together. In addition to ten baseball games, played on wet fields in chilly weather, we attended prom and baccalaureate before graduation day.

Cam had a great season, pitching six complete games and being the reason that we went 8–2 before losing in the third round of the tournament. I had a good season, but Tim was outstanding and was voted the team MVP. He hit close to .500 and had seven extra base hits in ten games. Smokey approached him before the season was half over, offering him the second base position on the Jewelers, replacing Sherm.

At graduation Candy was salutatorian, and Tim and I finished in the top ten academically, which wasn't exactly the greatest accomplishment in the world since there were only 122 in the class of 1953.

The big surprise at graduation was the announcement that I had won the Wahissa Warrior Award, which was new that year, presented to a graduating senior who exhibited outstanding leadership in academics and athletics. Mr. Singer, the principal, held a plaque high in the air and said, "This award carries a two-year college scholarship worth $500 a year. The winner for the class of 1953 is Jacob Joseph."

I almost fell over. Five hundred dollars in 1953 was nearly half the cost of a year in college. To put this in perspective, most high school teachers made between $4,000 and $5,500 a year. During my first year at the University of Wisconsin I spent just a bit over $1,400. Someone had provided me with nearly 40% of what I would need to attend Wisconsin's premier educational institution. The donor, Mr. Singer said, wished to remain anonymous.

On the Tuesday following graduation I visited Mr. Singer, to ask how I was to write a thank you note to Mr. Anonymous. He told me to write a note and give it to him. He would put the letter in the hands of the donor.

Next, I asked how I was chosen. He told me that he was not at liberty to reveal either the process or the committee who had made the choice. The gift was shrouded in mystery.

I spent hours talking about the identity of my benefactor. Tim speculated that the donor was Ken Brown. Candy guessed that it came from Judge Swiggum. At home Dad told the family he thought the donor was Ted Towne while Mom theorized it was a graduate of Wahissa High who no longer lived in the area.

None of the speculation rang true to me, so one day, in the middle of June, I visited Pastor Hauge to ask if he knew anything about the scholarship. He said he did not, but I left thinking he wasn't telling the truth. It may be a terrible thing to accuse your pastor of lying, but he looked like he was hiding something. Actually, I took it as a positive, concluding that Pastor hadn't had a lot of practice lying, and therefore wasn't very good at it.

. . . .

All year long Candy and I talked about the beatings wondering what had happened when Pastor Hauge met with Woody. We wondered if Pastor had found it necessary to tell Woody what part we had played in providing him with information. Whenever we met Woody in the hall at school or nodded to him at church, we asked each other, "Did he seem to look at us differently?" The answer was always, no.

I had hoped to work for Moose again in the summer of '53, but Charlotte wasn't planning to travel so Moose really didn't need me. About the first of June, Ken Brown stopped by the house to offer me a job working with his apartments. He informed me that he planned to spend most of the summer at the lake. He needed someone to collect rent and deal with maintenance issues. It was an easy job and the pay was quite generous. I think he could have driven to Wahissa to take care of it himself every two weeks, but I accepted the job with gratitude. I had no set hours and I had a car at my disposal, a green 1952 Studebaker, a car that was designed to confuse people. The front and rear ends looked nearly identical. In addition, the car had something called *overdrive*. Once you reached a certain speed the driver stepped on the clutch and pulled a rod. The car then was freewheeling. It was terrific for coasting down hills, something that our part of Wisconsin had in abundance.

· · · · · · ·

The Jewelers had a great summer winning the league championship by three games. Buck was awesome, but announced part way through the season that it would be his last year. Cam, who had grown two inches and put on ten pounds, became the number two pitcher. He pitched into the seventh inning several times and threw two complete games. Tim started at second and hit just over .300. I led the team in batting average and stolen bases, and the Zitzners hit a total of fifteen home runs between them. Mom, Dad, Jumpy, and Melinda never missed a game.

In August, Candy told me that she thought we ought to break up before we left for school. "This fall we won't see each other except for Thanksgiving and Christmas. With you in Madison and me in La Crosse, we will be 135 miles apart," she reasoned. "We ought to be free to date other people without feeling guilty."

I was very unhappy with Candy's decision. She was the only girl I had never dated. Though we had never talked about it, I just assumed that we would get married when we finished college.

As it turned out, I had no voice in the decision. On a tearful night the third week in August, she removed the tape from my class ring and handed it back to me. I took her ring off my pinkie and gave it to her. We both wept. Then we made out for over an hour and experienced the heaviest petting in our two-year experience. As I look back on it I think it was a strange way to end things, but that is what happened.

Dad said it was a smart move. "Jake," he said, "now you can spread your wings."

The last week of the summer Tim arranged for us to go north to a friend's cottage near Rhinelander. The announced purpose of the trip was fishing, but we only cast a line once during the three days. As difficult as it was to say good-bye to Candy, my last days with Tim were worse.

When I moved into a men's dorm along the shores of Lake Mendota on Labor Day weekend, I discovered that my roommate, Pat Ryan, was from Kenosha. We were friends from the first day on campus and roomed together four years.

The baseball team held fall tryouts in early September. I was cut on the third day. The coach told me he expected to get more power out of the outfield than I could provide. I guess they could tell by looking at me that I was a singles hitter.

Just before Christmas I received a call from a man who identified himself as Mr. Coleman. "I'm the Sergeant at Arms for the Assembly," he told me. "I have an opening for a page on my staff. It's yours if you want it. You'll work twenty hours a week. You can study when you aren't running errands for the members of the Assembly." He told me that some days when I worked there wouldn't be any people in the chambers, but that he needed someone to do odd jobs just in case something happened.

I took the job and held it for three years. It paid well and provided a great place to study. The day I quit the job at the end of my junior year Mr. Coleman told me that he had hired me at the suggestion of his friend, Judge Erling Swiggum. "Anyone the Judge recommends, I hire," Mr. Coleman said. That night I wrote a thank you note to the Judge and told him that he had more than paid for any act of kindness I had shown to him.

During the first two and one half years, I was completing all the course work that would allow me to teach English and coach at the high school level. I was scheduled to student teach the second semester of my senior year. In January of 1956, my junior year, two of my English professors approached me with an offer. They wanted me to make an early application to the graduate school to study American literature. I did what they suggested and was immediately accepted.

The summer after my freshman year, 1954, I returned home to play for the Jewelers, work for Ken Brown, and to date Candy. Ken expanded my work from the previous summer, again providing me with the 1952 Studebaker. He increased my salary. When I returned to Madison the end of August he gave me the Studebaker as a gift.

The loss of Buck made Cam the lead pitcher for the 1954 Jewelers. We finished third in the league. It was great to play another summer, my last, with Tim.

Candy and I had a great time in June and July, but in August she told me that she didn't want to date me any more. She told me she had met a guy, a year older, from Onalaska, Wisconsin. It was the last I saw Candy for several years.

· · · · · · ·

I received my PhD from the University of Wisconsin in the spring of 1963, writing my thesis on the works of Hemmingway. Just before graduation I was interviewed by the English department at the University of Kansas in Lawrence. They were looking for a young teacher who could teach writing and twentieth century American literature. I was hired and, along with my wife, moved to Lawrence where I began teaching in the fall of 1963.

In 1958 I had begun to date Charlene, a woman from New York who was enrolled in the same program. By 1961, though we were not engaged, we talked frequently about getting married.

That summer I drove up to Wahissa alone on a Friday night to spend the weekend. When I arrived Dad informed me that Mom was at a shower, and that we were invited to have dessert with Jumpy and Melinda. We were sitting on Jumpy's front porch when Mom drove up in our car, leaned out the window, and shouted. "Jacob, would you please come home? I need to talk to you right now." She was clearly upset.

I followed her briskly up the hill, wondering what in the world had happened. Dad walked a couple of steps behind me. We entered the house to see Mom sitting, steely eyed, on a footstool in the living room. I hadn't seen her for nearly a month, but before she greeted or hugged me, she motioned that I should sit down. "Do you think that I am the kind of mother who tries to run her son's life?" she asked.

I was confused, but shook my head and said, "No. You have given me a lot of freedom."

"When you started dating Candy, did I try to interfere?"

Still puzzled, I responded, "No."

"What about when you broke up. Did I intervene?"

"Mom, what is this about? When Candy and I broke up you seemed sad, but you said nothing. That was seven years ago."

"Then you must not think of me as a dominating mother for what I am about to tell you. I will say this once, and then I will not repeat myself. I just returned from Candy Paulson's shower. She is getting married in a month to a man she does not love. Jacob, she still loves you. She didn't tell me that, but I know it as sure as I know that your father loves me. I also know, or at least believe, that you love her. Charlene is a fine woman, but it is clear to me that you do not feel the same way toward her as you did toward Candy. Candy is making a terrible mistake. Tonight when she described her finance, Darren, she talked with very little enthusiasm. I saw no spark in her eyes. Before we ate she asked about you. When I told her what you are doing she lit up like the morning star."

I had never heard my mother talk like this in my life, nor had Dad who looked at her in total astonishment. In addition to all the straight talk I noted that she was calling me by my formal name for the first time since I came home in third grade and announced that my name was Jake.

"Jacob, over the years I have watched you with Candy and later with Charlene. When you were with Candy you could hardly wait to leave us so you could be alone to touch and kiss. When you are with Charlene it is as if you are sitting with a valued colleague. Nothing more. You are proud of Charlene and respect her, but you were in love with Candy. I never get the sense that you can hardly wait to be alone in a dark room with Charlene. Your relationship lacks passion. If I am wrong, tell me."

Mom was not wrong. She had called it exactly right. What was frightening was that until that moment I didn't realize that my relationship with Charlene was a professional one. I respected her, but I wasn't sure I loved her. Even though I had been far more intimate with Charlene than I ever had been with Candy, it was not nearly as passionate. Mom made me realize that I did not love Charlene the way Dad loved Mom. As I stared at my mother in amazement I realized that I loved Candy. I had always loved Candy.

"What . . . ?" I didn't know how to finish the sentence.

"Go over there now. Tell her you love her. Be gentle, this is going to come as a shock to her."

That may have been the only thing that Mom said that night that wasn't the straight-on truth. I got up and walked over to where my mother was sitting, lifted her up, and hugged her. Normally she loved it when I played with her. Not that night. I started to tell her she was the most amazing woman I had ever met, but she pushed me away and said, "Go! Go now!"

I did. I arrived at Candy's house and found her and Melissa, a friend from high school days, sitting on the back porch. I walked up, greeted Melissa, and asked about her husband. Then I said, "Melissa, I'd like to borrow Candy. Do you mind?"

Melissa shook her head, hugged Candy, and stepped back. I then took Candy by the hand and gently led her, without speaking, toward the park. When we arrived we found a very dark place where we were utterly alone. The first words she spoke to me were, "Jake, did you come to save me?"

I kissed her and said, "I came to marry you."

She said, "I love you Jake."

I said, "Candy, I have always loved you. You are the only girl I have truly loved in my entire life."

We walked and talked for nearly three hours. Somewhere around one in the morning, I said, "The day you give Darren back the ring I will ask you to marry me."

She said, "The day you ask me to marry you I will say yes."

Before I left her, a long time after midnight, Candy kissed me and then said, "Tell your mom thanks." Then she shook her head, "No, I'll tell her. I've always had your mom in my corner."

On Saturday, December 30, 1961, six months later, Pastor Hauge married us at Maple Street Lutheran Church.

Epilogue

. . . .

*I*n July of 1988, Candy and I, along with our daughter, Mary Catherine, came home for our annual summer visit. Our two sons, Dave and Bill, who lived near Milwaukee, joined us. Tim, who had moved back to Wahissa to start his own engineering firm in 1986, had room enough to host our entire family.

Shortly after we arrived on a Sunday, Tim pulled me aside and said, "Woody Carlson died yesterday. The funeral will be at our church on Tuesday. Pastor Hague is coming. He called to ask if you would be there."

Dad and Mom, who were in their 80s, along with Tim, his wife Ruth, Candy, and I attended the funeral. The pallbearers were all former teachers.

We were all delighted to see Pastor Hauge, who had retired and moved to Eau Claire. He looked terrific. When the service at the graveside was complete he took Candy by the hand, looked at both of us and asked, "Will you take a walk with me?"

As we walked he asked about our children while holding Candy's arm tight. I had never thought of him as affectionate, and I was moved by his kindness. We stopped several times, I believe, in order that he could look at us while he told us about his wife, children, and grandchildren. It soon became apparent that his goal was the gazebo that was located in the middle of the cemetery. When we reached his destination he reached into his vest pocket, took out an envelope and said, "Woody wanted me to give this to you after he died. I have a copy at home, though it is well over a decade since I read it."

The outside of the envelope read, "Dr. Jacob Joseph." Inside was a two-page letter. I asked Candy if she wished to read with me. She shook her head and said, "I'd prefer that you read it out loud."

I began,

Dear Jake,

I am writing to thank you and Candy for saving my life.

I was a very angry man in 1952. Few people know this, but Linda, my wife, was married once before. We had dated in college, but another man, Lawrence, convinced her to marry him. Though he had never threatened her or touched her violently before they were married, after the wedding he became brutal. He beat her several times before she left him.

It was years before she was able to deal with the trauma of that first marriage. I'm convinced that her abuse is the reason that we never had children.

Though Linda pressed charges against the man, he never was arrested or tried in court. The court's inability or unwillingness to act against abusers frustrated me to no end.

When my sister called me in March of 1952, telling me how her husband beat her, it added to my frustration. Meanwhile, ironically, Linda was assigned by the court to work with several abuse cases. Though there was clear evidence that her clients were abused the district attorney refused to act.

One afternoon, afraid to visit a man near Paradise, Linda asked me to accompany her. I stood in front of the car about twenty feet away and listened to Lloyd Swenson shout at her, saying, "It is none of your damn business what takes place in my home. My home is my castle. You have no right to invade my privacy." It was all I could do not to run up and take him down on the spot.

When Linda wrote her report nothing happened. Shortly after that I decided to take matters into my own hands. I wore a disguise and started visiting country pubs where that man and the other abusers hung out. I never stayed long, and I spoke only enough to identify the men I was seeking. Virtually no one, not even the bartenders asked me any questions. Later, Pastor Hauge told me that I was spotted on one of the nights of the beating, but at the time I didn't think anyone recognized me. Nor did I think anyone paid attention to my car, which I parked a few blocks away from the bars. At least no one ever commented about seeing the car.

That first night in Vang, the only night I traveled without a disguise, I was actually looking for another man when I ran into Lloyd Swenson. I listened to his filthy mouth, the same filthy mouth that I heard while standing in his driveway. I observed him from a distance, and when he went out to urinate I decided to take him down. I had taped my hands and I wore gloves. When I first hit him I felt a fury that I had never experienced. My anger poured out so hot that it almost scared me.

When I finished I took off my gloves and felt his pulse. For a moment I was afraid I had killed him. After I detected a heartbeat, I went back streets to where I had parked my car and took side roads back to Wahissa.

At no time did Linda ever know what I was doing. She often commented, "You've been gone quite awhile," but she never asked where I had been.

The few days after I beat Lloyd, I listened with interest to all of the talk at Little Oslo. I felt a great sense of relief when I heard the Sheriff say that he had no clue as to who was behind it. I also heard him say he suspected that the perpetrator lived near Vang. This emboldened me, and I decided to square things with Fuzzy Kvamme next. The problem was that I couldn't find him, so I focused on Kid Hill. He was probably the biggest abuser of the entire group, so it was satisfying to take care of him.

After the Kid Hill beating I felt no shame at all. I firmly believed that I was doing what the courts refused to do. When they started calling me Superman I began to feel like I was fighting for truth, justice, and the American way.

My problem in locating Fuzzy and the three others on my list was that I had never seen a picture of any of them. In Fuzzy's case you would think that it would not be difficult to find a man with a full beard, but that description described a half dozen men from that area.

About that time Sherm Lewison began to talk to me about how Tom Knight was abusing a female friend of his. At the time I had no idea that Sherm was having an affair with Tom's wife. All I knew was that there was another wrong to be righted. Without telling Sherm everything, I offered to help him take care of Tom.

Sherm, who wasn't very strong, wanted to do most of the hitting himself. We found Tom staggering down the street outside the Minuteman. I took a pillowcase, which I carried in the backseat of my car, and put it over his head so that he couldn't see us. As I held him Sherm beat him. Though Sherm hit him several times he was still standing, so I took a couple shots at him, and he fell to the ground.

Later, I found out that Sherm had played ball with Fuzzy. When I asked if he would help me find him, he said yes. One night, without much planning, we left after a ball game and drove to Fuzzy's house. He was home alone, drunk. When we offered to help him find more to drink he went willingly with us in our car. We drove him to Paradise, thinking that it would confuse the police. When we determined that there was too much traffic close to the dance hall, we beat him about five blocks away and carried him to a corner near a streetlight so someone would find him. If the police knew he had been moved, nothing was ever reported.

That night was the only night that I didn't wrap my hands and wear gloves. Sherm and I both severely bruised our hands and needed to bandage them before work the next day.

I have one major regret about that encounter. We did not plan our trip in advance to find Fuzzy. Sherm had a couple of false mustaches in his car left over from a party. We put them on and wore red bandanas on our heads to change our looks. While we were transporting Fuzzy, Sherm's mustache fell off. I believe that Fuzzy recognized him. I also believe that Fuzzy was involved in the hit and run. I wish that I had found Fuzzy on my own, and I wish that I had found a way to tip off the police, though it didn't appear that they much cared about finding the driver.

I still had several people on my list, some as far away as Harden, when Pastor Hauge visited me. He spoke in a calm, quiet voice, and appeared to know almost all the details of the four beatings. He even seemed to know why I had beat up each guy.

At first I was afraid that Pastor Hauge was planning to turn me in. He told me that he hoped that wasn't necessary. He told me that what my victims had done was evil. He told me that I had every right to be angry. He then told me that the method I had chosen to fight evil would only perpetuate evil. He said that in two of the cases the men I had beaten had been beaten as children. He said that I was only fostering violence in the victim and probably in their sons. After several nights talking in his office he convinced me that to fight evil with evil only makes it spread.

I met with him twelve times during the 1952–53 school year. In spring of 1953, I entered a program in Minneapolis for men like me.

I began this letter by saying that you saved my life. Through treatment I became convinced that had I continued I would either have been caught and jailed or my violence would have been revenged. I am convinced that whoever hit Sherm (Fuzzy?) with his vehicle was involved in revenge. After treatment I became convinced that it was impossible for me to remain hidden for an extended period of time. My counselors told me that nearly every person who took the role of a vigilante either was killed or continued their violence until they were caught.

Now you know why I believe you helped save my life. Thank you for doing the investigation. Thank you for trusting Pastor Hauge.

It was March before he told me where he received his information. One of the steps in my treatment was to find a way to atone for my actions. I soon decided to establish the Wahissa Warrior Award. It was an honor to support you for your first two years at the university.

Jake, I have followed your career closely and have read all five of your books. I never finished the one on writing, but I did read the first two chapters. My favorite is your book on J.D. Salinger. It led me to read everything he wrote, which isn't that difficult since he didn't publish many books. I also have read what other critics have written. Your book is the best one in print.

You are a remarkable man, Jake. You had total trust in Pastor Hauge. For that I am most fortunate.

When Linda dies I release you from all issues of confidentiality. I have gone into detail in this letter so that if you think it wise to tell this story you will be able to do so with adequate information. If you think it is worthy, I hope you will write it.

God Bless You,
Elder (Woody) Carlson

When I finished reading we all sat in silence for several minutes. I felt a huge sense of relief knowing that the story that had begun forty-one years ago finally had an ending. The goal that Candy and I had set had been reached. Candy was the first to speak, thanking Pastor Hauge, "You were a mentor and guide for both of us during our formative years," she said. "Most important, you kept your promise. We are grateful beyond words."

He smiled and then quickly changed the subject. He asked about our family and finally, about our immediate plans.

I told him that we intended to stay for the rest of the week before we headed back to Kansas. Candy was to be at work at the main library on the University of Kansas campus the next Monday.

"And what lies ahead for you?" he said to me.

Epilogue

I thought for a moment and then said, "I am wandering a bit out-side of my normal focus of American literature and doing research on the place of God in the novels of the English author, Graham Greene, but I may put that aside for another project."

"Which is?"

"A novel about life several decades ago in a small Wisconsin city."